The Second S...

The Circle of Time

Liz MacRae Shaw

The Islands Book Trust

Published in 2024 by The Islands Book Trust

The Islands Book Trust, Community Hub, Balallan,
Isle of Lewis, HS2 9PN. Tel: 07930 801899

https://islandsbooktrust.org/

Copyright remains with the named author. Other than brief extracts for the purpose of Review, no part of this publication may be reproduced in any form without the written consent of the publisher and copyright owner.

© Liz MacRae Shaw 2024

ISBN: 978-1-907443-89-3

Typeset by Erica Schwarz (www.schwarz-editorial.co.uk)
Printed and bound by Martins the Printers, Berwick upon Tweed, UK

Photos: Front cover image courtesy of Cailean Maclean;
back cover images courtesy of Liz MacRae Shaw.

CHAPTER 1

Summer, 1968

WHAT A DUMP! I look around me at the huddle of dingy grey buildings as I stagger stiff legged off the bus in Portree square, and I glance at that picture of the Highlander strutting along the side of the MacBrayne's bus – such a cliché! I had forgotten how far Skye is from everywhere else. The slow train to London, the stuffy rattling sleeper to Inverness and finally the straggle of carriages shuffling into the tiny station at Kyle. Surely the station has shrunk since I last saw it. It seems like something from one of those model towns you see at the seaside. Then that ferry over to the island, stinking of engine oil, sea water and stale chips. And finally the rickety bus, wobbling round the bends in the road and grunting up the hills. The extra stop on the road as the driver hooted to get those stupid hairy cattle out of the way. He had to jump down from the bus in the end to shoo them off. If they didn't have horns like handlebars, you wouldn't be able to tell the front end from the back.

At last, I'm here. I sigh and start to walk up the steep brae. It's shorter than I remember it but still a struggle hauling the case. I dump it down half-way to ease my cramped fingers. How many years since I was here last – six or eight maybe? That would be with my mother, and Pappa would be at the bus to meet us, pipe in mouth and shouldering the case as if it was a kitbag. I'm worried about seeing him again. Will he be shaky and mumbling? Mum said that he had failed a lot and it would be my job to help Granny round the house – ugh! And cheer Pappa up. How am I expected to cheer other people up when it's all gone wrong for me? No summer job so no money, no chance to see Neil over the summer and "You won't be allowed to go to university next year if you don't buck your ideas up."

I kick the case before picking it up. It's not dark yet but the road is deserted. No, it's not. There's a figure walking unsteadily towards me – a drinker staggering home I expect. He's bow legged and carrying a heavy sack over his shoulder but it's no Father Christmas. Something is dripping from the bottom of the sack and leaving a dark trail. It stinks too. Blood! I shudder as I remember those tales of the Celtic heroes who were always chopping off the heads of their enemies and dangling them as trophies from their belts.

'There you are!'

Oh no! The creature is speaking to me. Or is he? But there's someone else, waving a stick. Some old man. That's all I need. I turn away in disgust. The other figure trudges on. Then I hear a voice behind me and peer again at the figure behind me. There's something familiar about him but no, that shrunken figure can't be Pappa. I find myself stumbling forward, the case bashing my legs.

'*Eisean*,' he calls out and spreads his arms wide. 'Here's my favourite grandchild.'

I feel a flood of warmth although I'm much too old to be called a chick, like he's just said. I wonder if he can read my mind with its grudging thoughts. I inhale the smell of pipe tobacco.

'I couldn't let you carry your bags all by yourself,' he says when he lets go of me.

'The case is very heavy. Shall we carry it between us?'

'We'll do no such thing,' he says, his knotty hands reaching for the handle. He staggers as he straightens up and we start to plod up the hill together.

'Who was that, carrying the sack?'

The Second Surge of the Sea

'Don't you remember John Iain? The man who pulled down the stairs in his house and put them on the fire when he ran out of coal?'

I shake my head.

'He's the slaughterman. He'll be taking sheep heads home to boil up.'

I have to swallow to stop myself throwing up. On the bus I had been thinking about the lamb chops Granny always made when we came, melting flesh flavoured with onions and a mountain of buttery potatoes, but now I feel sick.

'You must remember all the stories about him. Like the time he was brought a pig to slaughter. He fancied a drink before doing the deed and shared his whisky with the beast. His neighbour found the pair of them lying down together snoring their heads off.'

I can't bear to ask what became of the pig.

Pappa lifts the gate that has dropped on its hinges. There's Granny, waiting outside the front door. We go inside and she steps forward to hug me. She's smaller than I remember, her sparse grey hair pulled back into a bun but her dark brown eyes are bright. She stands back, hands on hips, looking me up and down, shaking her head.

'You're taller than ever. You must take after the English side of your family.' And I feel myself stiffening. Surely now that I'm adult we can put a stop to all those boring discussions of how much I've grown. It's not my fault that all my Mum's relations are midgets.

'You're in the back bedroom,' she says. I nod and pick up the case, heaving it up the stairs. The room is as I remember it before, with its horrible floral wallpaper and the slippery pink eiderdown on the bed. There's a chest with an old-fashioned amber glass tray with little dishes on it and a few old books stacked in the corner.

I remember looking through them on one of the many days when it was pouring with rain. They were all prizes from school and Sunday school that Granny had won. Unreadable stuff by Sir Walter Scott. I'm relieved to know that I'll have the spare room to myself. When I came before I shared with Mum – Dad never came up with us. He said that he had to keep earning money, doing clients' accounts. Now I wonder if he felt that he didn't fit in, being English. What does that make me, being half and half?

One time I had to share with Granny – I can't remember why but I can see her sitting up in bed and reading her Bible, her lips moving as she turned the flimsy pages. I dump the case and run downstairs, hungry for my tea.

'I'm looking forward to my chops,' I say to Granny's back where she's stirring a pan on the hob.

She turns round and sighs, 'I've not had time to cook them with your Pappa being as he is. I've done stovies with corned beef.'

My face must show my feelings. I loathe corned beef and I'm not keen on heated up potatoes either.

'I can't be running down the brae to the butchers, with my legs as they are.' She lifts the edge of her apron and the hem of the tweed skirt underneath to show me her knees. They're swollen and misshapen, huge above her skinny Minnie the Minx's legs. I feel a stab of guilt.

'I can get some chops for you and cook them if you tell me what to do.'

She shrugs, 'You'll have to explain that the meat's for your Granny or the butcher will think that you're a visitor and give you rubbish.'

I feel deflated, 'Well, let me take the plates over to the table.'

When we're sitting down, I take a small forkful. It's halfway to my mouth and Granny looks sharply at me.

The Second Surge of the Sea

'We must give thanks to the Lord first,' she says and I drop my fork as if it's on fire. 'You say a prayer, one you use at home.'

You must be joking, I think.

'You'll know the Selkirk Grace?' Pappa says. His eyelid flutters in a wink before he starts the verse:

> 'Some hae meat but cannae eat
> And some would eat that want it.'

Then I remember it and join in.

> 'But we hae meat and we can eat
> And sae the Lord be thankit.'

By this time my stomach is so empty that it's fallen in on itself. At least it means that I can manage the stovies. Granny asks me about the journey and talks about the doings of relatives and neighbours, most of whom I can't remember. Pappa is silent and looks down at his plate, pushing his food around. We have dark brown tea and shortbread for pudding. I don't want to say that I only like tea weak with no sugar and try not to make a face as I swallow. Afterwards we hear the news on the radio. Radio! I had forgotten that there's no TVs up here.

'We'll go to the ten o'clock service tomorrow,' Granny says.

I stifle a groan and nod.

'I won't come but your Granny will be glad of your arm to lean on,' Pappa says.

After our meal I clear up the plates and take them into the kitchen, piling them up on the wooden draining board beside the stone sink. How cramped and out of date it all is. The cooker with its chipped enamel front and a couple of cupboards take up all the space. And no fridge.

'I'll wash and you dry,' Granny says.

I shake out the ironed tea towel. Who on earth bothers drying up dishes or ironing tea towels? But I wipe them carefully as I know she's watching me. When I've finished, she shows me where to put them all, granting me a small smile but no 'thank you' for me being here. I suddenly feel very tired.

'I'll go to bed if you don't mind.'

'You've had a long day.' She sighs and pushes her face forward for me to kiss her cheek.

I clean my teeth quickly in the cold bathroom and get undressed. When I pull away the tightly folded sheet and slide under the heavy blankets it all feels so strange that I think I'll never go to sleep but the next thing I notice is the light pouring in through the gap in the curtains.

'Just the day for a walk by the sea,' I think, but then I groan as I remember that it's Sunday. My watch says nearly 9 o'clock so I'd better get up. I'm sure Granny won't like me coming down in my pyjamas. She's putting the kettle on as I walk into the kitchen. She looks me up and down and nods. Mum had insisted that I take a "nice dress and stockings. You can't wear those dreadful jeans to church and you better take a beret or something too. You're too old to go bareheaded!"

Granny insists that we set off early just like Mum who always nags me to hurry up and then we arrive far too soon. She takes my arm as we plod down the brae, the same one that I climbed up yesterday. She greets other people, some in English, others in Gaelic, some like her, carrying a bible nestled in their hands. We arrive before the bell starts ringing and she leads me to a pew half-way down the aisle. I look up at the balcony and suddenly remember how I wanted to sit up there when we came before.

'We only use upstairs when the church is very full, for a big funeral or a communion Sunday,' she hisses in my ear.

The service goes on for ever and I find myself gazing unseeing through the window. Most of the windows are plain glass. There's

The Second Surge of the Sea

just the one stained glass picture at the front. I really don't believe in all this religious stuff. I don't think Mum does either because she never goes to church at home. I like singing hymns at school assemblies but I don't know the tunes here and some of them are strange wailing psalms that send prickles down my spine. The minister is a slight man with a soft voice but an insistent one you can't ignore. Like Miss Jones, the maths teacher at school. You could imagine that it would be easy to mess around in her classes as she never raises her voice. Nancy tried it on once, talking in a joke Welsh accent while she had her back turned, writing on the blackboard. She never risked it again after Miss Jones hauled her out to the front and tore chunks out of her until Nancy was in tears. The minister's talking about how the world has been redeemed by Christianity. That's a big claim I think to myself. What about all those people burnt at the stake for being Catholics in Protestant countries and the other way round?

'And we must remember how fortunate we are when we think of the heathen peoples, past and present who know nothing about Christianity.' And maybe they would have preferred to be left with their own beliefs, I think.

'The Venerable Bede tells us about how England became a Christian country. He writes how Saint Augustine was in the hall of an Anglo-Saxon chief one night when a small bird came in through the window and in a panic sped across the building to fly out the other side.

The Anglo-Saxon chief said to him, "That is how our lives are – a brief time in the light but beginning and ending in darkness."'

That makes sense to me but of course the minister has to drag Christianity into it and say that the Church knows better and it's not true if we believe in the kingdom of Heaven.

It was the mention of the Venerable Bede that caught my attention. Our keen new History teacher, Miss Greaves, keeps saying how we shouldn't just read about the Tudors and Stuarts on the syllabus but look at other important times in history. I used to love History when I was younger, but I had lost my taste for it after Mum wouldn't let me go to the Tech to study for 'A' levels. Being fed up with being at an all-girls' school wasn't a good enough reason to change, she said. But I know that if I don't get good enough grades I won't get to university and will end up stuck doing a boring job like Mum does, at the Ministry of Ag and Fish.

I feel Granny poke me in the ribs. Everyone is getting to their feet. More greeting everyone and shaking the minister's hand on the way out. I'm helping Granny down the steps when I hear a voice behind me: 'You must be Margaret.'

I turn round to see a small woman in fusty black, her reddish grey hair pulled back under a hat like a pudding basin. I force my lips into a smile that's more of a snarl. I remember Flora MacKinnon from the last time I was here. That time I came up with Mum and I was so excited about hearing that my cousins, John and Anne were coming up to Skye with Auntie Beth. Mum was furious, "It's not her turn to come! There's not enough room for them. Where will they all sleep?"

But I didn't care. I took them down to Scorrybreac and we rushed around, throwing great slimy ropes of seaweed at each other, paddling in the sea and shrieking at the cold and the sharp rocks jabbing our tender bare feet. On the way back we were ravenous, and I suggested that we stop at the Caley, a café with shiny chrome fittings that my Granny disapproved of because they sold drink. We bought chips and walked home eating them – luscious, fat chips nestled in greasy paper, crisp on the outside and soft on the inside. That's when we saw her, Mrs MacKinnon, and I said 'Hello'. I thought no more of it until we went in the backdoor and were swept up in an Arctic gale.

The Second Surge of the Sea

"You've been seen eating chips in the street like ragamuffins," Mum had said.

"My two would never have done that. Your Margaret led them on," Auntie Beth had added, all flushed and with her blouse buttons done up in the wrong order as if she had got dressed in a rush.

"We have as much right to stay here as you do. You just like ordering everyone around. You always have."

The injustice of it! I wasn't even the oldest and they were keen to come. And all this anger coming from Auntie Beth who was usually so mild.

"It's a pity that you don't come more often to help, rather than swanning off abroad."

"Children, children, calm down," Pappa had pleaded with them, but they took no notice. He gave up and went out into the garden. Granny disappeared into the kitchen while Mum and Auntie Beth went upstairs. There was more shouting and doors banging.

Part of me was pleased to hear Mum being told off but I sensed that somehow I would be punished for it. Granny made a heap of pancakes for us children. Usually I loved them, hot, squidgy and oozing butter but this time they clogged my throat. My aunt and cousins left on the morning steamer. What was it all about? The chips were just an excuse for a fight. As an only child I find it hard to understand rows between brothers and sisters, but I know if that awful old witch, the great churchgoer Flora MacKinnon, hadn't caused trouble none of this would have happened.

Granny prods me, 'You're away with the fairies. Let's get home. You're not hungry, are you? I thought we would have boiled eggs for lunch,' she says as she reaches up to her maroon hat with the wide brim and the black ribbon and removes the pin. She brushes the crown and asks me to put it away, 'carefully, mind', on the shelf by the front door.

I'm hungry but decide to keep quiet. I remember that I have a chocolate bar in my case, left over from the journey.

'You know that your Pappa and I both have a nap on Sunday afternoons,' Granny says after we've eaten.

After all that excitement of the service, too, I think to myself. I decide to lie on my bed and see if I can tune into Radio Caroline. I tinker around with the dial but there's a lot of interference. Crazed with boredom I get up and look out of the window. The house is on a corner and I can see the road ahead leading up to the moor. The front gardens are all tiny and fenced in to stop wandering sheep invading and eating everything. There's space at the side where Pappa used to grow vegetables but it's all overgrown now. I decide to slip downstairs and go out for a walk. I suppose that's forbidden too. As I close the gate behind me, I feel something pushing against the back of my leg and look around to see a small dog with shaggy whitish hair, a long back and dumpy little legs. It tilts its head on one side and wags its frond-like tail.

I crouch down, laughing, 'And who are you?'

It's a Skye terrier, I think. I remember that most of the dogs here are either working collies or terriers of some sort, usually small grey mixtures of different breeds. I crouch down and ruffle the hair on its head. It nuzzles me and I think how I've always wanted a dog but Mum isn't keen because we're all out during the day. This animal hasn't a collar and when I stand up it starts to follow me.

'I can't take you home with me and I don't know where you live.'

The dog tilts its head again. I don't want to wake Granny and Pappa up to ask them and decide to carry on down the road,

The Second Surge of the Sea

hoping that it will show me its home. It trots along happily beside me, stopping now and then to cock its leg but shows no sign of wanting to go into any of the gardens. I bend down again and eyeball it.

'Where do you live then?'

The dog stares back, its tongue hanging out.

'Down the brae, at the Matheson's.'

I jump out of my skin and look round.

'It's you, Pappa. I didn't hear you. I thought for a moment that the dog had learnt to talk.'

He chuckles, 'Come on, Margaret. We'll take Dileas back home. His name means "faithful" but he's a bit of a rascal and always escaping. We'll tell your Granny we were out on a mission of mercy if she asks.'

I notice that he's limping and wearing his slippers. He sees me looking.

'I can't bear shoes or even welly boots these days. The doctor says it's the circulation not working properly in my legs, but I can't bear sitting inside all day.'

I don't know what to say. It's difficult when old people talk about their ailments. So, I just nod.

'It's why I had to give up the fishing and I'm supposed to stop smoking, too.'

'The boat, "The Brothers' Pride" it was called, wasn't it?'

'Aye. We left her to rot on the shore in the end.' He sighs.

'We always had a Skye terrier when I was growing up. One of them, Bobby, used to come out on the boat. He was a fearless wee dog.'

'Well, I've heard of a ship's cat but not a ship's dog. His name rings a bell. Wasn't there a famous Skye terrier called Bobby?'

His face lights up making his blue eyes crinkle at the edges so that they almost disappear.

'Aye, he was the second Bobby, named after the one at Greyfriars, in Edinburgh.'

I'm curious. All the family stories I know have come from Granny. Pappa was the quiet one, always sitting smoking his pipe, out in the garden or down at the shore, watching the boats.

'Tell me about your Bobby.'

He looks hard at me, 'Are you sure?'

'Yes, I would like to hear. I've always wanted a dog but we've never had one.'

I reach out to touch his arm.

He smiles again, 'It's a way of passing a boring Sabbath afternoon, right enough.'

I smile back, feeling as if we're fellow conspirators.

CHAPTER 2

Pappa closes his eyes for a minute, before speaking.

'You know our old family house, down by the shore?'

I nod, thinking of the row of narrow stone fishermen's houses at Bayfield, built so close to the sea that they seem to lean over to gaze at their reflections in the water.

'I was running home from school one day…'

'How old were you?'

He frowns, 'I suppose that I was about ten or eleven, just before the First War. My Pappa always said it was good luck to be born near the start of a new century. And now, of course, I'm nearing my three score years and ten, my life span as the Bible tells us.'

I smother a sigh. It's so boring when old people go on about their age.

He half smiles as if he's read my thoughts and carries on.

'I always ran back all the way – glad to escape. I stopped to catch my breath as I reached the shore. Something small, with long hair, streaked grey and white like a winter sky, came bouncing towards me. He was tripping over his paws, his long tail streaking behind him and bat's ears twitching. He danced in circles round my feet and jumped up to lick my nose. I bent down to rub my face against his.'

'Bobby?' I ask.

'The same. I always talked to our dogs. That's what reminded me when I saw you with Dileas. I've found a name for you, wee one. I'll call you "Bobby", I told him. I rushed inside to tell Mamma. She was wiping her hands at the sink, "Don't give him a name. You know we can't keep him."

Well, I turned away because I didn't want her to see the tears in my eyes. I knew she was right. Raising pups and selling them brought in money but it was so hard to lose the last one in the litter.

"Have a glass of milk and a scone. I've just this minute taken them out of the oven."

She ruffled my hair but her kindness didn't take the hurt away. I nibbled at a scone but didn't taste it.

"Bobby's an odd name for a dog, mind."

I explained that Miss Matheson had told us a story today about a dog called Bobby. He was a Skye terrier too. He belonged to a shepherd called Old Jock who was down in Edinburgh when he took ill. He was buried in Greyfriars kirk yard and the wee dog wouldn't leave his grave.

Mamma stood up and went to the sink to peel the potatoes for tea.

"I wonder what a shepherd was doing in Edinburgh. Off you go now from under my feet."

The pup soon learnt his name as he grew bigger. I caught mackerel to feed him and no-one came to buy him.'

'That was good, wasn't it? That you kept him, I mean.'

'Yes and No. If Bobby was sold, I would lose him, but he would be safe. If not? Maybe Mamma would let me keep him but I couldn't be sure. He might disappear one day, like other kittens and puppies had.'

He sees the question in my eyes.

'My big brother Iain told me that sometimes Dadda took a wriggling sack out to his boat and came back home with it empty. I didn't want to think about that. But we had fun, Bobby and I. We had stepping-stones from our house over to the opposite shore that we used at low tide. Bobby often fumbled with his feet and fell in. The mud turned his white hair black. He loved

The Second Surge of the Sea

to chase the gulls and got seaweed tangled in his hair so that he looked like a sea monster. When he got really dirty I took him for a swim so that Mamma wouldn't complain about him bringing mud into the house.'

'So, he stayed safe with you?'

Pappa shakes his head.

'One day we were sitting on a rock, letting the sun dry us, after a swim. I heard footsteps behind me: "Good day, young man. Is that a Skye terrier puppy you have there?" I turned round, wondering who was speaking in that funny voice. It was a tall lady, wearing a broad hat that hid her face. Her bright blue gown flowed down over shiny brown shoes and the lace at her neck frothed like sea spray. I could feel my face redden like a furnace. There I was sitting with just my drawers on! I jumped up and hopped on one leg to pull on my breeks.'

I smile at the picture he is painting. Why would he be so upset when he was only a boy?

'Crash! Ouch! My feet slipped on the wet rock, and I landed hard on my bottom, feeling even more silly. Bobby made it worse, rushing around in circles, barking. The lady turned away until I got dressed.

"I'm sorry to startle you but I've been reading the story of Greyfriars Bobby," she said, with a smile. I tried to pull my wits and my dignity together and answered, "Our teacher told us the story. He was such a faithful wee dog," I explained to her.

The lady replied, "I'm so pleased because I was hoping to find a Skye terrier before I return to Canada. Do you live nearby? I would like to speak to your parents."

My heart was pounding now. Did she want to buy Bobby? But he couldn't go away over the ocean, could he? Mamma was flustered when she saw the grand lady on her doorstep. She invited her into the front room and dragged me into the kitchen,

"*Oh mo creach*! The house is a mess! Go and brush your hair and then talk to the lady while I make the tea."

I felt shy, but I needn't have worried because the lady did all the talking. They're like that, aren't they, the folk from over there? They have plenty to say for themselves.

"My Grandaddy came from Skye, you know, many years ago. He told me stories about the long-haired cows but especially the long-haired dogs. I've seen the cows, but these are the first of the dogs I've seen."

Then she picked Bobby up and he nuzzled against her neck. I clenched my fists. No-one but me ever picked him up! Mamma called me to bring the plates through. They were piled high with oatcakes, scones, and shortbread. Usually enough to make my mouth water but I felt sick at the sight of them.

"Off with you outside while I talk with the lady," Mamma said.

I walked on tiptoe round the side of the house and crouched down under the window to listen to what was happening. I could hear Bobby whining. I couldn't bear to stay any longer and wandered down to the shore. I skimmed stones out to sea with all my strength. At last, the front door opened and there was the lady. How I hated her when I saw Bobby struggling in her arms. She shook Mamma's hand. Then she turned to me and said, "Don't fret young man. I'll take good care of him. He'll be very happy."

Mamma glared at me, but I couldn't make myself smile or say a word.'

Now, Pappa stops talking and bends down to pat Dileas.

'Off you go, now. You're back home.'

He opens the gate for the dog which trots inside, tail up without a backward glance.

'Is that the end of the story, Pappa?' I sigh, realising that I've been holding my breath.

The Second Surge of the Sea

He laughs and carries on.

'Well, Mamma was very happy. She'd paid us well. She really wanted that puppy, she'd said. But I couldn't bear to watch as the lady left, Bobby tucked under her arm, his fluffy tail round her waist.

"The wee dog will be fine," Mamma said as she tried to take my hand, but I pulled away.

The next day I didn't run home from school as usual. I slouched along with my hands in my pockets. I didn't want to go inside the house with no Bobby there. So, I walked past the other houses towards the headland. I kicked a few stones and looked out to the bay. I could see the steamer heading for Kyle. I liked watching it usually, but not today. The boat left a trail of foam, stretching out like a tail as it sailed away. The water settled down, but I could see something moving towards the shore. What was it? I screwed up my eyes to see. A seal? No, it looked too small. A seal pup? An otter? A big fish? I couldn't make it out. What did it matter anyway? I shrugged and plodded home. I was almost there when I heard a sound.

"It sounds like……," I thought…but no – my mind was playing tricks.

But there it was again. I ran down to the shore and waded through the waves, shouting, "Bobby! I don't believe it. Is it really you? You've come back home!"

It was Bobby himself – tired, soaking wet and hoarse with too much barking. But his eyes were shining, and his tail wouldn't stop wagging. Later, when we were all sitting down after supper and Bobby was fast asleep on my lap, Dadda said, scratching his beard, "Well, I've never heard of a dog jumping ship like that."

"Bobby's such a clever dog and it was me who taught him to swim. Will the Canadian lady come back to get him?" I said, my heart in my mouth.

"I doubt it," Mamma said. "She would likely think the dog was drowned after it jumped overboard."

"You got a good price for him so…", I whispered.

My parents looked at each other and then at me. Dadda nodded.

"Aye, you can keep him. He's as loyal as yon first Bobby," Mamma said with a smile.

Bobby barked and wagged that long curly tail when he heard his name.

"See, he understands," I said.'

Now, Pappa falls silent. I sigh, not wanting to talk and break the spell. I don't think that I've ever heard him talk so much at one time, ever before. I have a sudden memory of sitting on the floor at infant school when Miss Pratt used to tell us a story at the end of the school day. When it ended and she closed the book, I used to sigh that same sigh with the feeling that I was suddenly bumping down to earth before we leapt to our feet to scurry out of the classroom.

I feel that bumping down again now. 'I really enjoyed hearing about Bobby.'

Pappa shrugs and looks down, 'We had better get back or your Granny will be thinking we've made a run for it.'

'Can we do this again? I would like to hear more stories.'

I feel sort of awkward asking him. I don't know why. Maybe because I wonder if he'll think I'm being childish, but he smiles shyly and nods.

CHAPTER 3

We arrive back to a chilly reception. Granny is standing in the doorway, arms folded, eyes blazing, and mouth clamped tight. She doesn't speak until we're inside and the door closed behind us.

'Where on earth have you been? Gadding around on the Sabbath!'

Pappa looks hangdog so I speak up.

'I went out to stretch my legs and saw Dileas wandering around. Then Pappa appeared and we walked along together to take him home.'

I keep quiet about the story of Bobby. I'm not sure why but I notice Pappa's shoulders relax and I sense that I've done the right thing. I'm cross with Granny. I thought that she wanted me here to cheer Pappa up and now I'm being told off for doing just that. She goes off to put the kettle on and when she brings the tea through, she seems to be in a better mood.

'Here's some pancakes. I remember you preferred them hot from the griddle, but I couldn't make fresh ones today.'

"I know, the bloody Sabbath", I think to myself, but I smile and take one. It's OK but not as I remember the fresh ones, butter dripping off the sides as I juggled them in my hands so that I didn't burn my fingers.

'Are you going to write to your mother tomorrow?' she says. 'I saw that you had some postcards, but you'll need to send a proper letter.'

My mouth is full, so I make a sort of grunting noise. It's none of her business! She must have been poking around in my bag. The cards are for friends at school and maybe one for Neil.

Mum doesn't need a letter from me when Granny sends one every week and, anyway, I'm still cross with her for packing me off up here.

Later on, I go upstairs and look through the cards. I decide to send one with Highland cattle on it to Neil. I'll write it now and post it tomorrow when I go out with Pappa. Maybe I'll send a letter later, but I want to keep things cool, not to sound desperate about missing him, even if that's what I feel. We've only been going out for a few weeks. He's my first proper boyfriend. We've been for walks, holding hands with me worrying about my sweaty palms, cuddled in the pictures, bumped noses and kissed awkwardly a few times, our teeth getting in the way. Mummy doesn't approve of him because he lives in a council house. What a snob! What does she think Granny and Pappa live in? Years ago, when I didn't understand what she was talking about, she said that I mustn't tell anyone ever on pain of execution, that they lived in a council house.

Dear Neil,

I thought that you might like a picture of some of the hairy locals. The bus got held up by a herd of these on the road. It's a good job that they have horns, or you couldn't tell what was the back and what was the front.

I stop and chew my biro. Postcards are awkward. Two sentences aren't enough to fill the space, but you can't say anything important either.

I go out for a walk each day with my Grandad and he tells me stories from the past. Maybe I will write them up as an oral history project.

That idea only pops into my head as I write it down. Miss Greaves said something about oral history being a newish idea, a way of preserving true accounts that would otherwise be lost, although of course memories aren't always reliable.

The next morning Pappa and I set off down the hill.

'Maybe I can manage to walk down to Scorrybreac if I have a few stops on the way,' he says.

'I was wondering if you heard from the Canadian woman again,' I say.

'Not a peep, but I was on a knife edge every morning when the postie came in case she wrote a letter asking for her money back. But then I forgot because it was soon my birthday. Mamma made me a sponge cake and I blew all the candles out in one go so that meant good luck for the next year. Dadda gave me a collar for Bobby, made out of an old leather strap that he oiled and polished until it looked like new. Mamma plaited lengths of rope together for a lead. Even Màiri gave me something for Bobby, an old hairbrush to groom him.'

I'm about to ask a question but Pappa gets in first, 'Màiri was my big bossy sister and Iain was the oldest. He gave me a ball for Bobby to chase.'

He looks thoughtful and I wait a moment before prompting him.

'What happened then?'

'A few days later I was asleep with Bobby curled up at my feet. I woke up with a jolt and once I was awake, I felt hungry. I padded down the stairs to get an oatcake to eat but as I put my hand on the kitchen door I heard voices. I touched Bobby's muzzle to keep him quiet and listened. I could hear Dadda's voice.

"Once I'm back from the herring fishing, we'll need to think about moving away."

I nearly gasped in shock. Then Mamma spoke, "Well, we've talked about following your brother to Canada but it's so far. We would never see Skye again."

She sounded close to tears.

"Or else we go south", Dadda went on, "I could earn good money as a cooper down in the Lowlands. The distilleries always need barrels. I'm sick of living hand to mouth."

"Remember I'll earn money too when the salmon come." Iain piped up, "And Màiri's nearly fourteen. She'll be leaving school and getting work."

"Don't you tell me what to do, Iain. I want to stay on at school. Miss Ferguson says I'll make an excellent pupil teacher." My sister sounded angry.

"But it will be years before you earn anything. We can't afford to keep you all that time," Mamma said.

"But I've set my heart on it!" she wailed and flung the door open. I couldn't get up the stairs in time before she saw me and pushed me against the wall before I could get into my room.

"What are you doing? Eavesdropping on things that are none of your business."

I wriggled out of her grasp.

"It's my business too. I'm part of the family."

She followed me into my room and laid into me, "What do you do, spoilt baby? I do the milking, churn the butter, look after the hens, sweep the house. You just play around."

She caught sight of Bobby trying to hide under the bed.

"And that dog of yours eats us out of house and home."

"That's not fair! I catch mackerel for him and snare rabbits. He'll soon be big enough to catch them himself. I know you want to stay on at school but it's not my fault Mamma and Dadda can't afford it."

She let me go and, tossing her dark, curly hair, stormed down the stairs. I went back to bed with my stomach rumbling. Maybe getting older wasn't so grand. It made me old enough to worry about things but too young to do anything about them. I hated

The Second Surge of the Sea

the idea of leaving the sea and the mountains to live in a big, dirty city. I wanted to run free and grow up to be a fisherman, like Dadda and Iain.'

Pappa stops and leans on a gate post.

I want to hear more.

'And did you all move away? What about Màiri? Did she get to stay on at school? Girls didn't get many chances at education, did they?'

'So many questions! I can't make it down to Scorrybreac today. My leg is really bad. Let me rest a minute and we'll turn back.'

While I wait, I think about how much life has changed. I can't imagine leaving school at the end of the third year when you're starting to think what subjects you really like and which ones you hate. For me, it was geography I loathed. I couldn't even fold up one of those Ordnance Survey maps back into the fold marks, let alone make sense of anything inside them.

Granny seems in a better mood than yesterday, so when we get back I decide to ask her about her schooldays.

'Would you have liked to stay on longer at school, like we can today?'

She spends a long time swallowing her mouthful of tea before she answers.

'I didn't think about it because I knew I would have to leave. Most of us did.'

'But did you like school? I remember when I was small, you used to recite poems to me you had learnt by heart at school. There was one about a toy soldier who was gathering dust because the boy who owned him had grown up. I thought that was sad.'

Her face softens.

'You can't hold on to childish things. I was in the middle of a big family. Mamma needed my help. She took in washing to make extra money. It was hard work doing it all by hand and turning the big mangle to squeeze the water out. Then I got the chance to go to Glasgow, to work in a doctor's house. I started doing the rough work like laying the fires, but the lady of the house found out I could sew so I got to make the children's clothes. That was better.'

I can't think of anything worse. I loathed needlework at school. Luckily if you had any brains you got to do Latin instead.

'You're lucky to be allowed to stay on at school. You can get a nice, steady job in an office,' she says.

'But I don't want to do that. I'm going to university.'

'Won't that be wasted when you get married and have a family?'

'I have no plans to get married and be stuck as a housewife. I can't think of anything worse!'

She frowns. 'What nonsense! All girls want to settle down and have a family.'

I take a deep breath. 'The world is changing Granny. Girls can be independent these days, not hanging around waiting for some man to marry them.'

'Well, you're lucky to have that choice. You had better make sure that you work a bit harder at school.'

That proves that Mummy has been talking about me behind my back. I feel trapped and angry.

'I remember when girls didn't have much choice about who they married,' Pappa said, stirring more sugar into his tea.

'My own Granny married when she was only seventeen to her cousin who was thirty-three years older. He had come back home after going to Australia.'

'That's disgusting! He was probably older than her father.'

Granny shrugs.

'That's how it was. People had to live. It was either that or stay at home to look after your parents when they became old. Then,

The Second Surge of the Sea

when they died, the oldest son would get the croft and you had to hope that he would support you. Life was hard if you were a spinster or a widow. Unless you were the gentry, of course. You must thank the Lord for your good fortune, my lass.'

How sick I am of being told what I should think! Then Pappa looks up, his clear blue eyes meet mine and he winks.

CHAPTER 4

I wake up, finding myself looking forward to my walk with Pappa. Well, I have to make the best of things, I suppose. I hurry over breakfast and go out in the garden. I find him looking at the overgrown vegetable patch.

'I can clear that for you, and we can plant some tatties.'

He shakes his head and pats my hand.

'I can tell you live in a town. July is far too late for that.'

I shrug, 'Well, if the ground is ready, you can plant some next spring. Maybe I can come and help you.'

Where did that come from? Next spring I'll be busy revising for the exams, but I suppose I could do that here.

He sighs, 'We'll see.'

'I want to hear what happened next with Bobby. Màiri sounds like a horrible bossy big sister.'

'She wasn't so bad. Later I got to know her better. She had a lot of courage.'

I'm longing to ask him more questions, but I know I can't rush him. What's that annoying thing that Dad says, "Softly, softly catchee monkey"?

We walk slowly down the hill. I have to keep stopping for him as he shuffles along. Then he straightens up, bends his hand to his back and starts talking.

'I remember lying awake for a long time after she stormed out. Bobby jumped up on the bed and I lay there thinking. I couldn't get back to sleep because my stomach was churning. I hated the thought of leaving Skye. I had never known anywhere else. I felt sick at the idea of living in a dirty city without a blade of grass anywhere. I tossed and turned listening to Bobby snoring

The Second Surge of the Sea

and envying him not having any worries. Then I remembered my Granny always said that no worry looked so bad in the morning.'

'And was she right?'

'Aye. She was. "You're daydreaming this morning, Sandy. Stop dawdling over your porridge or you'll be late for school. Listen, MacDonald the milk is here already."

That was Mamma scolding me as she passed me the big jug and took a broken biscuit from the tin. I ran outside and there was Rab, his ears twitching. He tossed his head and snickered. I loved the way he always breathed into my hand with his whiskery nose and scooped up the biscuit with his huge tongue. I buried my face in his neck and his rough mane tickled my nose.

"I can't get him to walk past your door until he gets his *strupag* here first," Mr MacDonald said as he poured the frothing milk into my jug. I carried it carefully inside. "Hurry up, slowcoach." That's Màiri tripping down the stairs. Always pleased to be going to school. Not like me. I could think of a hundred things I would rather be doing – fishing for mackerel, running up the hills with Bobby, out in a boat with my friends, playing shinty. I slouched out the door.

The idea leapt into my mind like the flash of a salmon swimming upstream, right in the middle of doing long multiplication sums. I must have gasped aloud because Miss MacGregor stood up from her tall desk at the front and strode towards me. She snatched up my slate, peered at my work and then dangled it at arm's length.

"I thought for a moment, Alexander MacPherson, that you had discovered a correct answer, but I'm doomed to disappointment."

She slammed the slate down on my desk, making me flinch, an expression of disgust on her face as if she had just smelt a decaying fish.

"You'll never be a scholar like your sister Mary."

I hated it when she turned our names into the English. I was Sandy to my family and friends – Alasdair to everyone else. She had taken a dislike to me. Twice she strapped me across my hand for speaking Gaelic – the language I learnt at my mother's knee.'

Pappa stops dead and I nearly bump into him.

'That's wrong! She sounds like a nasty piece of work. But I thought that your teacher was Miss Matheson who told you about Greyfriars Bobby.'

'What?' He shakes his head like a horse bothered with flies.

'Bobby swam back home in the summer holidays. When I went back to school in August, I moved up a class. Miss Matheson was young and kind, but Miss MacGregor was a dried-up old maid.'

'I remember changing teachers and what a shock it was to get a nasty one. No escape – you had to sit in that same classroom all year. I got a nasty teacher, Miss Lugsden, who took a dislike to me and made my life miserable.'

'So, what did you do wrong? I thought you were good at your studies.'

'I stood up to her when she tried to make me learn to knit.'

'Well, I can imagine you doing that,' he says with a laugh.

'Friday afternoons we did craftwork. She said that we girls would learn to knit, and the boys would make wooden boats that they could sail in the stream behind the school.'

'Let me guess – you wanted to make a boat?'

'I did and I asked her politely if I could, but she wouldn't let me. So, I sat there every Friday afternoon with my arms folded and refused to do anything. Every now and then she would come along, grab the needles, and do a few stitches on the scarf. Making scarves in the middle of summer!'

'You didn't get the tawse?'

The Second Surge of the Sea

'Like the cane?'

'A leather strap, rather than a stick, very sore when it hit you.'

'No, but it was worse in a way because she kept picking on me – being sarcastic, making me do all the clearing up and listen to the slow readers. And she put me off knitting for ever. But what was the idea that leapt into your head?'

'Well, when Kirsty MacLeod who sat next to me got over her giggling and my red face faded, I decided that after school I would go up to Home Farm and find Mr Munro. He was there in the yard, watching the horses being led back to their stables. Lovely Clydesdales they were with glossy brown coats and feet like dinner plates, smelt of hay when you put your head against their flanks. Big beasts. I had to jump up to reach the bridle.

"You look out of breath, lad," Mr Munro said.

I gulped and said my piece, "Mr MacDonald says that I have a way with horses, and I was hoping I could maybe have a job. I'm still at school so I can't help with deliveries, but I could come early and help load up the carts."

Mr Munro looked me up and down. Then he stroked his chin. "Hold out your arm, lad."

He squeezed his big, rough fingers around my arm, above the elbow. It hurt but I didn't show it. "See how my fingers meet? Your arm's only a wee stick of a thing. You're not big enough to lift milk churns. Come back when you've grown."

His smile was kind but that didn't help. Everyone thought that I was too young, too wee, or too stupid to be any use at anything. I wandered home, with my head down but when I reached the shore, I heard a bark. There was Bobby running towards me, his tail spinning and his tongue hanging out as if he was laughing. I bent down to pat the dancing dog.

"You're always in a good mood. To you, I'm the best lad in the world."

Mamma's scones cheered me up.

"His lordship came for his kilt socks, today. He paid me a few shillings – not what they're worth."

"That's not right when you spent so long knitting them."

"That's how it goes but he did give me something else."

"What?"

"Go and look in the pantry."

I opened the door and found a basket, covered with a cloth. Bobby had a good sniff, and I could hear cheeping noises. I lifted the cloth and found four, no five balls of fluff with gaping beaks. Chicks! But they weren't the usual yellow ones. They were speckled dark brown and had spoon shaped beaks.

Mamma came out, "Do you know what they are?"

"They look like ducks but they're not white."

"His Lordship said that they're fancy ducks – 'Indian Runners'. They're kept for laying eggs, like hens. I thought you could look after them and sell their eggs. They're bigger than hens' eggs and good for baking.'"

'So, the day turned out not so badly, after all. And did you make money from them? Did Bobby chase them?'

'Well, he knew not to chase the hens. He used to guard the ducklings while I was at school. Barked at the seagulls and rounded them up in the evening so they could sleep in the shed. When the fluff came off and they grew proper feathers I could see why they were called 'Runners'. They stood upright and trotted along.

"They'll be ready to lay soon. We'll leave the first eggs to hatch and build up the flock," Mamma said.

I couldn't wait for them to lay their first eggs. A few days later I spotted two big, blue-green eggs in a patch of grass near the shore. I was surprised at how cold they were when I picked them up and took them inside to show Mamma.

"That's ducks for you. They don't get broody like hens."

The Second Surge of the Sea

"But the poor wee ducklings could die before they hatch."

"Well, you could always keep them warm inside your shirt."

"I can't do that! Everyone at school would laugh at me and poke the eggs until they broke."

Mamma laughed and dug me in the ribs.

"I'm only teasing. We'll put the eggs under old Dolly. She's a good broody hen."

That's what we did, and the ducklings hatched, looking just like the first ones. Dolly the hen looked after the ducklings as if they were her own chicks, clucking at them to follow her as she pecked the ground for seeds and insects to eat.'

'And did you sell plenty of eggs in the end?'

I'm getting a bit bored with all this talk of poultry. But Pappa won't be rushed.

'I did in the end but there were a few problems first. Not long afterwards I heard a terrible racket when I was coming home from school. Squawking, clucking, and barking. It sounded as if a war had broken out. What was attacking the birds? I found Dolly running up and down along the shore as if she was demented. Bobby was running along the shore with a duckling dangling out of his mouth. He dropped it and rushed into the sea again, barking his head off, chasing after another of the ducklings. I shouted at him, "What on earth are you doing?"

I would have to tie him up if he was harming the birds. What had come over him?

Mamma rushed out and laughed.

"Well, it was bound to happen. The poor wee dog was only trying to help. The hen is frantic because she wants the ducklings back on dry land but they're following their nature. Let's get them back and shut in for the night."

That took a long time because the ducklings kept trying to get back in the water. When I had my tea, I fell asleep with my nose in my bowl of rice pudding and Bobby was snoring at my feet. That wasn't the end of it all, though. I woke up in the middle of the night with Bobby barking in my ears. I thought at first that he was dreaming about the ducklings, but he ran downstairs and started scratching at the back door. He was growling and the hairs of his neck were standing on end. I followed him as he charged ahead towards the hen house. There was a scrabbling at the door and Bobby leapt forward, sinking his teeth into a long tail. A fox! It ran off, snarling and something fell from its mouth, something that rolled over and quacked. I picked up the duckling. It had lost some feathers but didn't seem to be hurt. Heart pounding, I opened the door of the hen house. Had the fox got inside and killed all the birds? But I could see them all roosting inside. I must have forgotten to count the ducklings and this one got left outside. I put it with the others and crept back to my bed as quietly as I could, but Mamma had heard the barking. While I was telling her, Màiri appeared rubbing her eyes.

"Why was that silly wee dog of yours barking?"

"That silly wee dog has just earned his keep by seeing off a fox," I replied proudly.'

Pappa smiles, so I do too, but inside I'm feeling bored. When I asked him to tell me stories about his youth, I didn't mean Beatrix Potter type stuff. Jemima Puddleduck might have been my favourite story once but that was a long time ago. I'll have to find a way to move him onto the First World War.

CHAPTER 5

Next day, after lunch I'm desperate to escape the house so I offer to go down to the Post Office and see if there are any letters. Granny is pleased, of course, because she thinks I'm being helpful, but it gives me a chance to see if Neil has replied to my postcard. It's a strange system I think as I queue up for the letters. Why don't they get delivered to the houses in Portree? The Post Office is a huge building, much too big for a small place. I suppose that people in more outlying villages manage to get a delivery.

The woman smiles at me and hands me a letter, but I can't manage to smile back when I see that it's addressed to Granny and I recognise my mother's writing on the envelope. I'm wearing a mac because it's showery again and go to mooch down on the shore before going back. There are a few tourists around, but I don't bother to look at them. I reach as far as the Black Rock. It's low tide, so the last part of it sticks out like a bony finger. If you wait for the sea to come in, it disappears. Maybe I could tell Neil about it – how Bonnie Prince Charlie got a boat from there to the Outer Isles when he was a fugitive after Culloden. A tatty looking cormorant is perched at the highest point, fanning out its wings and giving me a suspicious look. I remember Granny saying that she used to eat cormorant as a child. It had black flesh and tasted strongly of fish – sounds disgusting.

A cold wind is battering my face, so I turn back and it's then I see a girl about my age, with a collie at her heels. Her hood is up so I can't see her face properly but when she smiles, I smile back and say 'Hello.'

'Not much of a day, is it?'

I agree, 'But that's Skye weather, isn't it?'

She nods, 'Are you walking back to the village?'

I say that I am, and we talk as we head back. Her name is Catriona, and it turns out that we have quite a lot in common.

'It doesn't sound as if you have a Skye accent.'

'No. I was brought up in Inverness although my Granny lives on Skye. It was quite hard when I started at the High School here because everyone else has known each other since they were in their prams.'

She doesn't say why she's on Skye now and I don't want to be nosey and ask. She's small and dainty, unlike me, and has brown eyes and a tanned skin. I don't envy her being small. I'm glad that I'm tall and strong but I wish I could tan rather than having a white skin, splodged with freckles. We walk to the end of my road together because she lives further up Stormy Hill Road.

'We could meet up again if you like?' I say, trying not to sound desperate.

'Why not? I have to take Bracken out anyway. I'll see you tomorrow.'

I'm skipping as I push the back door open and almost bump into Granny who is hovering there.

'Who was that you were talking to?'

'Her name's Catriona. She used to live in Inverness.'

'I know! You're not to mix with that family.'

'Why not?' I can feel my heart thumping and my face turning red.

'They're a tinker family, that's why.'

'How come they live in a house then, like everyone else?'

'That doesn't change their spots. They're still tinkers and you can't trust them. And they don't go to church – not any church.'

I bite my lips hard. I don't want to risk answering back. 'I'll just go upstairs. Here's your letter.'

Later on, when I come downstairs for a cup of tea, I get the

The Second Surge of the Sea

frozen treatment. Pappa winks at me while Granny is putting more water in the pot.

'You didn't write to your mother,' he mouths behind her back.

I wait until she's sitting down again and then ask, all innocent, 'Did Mum have much news?'

She takes a deep breath and then spits out, 'Why didn't you write to her?'

I open my eyes wide. 'I knew that you would give her all the news.'

'But she was hurt not to hear from you.'

'Too bad,' I think, 'I was hurt to be exiled to the Gulag.'

'I can understand why she was cross with you. You're not a nice, thoughtful girl like you used to be. You'll have to work very hard to be as good and clever as your mother.'

I clench my jaw to stop myself making retching noises. I'm good at keeping a poker face. I'll find a way of seeing Catriona again. I worked out a plan when I was determined not to play hockey at school anymore. I hated all that running around in shorts, getting corned beef legs from the cold and bruises from the hard ball. When I started in the Sixth Form, I deliberately missed the first lesson with the new P.E. teacher so that my name never went on the register. Plan worked! No more hockey.

Now, I nod to Granny and say, 'I'll write to her.'

I do write, too, although it's a short letter, saying nothing much. What does Mum expect? Tear-stained pages about missing home? The next morning I'm down at the Post Office early. Surely Neil will have written? I pick up the two letters, something official in a brown envelope for Granny and Pappa and one for me. My heart leaps into my mouth. The postmark is right. I stuff it into my pocket and hurry down to the shore. I don't want to read it anywhere public with so many nosey people around. I perch myself on a rock and tear it open.

Dear Mags,

Hope you are alright in the wilds.

I gasp when I realise it's not from him. Of course not. I don't know what his writing is like. We either meet on the school bus or phone. I should have realised that it's Sue's writing, my friend from school. I read on:

Nothing much happening here but there is something I need to tell you before anyone else does. Neil has been avoiding me in the street and looking shifty. Then I saw him in town with that snooty Jill. They didn't see me, and they were holding hands! They used to kill a messenger who brought bad news, didn't they? But I thought you should know.

I scrunch the page up but it's no use. I can't pretend that I haven't read it. I'm shaking with pain and rage. What a coward he was, not to tell me! I pick up stones and hurl them into the sea until my arm aches. Then I walk back, feeling alone in the world. There's no-one I can talk to and even worse, I have to pretend that I'm fine. So, when Pappa smiles at me and asks if I want to go out for our walk, I find myself snapping at him.

'I hope that you've got a more interesting story this time. I wanted to hear about what happened in the First World War, not stuff about dogs and ducklings.'

I feel really bad when I see his eyes widen and his lips shrink into a thin line.

'I didn't know I was boring you.'

'I'm sorry. You weren't boring me. I'm feeling grumpy because I've heard some bad news from a friend.'

'About a lad, maybe?'

'How do you know?' I gasp.

The Second Surge of the Sea

'Well, I was young once although it's hard for you to imagine it.'

'It is about a boy, but I can't bear to talk about it.'

'Let's go for our walk then but you'll have to give me some time to work towards the War. Let me untangle my thoughts first. They're like nets full of holes.'

'I do like Bobby, but I want to know about the people too. Did your brother, Iain, go to war?'

CHAPTER 6

'I can't go straight to talking about the war because it's tied up with Iain's new job and so much else.'

'I'm sorry, Pappa, for being so grumpy. I've nothing against the poor wee dog. I like dogs.'

'You've got the impatience of youth.'

We walk towards the shore, and I try to slow my pace to his.

'Anyway, over to Iain. I've been thinking a lot about him. "How would you like to come to Inverness with me?" he'd said to me one day.

'I jiggled with excitement. I'd never been there – never even crossed to the mainland.

"Will we go on the train?" I asked.

"Stop jumping around like a fish on a hook and I'll tell you. We'll go down on the train but come back a different way."

"On a boat? That would take a while, but I don't mind missing school."

"You like school as little as I did but not on a boat."

"On a cart?"

"No, guess again."

"On horseback?"

Iain smiled and shook his head.

"I give in. It can't be on foot. It would take us too long."

"Well, wait and see. If you stop pestering me with questions you can bring Bobby."

The next day we caught the steamer for Kyle. Mamma packed oatcakes, cheese, and scones for our lunch.'

'I notice how you always remember the food you ate,' I tease Pappa.

'Well, I was always hungry. We were lucky. We weren't rich but there was always enough to eat. Not like many, who had only a barrel of salted mackerel to last all winter. It was a sunny day, I remember, so we stayed up on deck. The wind blew Bobby's long hair as we leant on the rail.'

'I bet you held onto him tightly.'

'I did! But he showed no sign of leaping overboard. Then the excitement of the train. You're used to it but for me it was all new. We found seats in the front carriage and my face was glued to the window as the engine went clackety-clack over the rails, winding its way along the shore and then back over the moors. I even forgot about my stomach. Then at Inverness there were so many people hurrying along the platform. "Don't stand gawping. We have to get a move on," Iain said.

He took me round the back of the station where there were workshops, men hammering iron to make engine parts. I had to put my hands over my ears because of the racket. We stopped at a big shed made of rusty corrugated iron. It looked ready to fall over but Iain opened the door, and I had a glimpse of something black and gleaming. When I got closer, I could see shiny lamps, glowing like owl's eyes, big wheels and a door opening onto glossy leather seats. A man wearing overalls appeared, wiping his hands on a rag.

"Have you not seen one of these before? Hop up laddie and have a proper look."

I wiped my hands on my trousers, put my foot on the ledge under the door and lowered my backside down carefully on the red leather.

"It's like a carriage but without a horse to pull it," I said running my hands over the wood.

"Well sometimes folk call them, 'horseless carriages' but they're much faster than a horse and don't need to be fed hay. Why don't you blow the horn?"

I did – and made Bobby bark in surprise.

"Did you build it yourself?"

"No, laddie. I just look after the engine." He stroked the metal as if it was a horse. "This beauty is an Arrol-Johnstone, built in Dumfries, the only motor car made in Scotland."

"It's the most amazing thing I've ever seen but who does it belong to?"

"I wondered how long it would take you to ask, Sandy. It's the doctor's new car," Iain laughed as I jumped in the air.

"So, we're taking it back to Skye!"

"We are indeed. You and Bobby can sit in it like lords while I drive. It's the first car in Portree and the doctor will use it for his rounds and guess who's going to be his chauffeur."

"His what?"

"It's the posh word for 'driver'."

"You are! Do you know how to drive it?"

"Of course. It's easy enough."

But I knew that he didn't.

"I'll show you the ropes," the mechanic said.

"Move along the seat with the wee dog so your brother can get in beside me. First though he has to start the engine."

Iain bent down to turn a handle at the front while I watched with Bobby. All three of us jumped in surprise when the engine roared into life. Iain hopped in.

"I'll be fine steering it. I've been steering boats all my life."

"Aye, but it will take you a while to get the hang of the brake and gears."

He was right. As Iain drove the car it wobbled and jerked like a new lamb unsteady on its feet. But once we were out of the town it got up speed until I could see the waters of Loch Ness shimmering through the gaps in the trees. All the people on foot or riding on carts turned back to stare at us.

The Second Surge of the Sea

After a while Alick, the mechanic, said, "I think you know what you're doing now. We'll turn back to the garage."

Before we left for home Alick drew something on a piece of paper before handing it to me, "The hardest part of driving is changing gear. I've done a plan of where the gears are so you can help your brother."

Iain scowled but he didn't say anything. We drove safely back past Loch Ness and people waved at us in all the villages.

"So, this is what it must feel like to be Lord MacDonald," I thought.

When we reached Dornie I remember how beautiful Loch Duich looked as the wind ruffled the surface of the water. It was liquid held in a bowl formed by the hills around it. I didn't say anything to Iain in case he laughed at me for being fanciful. I noticed that a ferry boat was about to sail, carrying passengers across the loch. It was just a big open rowing boat.

"How will we get the car aboard? It's only a wee boat."

Iain shrugged. "The ferryman will show us what to do."

I noticed that his fingers were clenched hard on the steering wheel. He braked and we waited for the boat to come back. The ferryman strolled over.

"That's a fine car. Were you wanting to take it over the other side?"

Iain pursed his lips, so I knew that he was irritated by the question.

"It's the doctor's new car. We're taking it to Portree for him."

"Are you now?" He tutted, sucked his teeth, and shook his head.

"I'll see what I can do. You'll have to drive it very steadily onto the boat. Help me carry the planks over."

Iain and I staggered under the weight of them while Bobby trotted alongside, thinking this was a new game.

"Get out of the way before I trip over you," Iain said to me through clenched teeth.

The boatman helped us balance the planks midships.

"Now all you have to do is drive the car up onto the planks."

Iain had gone white. I could hardly bear to watch as he drove towards the boat. What would we say to the doctor if his precious car ended up in the loch? Even Bobby looked worried. His tail drooped and he hid behind my legs.

"Steady, steady now. Forward a wee bit more," the ferryman said as the big car crawled up the planks, making them creak.

"Will you need to tie it down?" I asked.

"Aye, but you're lucky it's a calm day."

Bobby and I perched in the stern while Iain stayed in the driver's seat, still as a statue while the boatman whistled. When we reached the other side of the loch, he nudged the prow of the boat up onto the shore and guided Iain ashore. The car landed with a shudder.

"Thank the Lord that's over," I whispered under my breath.

Iain heard me.

"You didn't doubt me, did you, wee brother?"

"Of course not, not for a moment."

"That's as well because we'll have to do the same thing at Kyle to get over to Kyleakin."

"We're not going back to Portree on the steamer?"

"It would be too difficult getting the car on board."

I felt like groaning, but I laughed instead,' Pappa says, smiling at the memory and letting his gaze drift out to sea.

'That's incredible!' I say.

'All true though. There's old postcards showing cars being taken across like that.'

I remember Miss Greaves saying how you need to check oral history against other sources.

The Second Surge of the Sea

'I can't imagine living through all the changes you've seen in your life, Pappa.'

'Well, you'll live through many more yourself in your lifetime, I dare say. That wasn't the end of the adventures before we got home. I'll tell you the rest tomorrow, if you like.'

'I would like that.'

I realise that Pappa has the gift of building suspense, and he's stopped me feeling miserable for a while. After lunch I decide to walk down to Scorrybreac and see if Catriona is there. I spot Bracken first and he comes rushing up to shove his nose into my palm.

'You've made a friend there,' she says.

'My Pappa has been telling me stories about the Skye terrier he had as a boy. Have you ever had one?'

'No, always collies. They're more use really. Skye terriers look so odd with their funny wee stumpy legs and their big sticking out ears.'

I feel a bit protective of Bobby. He might have been small but he was smart. So I change the subject and ask Catriona what she studies in her history course.

'Well, a lot of Scottish history, of course.'

'I don't know much about it, except Mary Queen of Scots and Bonnie Prince Charlie. Was Macbeth a real king?'

She laughs, 'I bet your course is called British History.'

'Well, it is.'

'Not when you leave out everything about the rest of Britain, it isn't.'

I have to admit that she has a point and ask her to lend me a book so I can read up about Scottish history.

'I'll lend you my wee brother's book to give you an idea.'

I must look offended because she laughs and squeezes my arm.

'It's just something to get you started. It's all a bit bloodthirsty and there's eight kings called James.'

CHAPTER 7

'Well, what about the next instalment, Pappa?' I ask as I take his arm the next day for our walk.

He pushes up his cap to scratch his head, 'Well, where were we?'

'About to get across from the mainland to Kyleakin.'

'That's it. Well, I could see Iain's knuckles clenched white as we got near Kyle but he relaxed when he saw that the ferry boat was bigger this time. He didn't have to wiggle the steering wheel so much to steer the car aboard.

"Well, that was a piece of cake," he said, grinning when we passed the ruins of Castle Moil and landed on Skye once more.

"Just thirty miles to go now, but a few steep climbs. You and the dog will have to get out and help push."

"But Bobby doesn't weigh much."

"I'm only teasing, wee brother," he said, ruffling my hair.

I hated it when he did that, but I was pleased that he was in a good mood again. We sped through Broadford and wound round the road past Moll with no problems and I held Bobby up so that he could wave a paw at people who turned to admire the car.

"This driving business is easy," Iain said but I was thinking about the steep hill going up from the Sligachan Inn.

We crossed the old bridge and looked north. Just the hill and a few tight bends to see us to Portree. Iain swore under his breath as he struggled to find the right gear. There was a horrible grinding noise when the engine nearly stopped but after some splutters it lurched forward again. We were nearly at the summit.

"That's it. You won't have to push after all, Sandy."

The Second Surge of the Sea

Then I saw it. "Watch out! There's a huge hole in the middle of the road."

Iain hauled on the steering wheel, but it was too late. One of the front wheels banged down into the hole. He slammed on the brakes and the car bounced, slipping down towards the ditch. Iain groaned.

"What's the doctor going to say when he sees I've wrecked his brand-new car?"

He was always a bit theatrical, Iain, just like our sister. Meanwhile I jumped out to look.

"I don't think it's damaged, just stuck in the ditch. We could push it out."

So, we scrambled down into the ditch, with cold mud splashing on our legs. It was a heavy thing and push as we might it was wedged tight.

"It's no good. We need a horse to pull us out," Iain said after a lot of cursing.

"I could run back to the inn and ask Hector to help."

"Then we'll be very late, and the doctor will be wondering what's happened."

Bobby was standing, looking from one to the other of us and wagging his tail.

"I know! I'll send Bobby ahead to Malcolm at his croft just down the road, asking him to bring his horse."

"What good will that do? He's a dumb animal!"

I put my hands in my pockets while I had a think. That's when I felt something crackle. I pulled out the piece of paper that Alick had given me. When I rummaged in the other pocket, I found a stub of pencil.

"Look. I can write a note and put it round Bobby's neck in the bag we had our lunch in."

"Good lad!"

So, I wrote: *Malcolm, we need your help, please. Could you bring the horse and a long rope? The doctor's car is stuck in a hole.*

I put the note in the bag and bent down to talk to Bobby.

"Off you go," I said, pointing down the hill.

He set off and then looked back.

"You really think this will work?" Iain asked.

"Of course, it will."

But I had my doubts as the dog went trotting off.

I followed behind him, but I was soon left behind. I got a stitch and stopped for a rest. All the worry and pushing the car had worn me out. I wiped my brow and shut my eyes for a while. Then I heard hooves and saw Bonnie, big and shaggy with Malcolm on her back and Bobby sitting in front, tongue hanging out and looking pleased with himself.

"Hello there, young Sandy! I was having a *strupag* when I heard your wee dog barking its head off at my door. Show me where this new-fangled motor car is stuck."

We found Iain, pacing up and down with worry.

"Bonnie will soon get you out," Malcolm said, as he tied the rope round the harness. "You should stick to boats. I don't trust these new inventions."

The horse strained but nothing happened.

"You lads push from the back while we pull again. Come on lass."

Suddenly there was a sucking sound as the wheels pulled out of the mud. The horse whinnied, the dog barked, and the car was ready again, dirty but undamaged.

"Well, well!" said Malcolm, scratching his thick, black beard.

"The motor car is the new wonder of the world, so they say. Much faster than Bonnie here. But it was the horse that rescued the car. Cars will never take over from horses, you see, because you can't rely on them."

The Second Surge of the Sea

Iain raised his eyebrows.

"Well, you and Bonnie saved the day. Just let me know if you would like a spin in the car one day and you can see how fast it goes."

Malcolm shrugged.

"Faster than a horse, I dare say, but you can't talk to an engine like I can to Bonnie here."

The horse twitched her ears and nodded as she heard her name.

"Get her started," Iain ordered me.

Once the engine had sputtered into life, I said, "It all turned out well in the end."

"I don't want to talk. I need to concentrate."

He sounded grumpy and this time it was me who raised my eyebrows, but I said nothing. Iain drove very carefully, and I concentrated on looking out for potholes. When we arrived at the doctor's house, we could see him pacing up and down, swinging his battered bag.

"I'm so sorry to be late but the car is safe and…"

"Never mind that. Drive me at once to the MacLean's croft. I've just had word that Mrs MacLean's baby is on the way. It's her eighth and it could come quickly."

So off we went for several miles over a rough track with Iain biting his lip in concentration. The doctor hurried inside, barking out instructions for hot water and towels. We hung around outside, kicking our heels until Anna, the eldest daughter, brought us a heaped plateful of oatcakes and cheese. We fell on them like starving men. As I wiped the last crumbs from my lips, I noticed that all the other children were crowding around us, looking lost. I nudged Iain.

"Why don't we all go and look at the doctor's new car?" I said.

So, everyone had a go at turning the wheel and tooting the horn. After that excitement was over, one of the wee lads started to whimper and ask for his Mammie.

"I know. Let's wash the doctor's car and make it shine," I said.

We set to with cloths and a bucket of water.

"Take care. It's a very valuable car," Iain said.

When we were done, he checked all the bodywork.

"No scratches, thank goodness."

The children were starting to get fretful.

"I thought the doctor said that the baby would pop out at any minute," Iain muttered under his breath.

"Sometimes it takes a while," I said as if I knew what I was talking about.

"Let's play some games."

So, I got the wee ones to race each other and throw sticks for Bobby. We were all sitting down for a rest when Anna ran out, her face flushed.

"We've a new baby brother! Go and wash your hands and you can come and see him."

The children all streamed inside while Doctor Macleod appeared at the door, looking tired as he rolled down his shirt sleeves and put on his jacket.

"That car has proved its worth already. I arrived here in good time for the birth. Do you know what they're calling the wee boy?"

He grinned as we shook our heads.

"'Thomas' after me, 'Iain' after my driver – that's plenty you might think – but 'Arrol-Johnson' too after the car. That's quite a mouthful. Now, drive me home, chauffeur. And don't spare the horses!"

I laughed at the joke, but I was disappointed. I thought that Bobby's name should have been used too because of how he had saved the day, but I suspected that Iain hadn't told the doctor the whole story. As we drove the doctor home, I stroked the smooth leather seat. I liked the car well enough, but I agreed with Malcolm about preferring a horse that you could talk to. Suddenly my daydreaming was interrupted by the doctor's voice.

"Are you in the Reserves, Iain?"

"Aye. I enjoy the army camp each year. It's a change from the boat and we get paid too."

"That's what I thought. You're a good driver but I fear that there will be war soon and the reserves will get called up straightaway."

His words jolted through me. Iain was getting a good wage. What would happen if he went off to fight?'

Pappa sighs and I think about what I know about the First World War – so many men volunteered for a war that they said would be over by Christmas. Everyone was blind to the horror of death and destruction that followed. I don't feel that I want to talk about it. We began with jolly stories about a puppy and now the sky is darkening. Do I want to hear about the grimmer stuff yet? I decide to distract him.

'Could you just learn to drive then without taking a test?'

'That's right. I don't think that driving tests came in until the 1930s.'

'I want to learn, and I reckon I would be good but Mum says that she doesn't want to risk me driving her car. It took her for ever to learn and she's only got a licence for an automatic.'

Pappa says nothing. I suppose he doesn't want to criticise his daughter.

'I enjoyed that story, Pappa, but one thing puzzles me. How do you remember all those conversations from years ago?'

'Well, when you get old, the past seems much closer.' He smiles, 'I remember a lot of them. It's the story teller's art. Have you heard of the *seannaiche?* – the storyteller from back in the day when stories were told at the fireplace before they were ever written down. You listened to the same tale so often that you memorised it, like the summer travellers still do. And a lot of the talk in my tales was in Gaelic so I have to translate it as I go along. You never knew that your old Pappa was so clever, did you?'

I smile and squeeze his roughened fingers.

CHAPTER 8

The next day I'm looking forward to hearing the new instalment. At last, we're getting onto something more interesting.

'How did Iain feel about the War coming? Was he excited, like so many young men were?'

Pappa rummages around in his disgusting old pipe before answering.

'He was the same as usual, whistling through his teeth as he set off to the doctor's house. Mamma was thrilled with his new job, "Such a respectable, important job! No-one can look down their noses at us!" she kept repeating.

I never thought that they did but I had the sense to keep my mouth shut. Everyone seemed happy, except for grumpy Màiri and I decided to be happy too. My Dadda would be back soon from the east coast.'

'And why was your Dadda away?'

'Well, you could make good money on the bigger east coast boats, enough to put a bit by.'

Pappa is drumming his fingers on his knee, so I decide not to ask any more questions for a while.

'Where shall we start today?' I say, unable to hold the silence.

'Well, I like thinking about that same summer, and all the animals on the croft. One day I was woken up by Mamma's shouting, "Get out, you big, clumsy beast. Look at the mess you've made! I'm sick of that animal. Sneaked in when my back was turned and I find her sitting like a queen in my good wicker chair, with her feet sticking up in the air."'

Pappa laughs at my puzzled frown.

'It was Fraoch – it means heather, an orphan lamb that we had bottle fed. I remember Dadda bringing her in, a tiny shivering wee thing. I wrapped her in an old blanket and put her in front of the fire. As she grew, she used to tug on the bottle so hard that she nearly pulled you over but now that she was grown, she needed to stay outside with the rest of the flock. I kept telling Bobby to herd her outside, but she put her black head down and pointed her horns at the dog. She had no fear of dogs or people. "What was that you said about Bobby making a good sheepdog?" Mamma said, laughing but in the end, he chased her out.'

I'm sitting on my hands to stop me twiddling my fingers. Pappa laughs.

'Just be patient. Fraoch is important in the story.'

I nod. 'OK, seannaiche. Whatever you say.'

'There was no sign of Fraoch for the next few days. I missed her coming up to butt me on the knees. She liked you to rub her soft ears. Then one day when I was eating my breakfast porridge, Bobby started barking and scratching the door. I opened it and what a sad sight was there! A big lamb but it didn't look like Fraoch with her white coat and neat black feet. This sheep was drenched in mud and her fleece was tangled. She had a bad cut near her eye. She limped inside and stood, shivering while I washed the cut. She wouldn't stop shaking but then I had an idea. I hunted through the cupboards until I found her old bottle and filled it with milk. She gulped it all down and gave a big belch. She calmed down enough so that I could bend down to feel her injured leg. It didn't seem to be broken, just sprained. Something had scared her.

"Come on Bobby. We have to find the other sheep."

We climbed up to the top field but there was no sign of the other beasts. Bobby ran ahead, with his nose to the ground right up to where the field ended in a cliff. Fraoch had followed us out and stood munching grass as if nothing had happened. I was

The Second Surge of the Sea

really worried now and ran after the dog. Bobby stopped at the cliff edge and barked. I lay down to look over the edge and could make out white shapes perched on a narrow ledge above the waves. How was I going to get the sheep back up?

"Go on, Bobby," I said and scrambled after him. I was worried that he might scare the animals so that they fell into the sea. But he crept forward and gently nudged the legs of the nearest beast. I held my breath as it scrambled up the rocks. I inched my way down the slope so that Bobby and I could coax the other sheep to follow the first one. Fraoch strolled along above to watch, and her bleating seemed to encourage them to clamber up to the top.

One, two, three.... I counted, up to nine. There was one missing! But then I remembered that I hadn't counted in Fraoch. I lay exhausted while at the top the beasts started to graze.

When my heart stopped thumping, I got to my feet and called to Bobby, but he took no notice. He was nuzzling near a mossy rock and scrabbling with his paws until he pulled out an old, blackened bone. I called to him again but then my eye was caught by something gleaming in the hole he had made. Maybe it was an old coin?

I scraped off the earth and was disappointed to see that it wasn't a coin but some sort of ornament, a small golden horse that fitted into the palm of my hand. I turned it over and something jabbed me. It was a pin so this must be a brooch that someone had dropped. Not worth much but it was a pretty wee thing. I turned it over in my hands while I thought about what to do with it. It was Mamma's birthday soon. Maybe she would like it as a present. She could use it to fix the scarf she wore with her Sunday coat. I put it in my pocket and called to Bobby who was holding onto the dirty old bone. Well, I suppose that we had both found treasure. We set off for home and Fraoch trotted along with us.

"Where on earth have you been?" Mamma said, "And I told you not to let that beast in again!"

"Don't be cross, Mamma. Bobby has just saved the whole flock."

So, I told her the whole tale.

"Well, Her Majesty the Sheep can come in whenever she wants to and drink milk from a china cup and I'll get a bone from the butcher's for Bobby."

We laughed as Fraoch leapt into the chair and lay back with all four feet jiggling. At that moment Iain appeared, taking off the special cap he wore when he drove the doctor's car.

"There's that pest of an animal again. We should send it to market," he said.

"Wait until you hear Sandy's story."

"I wonder what scared the sheep," Iain said after I told him what had happened.

"We'll need to keep an eye open for stray dogs but with a boy, a wee dog and a sheep on the case we don't need a collie dog."

I was pleased. My brother wasn't usually one to dish out praise.

Later when I was getting ready for bed, I felt something jab my leg. I had forgotten about the wee golden horse. I looked at it again. Whoever had made it knew about horses. It looked as if it was galloping for the sheer joy of it. I lifted down a wooden box from the shelf above the bed. Inside it was a penknife with an ivory handle my Grandad had given me, a cast horseshoe and a piece of blue-green glass, worn smooth by the sea. When I looked through it, it made everything seem like a strange world, under the waves. I found a clean handkerchief and wrapped the brooch inside it before putting the box away. Who had the brooch belonged to? Someone who used to live on our croft? Could it have been from the time of the Vikings? Maybe Mamma would know.'

The Second Surge of the Sea

Pappa sat still with a faraway look in his eyes. After a while I ask, 'What happened to the brooch? Have you still got it?'

He smiles, 'I've got you hooked now, have I? You'll have to wait.'

I don't blame him for teasing me after I had been so impatient before. It was sunny so I decide to go out for a walk. As I walk down to the shore, I see Catriona ahead of me. She waits for me to catch up.

'I'm pleased to see you again so that I can pick your brains. I know that I'm a bit ignorant about Scottish history. My Pappa was telling me stories about when he was a boy and he said that he found what he thought could have been a buried Viking brooch. I didn't like to question him, but is that right? Were the Vikings on Skye, as well as the Celts?'

She raises her eyebrows.

'They sure were. You might have Viking blood yourself. They intermarried with the Celts.'

'I thought that the Vikings went in for rape and pillage.'

'At first, but then they settled down.'

'How do we know?'

'Because lots of placenames are Viking. Ones ending in "bost" for instance, like Skeabost, near here. I think it means "homestead."'

'And "Carbost."' 'That's it. We'll educate you yet.' She smiles and gives me a playful tap on the arm that takes away any sting from her words, 'Are you heading back home? I could walk back with you?'

'Eh....' I hesitate and feel the atmosphere freeze.

'Don't bother saying anything,' she hisses and strides away.

'Don't go Catriona. It's just my Granny being funny.'

She tosses her head and breaks into a run. Tears of frustration spurt from my eyes. Am I fated to have no friends, boys or girls? I hate Skye. It's cursed.

CHAPTER 9

The next day I feel really depressed but I don't want to tell Pappa about it because it's not fair to criticise Granny to him, but he's not fooled by my false smiles.

'Something is on your mind, lass', he says while he fiddles with his pipe.

'It's awkward.'

He waits, 'Is it that young man?'

'No.' I surprise myself by realising that I haven't thought so much about Neil in the last few days. Sometimes a memory jolts me, like a pebble stuck in my shoe, but quite a lot of the time I don't think about him. Now, though, this falling out with Catriona has made me feel really bad again. It seems like I can't keep any friends.

He waits and in the end I blurt it out, 'I started to get friendly with a girl called Catriona, but we've fallen out because I said that she couldn't come to the house. I knew that Granny would be cross and Catriona took offence and stormed off.'

'Aah.' He sucks on his pipe, making his lips all crumple up. I can't imagine being that old.

'She's one of the Summer Travellers. People more often call them tinkers of course. I knew her Granny well. They come later in the story, when everything went wrong, and it felt like all the plagues of Egypt were coming down on my head all together.'

His fingers are trembling, and I take one of his hands.

'Take your time. There's no rush.'

'Aye. Well, the good news first. One day I came back from school to find Dadda sitting by the fire. He was back from the east coast fishing, and we were all pleased to see him. When we had eaten, he lifted up his bag from under the table and gave us all presents. He had a pretty, silvery brooch for Mamma, nice enough but not as fine as the one I had found. There were ribbons for Màiri that matched her blue-grey eyes, tobacco for Iain and even a beef bone for Bobby.'

'What did you get?'

'Oh, some fish hooks in a wee purse. The fishing season had gone well so there was a good pot of money for the crew to share but there was a shadow there too that I couldn't put a name to. While everyone else was laughing and talking I watched Dadda. His face had turned brown with the sun and wind, but his cheeks seemed sharper. When he thought that no-one was watching his smile drooped. I told myself that he was probably tired and not getting Mamma's good cooking. Have you heard of the *dha shealladh* – the second sight?'

'Like foreseeing the future?'

He nodded, 'But then Dadda laughed, and I thought that I was imagining it. No-one else seemed to have noticed anything different. Iain disappeared quietly after we finished our meal. But he came back later, his face flushed.

"I've been having a dram with the lads."

"I can see that," Mamma said tartly.

"We're heading off in a few days."

"Where?" she croaked, her fingers clasped on the new brooch at her neck.

"An army camp, somewhere down in England," he said lifting his chin.

Mamma frowned and her eyes looked damp.

"You've joined up," Dadda said and again that strained look shadowed his face.

"I remember local lads going to fight in South Africa and they didn't all come back." Mamma put down her knife and fork and pushed her plate away.

"I'm in the Reserves, so we're the first to go abroad. It's only for a few months."

"Well, you've time to finish your meal first, then," Mamma said with a shaky smile.'

Pappa falls silent and I prompt him again.

'What did you think about Iain going to war, Pappa?'

'Well, part of me envied him going on an adventure. But I knew Mamma was worried about the danger and him losing his good job driving the doctor. The War didn't make much sense to me. It all seemed to be about an Archduke being killed in a faraway country. Some of the lads wanted to play a new game of Scottish soldiers against the Germans but I didn't want to join in. I preferred to fish off the rocks or play with Bobby.

Everyone lined the streets up to the Square to see the young men off. So, they had a fine send off, marching down the street to the sound of the pipes. We children were given a holiday and we made flags to wave them goodbye. We marched behind, waving and cheering as they boarded the steamer. The funnel boomed and off it sailed into the bay. Suddenly it all went quiet, like being in church. It was strange with him gone. My big brother would tease me and order me about, but I knew that he would always stand up for me. Meanwhile Màiri got even more unbearable – *"Ou est ton petit chien mechant?"* she would ask me when she came in from school.

When I looked blank, she would flounce and say, "Where's your naughty wee dog? It's a good job that someone in our family has the brains to learn another language."

"He's not naughty. And I can speak two languages already. What's the point of learning French when you will never go to France?"

She tried to kick me, but I dodged out of the way. School was a torment to me. She had spent all summer working as a chambermaid at the Royal Hotel and given Mamma all her earnings.

"You can stay on at school for just now – maybe until Christmas. Then we'll see if there's enough money to keep you there for longer. I'm not promising, mind you."

That was enough for Màiri. She couldn't stop herself gloating.

"I can't wait to start learning French and science again. Of course, you won't be doing that, Sandy. You'll be stuck with the hopeless cases, the big, stupid lads – like that fool, Archie MacLean who can't even hold his reading book the right way up."

I slammed my spoon down on the table.

"I'm not stupid. I don't want to take the exam to move up to the scholarship class because I hate school. And what good will your French and stuff do you when you have to leave and get a job in a big house somewhere?"

Màiri shrieked and leapt up, thrusting her hands round my neck and squeezing hard.

Mamma rushed in.

"Stop that at once! Don't I have enough to worry about already?"

That made me feel a bit ashamed for taunting my sister, but she was so annoying. The only thought that cheered me up was that Miss Henderson, who taught the top class, would be so busy with the scholarship pupils that she wouldn't have so much time to bother with the likes of me.'

'That Scholarship exam sounds a bit like the Eleven Plus exam that I had to do. I always thought it was unfair because it split our class up and then we all went to different schools. Mind you, Mum would have been furious if I hadn't passed it. It's a lot of pressure and I wasn't even 11 when I took it.'

'Well, you're clever like my sister and she was so angry not to get the chance of staying on at school.'

'That's true. I suppose I took it for granted that I could stay on and that I can go on to university as well.'

'The world has turned since those days.' Pappa stopped and reached out for my arm.

'I'm tired *isean*. Shall we go back home now?'

'Of course.' I could see that his face was tight with pain. I wish that I could make things up with Catriona and ask her how the schools work here but I can't think of a way to engineer a meeting. After we've plodded back home, I'll have a cup of tea with Granny and then make some notes on what I've learnt from Pappa.

Granny has a suspicious look on her face when we get back. Pappa says that he's going for a lie down and after we've heard him struggling up the stairs she says, 'I hope that you're not wearing him out with all this raking over the past.'

'I don't think so. He wants to do it. Shall we see if there's anything on the radio we could listen to?'

She grunts in agreement. 'You can help me wind some wool into skeins while we listen. I'm going to make an Aran pullover.'

I suppress a sigh and hold my arms out ready.

CHAPTER 10

Saturday, and it's pouring with rain and Pappa looks grey with exhaustion. He's certainly not up to a walk. What would I be doing if I was at home? Meeting my friends in town, having a coffee, going into Boots to hear the new releases in one of their listening booths until that grumpy supervisor chases us out – "You can't just hang around here all day girls. You put off the proper customers who really want to buy a record."

Silly old cow! Granny's words interrupt my thoughts.

'I want to go and see Mistress Ross down the road today. She's not been keeping well. Can I leave you in charge here for an hour or two, Margaret?'

I'm not sure if she's joking or not but I smile at Pappa and say, 'I don't think that we'll get up to too much mischief while you're out.'

'Do you want to carry on with the story?' I ask him after she's gone.

'Aye, I do but the next part will be like tearing off a bandage. I've never told the whole story to anyone before.'

'Well, if you're sure. We can always stop.'

I feel a bit nervous. What if he has a funny turn? But I want to know what happens next. So, I look pleased, bring through tea and biscuits and we make a start. He takes a few sips of tea and then holds the cup, swishing the liquid from side to side.

'When I arrived at school Miss Baxter was waiting for us in the classroom. Standing beside her was a stranger, a square shouldered, middle-aged man with a dark, frowning face. She glared at us until we stopped fidgeting.

"This is Mr Graham. He has come to instruct the children who won't be going up to the secondary division. That means that I can concentrate on working with the scholars who are preparing for the Qualifying Examination."

She strode off in her polished brogues. Mr Graham stared at us and drew back his lips, but it wasn't a friendly smile – more like the grin of the wolf who was pretending to be Little Red Riding Hood's Granny. He had been standing with his hands behind his back but now he brought them forward and I could see that he was holding a tawse. He swished it as he spoke in a rough voice.

"We'll all get on fine if you do what I say. Otherwise...." He left the words hanging in the air.

Archie MacLean, a brawny boy who could hardly fit behind a desk, gawped at Mr Graham with his mouth hanging open. It was Jimmie Beaton, a wiry troublemaker, who piped up with a cheeky grin on his face.

"What will you be doing with us, Sir?"

Mr Graham strode up to him, grabbed his collar and lifted him off his feet.

"The wee fella wants to know what I'll do with him."

Everyone else sank down into their seats.

"You'll be working outside and doing plenty of P.T. Will that suit you, laddie?" he said as he pushed Jimmie back down into his seat.

"Or would you rather do sewing with the lasses?"

The others sniggered. So, we set to. I didn't mind the outdoor work. We had to build a wall around the sports field and dig a vegetable garden while Mr Graham watched us with a scowl on his face. I noticed that sometimes by the end of the day he would start to limp but then stride out if anyone noticed. I took good care not to do anything that drew attention to myself.

One warm afternoon when we had finished a gymnastic drill Mr Graham allowed us to sit down for a few minutes in the sun.

The Second Surge of the Sea

I turned to speak to Archie who was next to me.

"*Tha mi sgith a-nis ach tha e math a'fuireach a-muigh.*"

'Do you understand what I said, Margaret?'

'I get the bit about being tired.'

'That's right. I was saying too about it being good to be outside. The school rule was that we had to speak English in the classroom, but Miss Baxter didn't mind about Gaelic outside. Anyway, I suddenly felt a hard grip on my shoulder, squeezing down onto my collar bone. I stopped myself yelping in pain when I looked up and saw that it was Mr Graham who had crept up on us.

"I won't have you speaking in that barbaric tongue, boy. It's only fit for ignorant tinkers."

I saw the sneer on his face and the spittle glistening on his lips. I was furious when I thought about Mamma singing Gaelic songs while she worked and the minister reading from the Gaelic Bible. They weren't barbarians but this man was.

"It's not a barbaric tongue, Sir. I learnt it at my mother's knee and the minister told me that it's an older language than English."

For a few seconds Mr Graham stared at me as if I was a dog that had suddenly learnt how to speak. The other boys froze, scared and excited at the same time.

"You dare to answer back!"

He wrenched my arm in front of him, prised my fingers open and, in a frenzy, beat my hand with the tawse. I was determined not to flinch although the pain cut through me. When the teacher turned on his heel and left, I could feel my whole arm throbbing. Jimmie came up and slapped me on the back.

"You're one of us now."

But I didn't want to be one of the bad boys.

The next problem was to get home without Mamma seeing my hand. I didn't want to worry her. I walked towards the school gate, flexing my fingers to make sure that they still worked. They did but the pain made me groan.

"What have you done to yourself?" As luck would have it my big nosy sister suddenly appeared.

"What have you done to yourself?" She asked me again, more gently.

When I explained she didn't tell me off as I expected but went to dip her hanky in the stream and pressed it on my hand.

"That should stop it swelling," she said as I winced in pain.

"Don't tell Mamma. It'll upset her."

"But she should know."

"I didn't tell her your secret."

"What secret?'"

I could see the flush on her cheeks.

"I saw you walking out with Kenny Morrison and holding hands.'"

'Why hadn't you told her before?' I ask Pappa.

'You're an only child, Margaret. You wouldn't know how secrets are like gold in a family. They give you power. Although Kenny was a tall, clever boy with wavy hair and a high opinion of himself, I knew that Mamma would not approve because Màiri was only fourteen. She huffed and puffed a bit but agreed to keep quiet.

"You could say that you dropped a rock on your hand when you were repairing the wall," she said.'

'No teacher would be allowed to do that now,' I say, horrified at his story. 'I think you were right to stick up for yourself.'

He smiled sadly, 'I paid a heavy price for my rash words.'

'He must have hated you for showing him up.'

'Maybe I'll tell you about the folk who saved me before I talk about him.'

I nod although really I want to hear more about Mr Graham because I sense that's the dramatic part of the story.

The Second Surge of the Sea

'Well, you know that I had found out about the boy that Màiri was sweet on? It was by chance. I was out with Bobby at my heels one day after school when I noticed some people ahead of me on the road to Dunvegan. Or rather I heard a clanging noise first. There was a woman with long plaited hair and two girls walking beside her. They were carrying baskets on their arms and the clanging sound came from the pots and pans that the woman had hanging from her belt. I recognised them because they came up to Skye every year. They were the travelling people who made all sorts of objects out of tin. Some people sniffed and called them "tinkers" but I prefer the older name, "The Summer Walkers."

"How's yourself, Sandy?" Mrs Stewart asked.

"I'm well, thank you."

"We're off to sell our pots," she said.

"And aprons, ribbons and pegs," the older girl said.

"Would you like a sprig of lucky white heather?"

"Why don't you come back with us and see the lads and the horses?" Mrs Stewart said.

I nodded. "I'd like to do that. If I don't go to sea when I'm grown, I would like to work with horses."

"And how is that kind mother of yours? And the rest of the family?" she asked as we walked along together. I found myself telling her all my worries – Iain about to go off to the War, Màiri bossing me about all the time and making an enemy of Mr Graham.

"And Dadda's not been himself since he came back from the fishing. I hear him coughing in the night."

"My goodness, you've got a cartful of woes. I can't do anything about most of them, but I can make up a potion for your Dadda's cough."

I was pleased to hear that. Mamma was always saying how the travelling people had kept a lot of knowledge about healing plants that everyone else had forgotten. We walked up the hill towards Borve where the Stewarts had set up camp.

"You go and talk to Jamie while I make us something to eat," Mrs Stewart said. He was busy putting down feed for the horses in a metal trough.

"That looks like porridge," I said.

"Aye. I steeped the oatmeal in milk and then added hot water to it. They need a good feed after they've been pulling the waggon. Mamma will fry up some onions with the rest of the oats to make skirly for us to eat. See the white horse? He'll make us good money. The folk in the big houses like a white horse to carry back the stags they've shot on the hills. I suppose that they show up better on the hillside."

Jamie was about the same age as me, but he seemed very grown-up.

"Do you have to go to school?" I asked.

"No, not me. What use is book learning? I find out all that I need to know from my family and from nature."

"You're the lucky one. I wish that I could live like you. When I have to go to school, I'm like Bobby when he's put on the lead. His tail sinks, his ears droop and he digs his heels into the ground."

"Why not come away with us?"

"I'd like that fine."

Then Mrs Stewart called us over to eat rabbit stew. I had smelt it cooking and I was starving. We all sat down at the entrance to their tent. The fabric was stretched over a framework of curved sticks. When I looked up, I thought that sleeping there would be like being inside a tunnel of trees. It was one of the best meals of my life – rabbit stew, skirly and tatties baked in their skins in the embers of the fire. Plenty of scraps too for Bobby. And afterwards a huge mound of clootie pudding, steaming and studded with raisins. I ate so much that I thought that I would never feel hungry again. After we had eaten, Jamie started to play his fiddle.

"You'll stay for the ceilidh," Mrs Stewart said.

"I can't. Mamma will wonder where I am."

As I ran down the hill, I could hear the gusts of music behind me. The tunes filled my head so that all my worries were blown away on the wind. That was when I saw Màiri, further down the hill. I would know her walk anywhere – the dainty steps and the gentle sway of her hips. And Kenny Morrison was holding her hand.'

Pappa takes out his pipe and I know that's the end of the stories for today.

'I remember seeing the tents with a chimney sticking out of the roof when I came up on the train.'

'Aye, the summer people are still around with their tales and their songs, if you know where to look for them.'

CHAPTER 11

'So, there was a kind of truce between Màiri and me,' Pappa says as we set off the next day on our walk.

'Maybe she felt sorry for you having to deal with that bully, Mr Graham.'

'Well, I wouldn't put it as strongly as that,' he laughs, 'I think she was trying to cope with her own worries. She knew that she would have to leave school soon.'

'She must have found that hard.'

'Aye. She kept kicking against it. She pleaded, stamped her feet, and shut herself away in her bedroom when she heard the news. Mamma went to talk to her through the door when she hadn't eaten for a whole day.'

'And you listened, I bet.'

'Of course! "I'm so sorry, *isean*. I hoped that you could stay but we can't afford to let you do that. Your Dadda's still not properly well and we'll lose Iain's good wage from the doctor."

"And my wee brother gets to stay at school when he hates it."

"That's how it is. Sandy does his best to help. He sells duck eggs and catches fish."

"Only to feed that useless dog of his."

Mamma's voice hardened.

"That's enough. Be grateful for your blessings. You're young, strong, and clever."

I crept away, thinking how unfair life was. If only I was 14 and leaving school while my sister was the youngest. It was her moods that were the problem. Sometimes she would laugh and joke but then she would lose her temper over nothing. Bobby and I got the sharp edge of her tongue.

"That dog's nothing but a pest," she would say when he went to greet her.'

'She sounds really bossy. Maybe I'm lucky being an only child.'

'It was just because we were children. We got on better later. Anyway, she insisted on showing me all the jobs she did.

"You'll have to milk Bethan when I'm away," she said.

"But that's lassie's work!"

She stood and glared at me, hands on hips.

"You drink milk, don't you? And plenty of it. And butter and crowdie so you'll have to do the churning too."

"What if the lads at school find out? I'll never live it down."

"They won't find out. I kept your secret about Mr Graham, didn't I? If anyone teases you, Bobby can bite their ankles."'

'Was Bethan a Highland cow or an ordinary one?' I ask.

'A Highland one and a gentle soul with big soft eyes and long curling ginger eyebrows. There was no need to tie her back legs when you milked her as you would have to with a grumpy beast. I would rest my head against her warm hairy flank and sing to her.'

"Your voice is starting to crack on the high notes," Màiri said when she heard me.'

'You couldn't win with your sister! What job did Màiri get?'

'Mamma had written to a relative in Glasgow who found her a job as a nursemaid for a Jewish family called Cohen. I doubted that she had the patience for the job but kept quiet.'

'I suppose it was a step up from being a kitchen maid.'

'She seemed to calm down and accept her fate. I even showed her the brooch. "That's one of the most beautiful things I've ever seen," she said, running her fingers along the horse's mane and tail.

When she came down for breakfast on the morning she was going to set off for the Cohens, I looked up from my porridge in amazement at the young lady standing in the kitchen. Màiri was so grown up. Her glossy dark hair up in a bun, her boots polished and her blouse a crisp, sparkling white with a frilled collar. Her long black skirt looked new and encircled such a tiny waist.

"Well, don't just stare. Say something." Her tongue was as sharp as ever.

"I don't know what to say. You look so…different. I hardly recognised you."

"Well, I suppose that's the nearest you'll get to a compliment," Mamma said. "We've both been busy with needle and thread this last week."

"You look grand," Dadda said, with a catch in his throat. "You could take your place anywhere in society."

"The only place I'm likely to be is in the nursery or the kitchen."

"But you'll soon be doing better things when they see how smart you are," Mamma said.

It felt very strange coming back from waving Màiri off on the steamer.

"I'm glad we've still got one bird left in the nest," Mamma said as she hugged me.

But I longed to be grown up enough to work. I felt stuck in the middle – too old to play and be carefree but not old enough to make my own way in the world. Old enough to worry but too young to be able to change anything.

A few days later I heard voices in the kitchen when I came home from a miserable day at school. Mr Graham had managed to corner me around the back of the school, shoving me hard in the chest so that I'd fallen over. I stopped to listen when I heard voices coming from the kitchen.

"Well, Morag, I do hope that the potion works. John doesn't complain but I know that he's not really feeling himself. That cough wears him out."

"You've a lot of burdens to bear."

I recognised the second voice as being Mrs Stewart.

"But I shouldn't trouble you with my worries. Life must be hard for you since your husband passed away. Your sons will be helping you though, I'm sure."

Mrs Stewart sighed. "Jamie is a sensible lad but I worry about Angus. He's left to go pearl fishing, down on the Tay. The freshwater pearls are highly prized, he says, and he has big plans to make his fortune, but he's got a temper and I worry that he'll get into fights. We'll be moving on ourselves soon."

I heard the sounds of their chairs scraping as they stood up, so I crept back along the shore.

"There you are Sandy," Mrs Stewart said as she came out and tied her row of pans onto her belt. "You must come and see us again before we're off on our travels. Would you like rabbit again or maybe a tasty bit of fish?"

"Thank you, Mrs Stewart. I would like that."

I felt sad after she left. Everyone else had somewhere to go but what had I to look forward to? Bobby trotted over and thrust his soft nose into my hand.

"You're never sad, Bobby.'"

CHAPTER 12

That evening I write down everything that I could remember from what Pappa had said and I found myself chewing my biro in frustration. It was obvious that he was avoiding launching into more troubled waters, but I didn't want to upset him by pressing too hard. So, the next morning I'm amazed to see him with a sparkle in his eyes and a spring to his step.

'I had a good night's sleep and no pain in my leg for once. I feel twenty years younger.'

He's right too. He strides along the shore so quickly that I have to speed up to keep pace with him.

'I'll tell you about the art competition.'

I suppress a sigh and wait for him to start. Still nothing about what's really on his mind.

'When I was crossing the playground, I heard a voice calling me, "Alexander MacPherson, come here."

It was Miss Matheson, one of the teachers who had taught me when I was wee. I hadn't enjoyed her classes but looking back I could see that she was a fair teacher, an angel compared to that brute, Mr Graham.

"Alexander, did you know that Miss Baxter is organising an art competition? You have to portray something to do with the Vikings. Her class has been studying them this year, but the competition is open to all scholars. And you always enjoyed drawing, as I remember."

I nodded. Art was the only subject that I enjoyed at school. I thought about how wonderful it would be if I were a Viking warrior. I would charge into the classroom with sword held high and hack Mr Graham's head from his body. Thwack! Like lopping a thistle.'

72

The Second Surge of the Sea

I smile and think of how I would have liked to stab Miss Lugsden with her own knitting needles.

"'Are you listening, Alexander, or daydreaming again? I know that you can draw well. I'm sure that Miss Baxter will let you look at the books she has about the Vikings so that you can get some ideas."

"I don't think that I'll enter the competition."

"Come on now. There's a prize for the best picture."

"I hope that it's not a book."

Miss Matheson shook her head in exasperation.

I spent the day avoiding Mr Graham and his fists, but that evening I suddenly remembered the brooch that Bobby had found when we were rescuing the sheep. I lifted down my special box from its hiding place and opened up the cloth where it gleamed. The horse looked as if it could leap into life. The brooch probably wasn't all that old, but I was curious enough to go and ask Miss Baxter the next day if I could look at her books.

There were drawings and even photographs of jewellery, on pages protected by sheets of tracing paper. I licked my fingers and turned them over carefully. There wasn't a horse but there were other animals – deer, wolves and hares that leapt into life off the page. When I saw Miss Baxter, she surprised me by giving me several sheets of paper and a box of watercolour paints. Now I had to do a painting.

That evening I settled down to paint in my room, with Bobby curled around my feet. I made several attempts until I felt that I had created a beast that looked as if it might leap off the page. I handed it to Miss Baxter the next day before I could change my mind.

"Well done, Alexander. All the teachers will take part in judging the entries and we'll announce the winner soon."

Well, I thought, I know one teacher who would never choose my work. Mr Graham picked on me again that day, making me clean and tidy away all the gardening tools and cuffing me round the ear. He followed me as I was shutting the door of the shed.

"I saw your painting. You're a cheat, lad. You never painted that picture. Did you get your sister to do it for you?"

"No, Sir. Màiri's away to Glasgow. I did it all myself."

I kept hold of the spade I was putting away. I felt scared because there was no-one else there and the teacher was edging closer all the time.

"Well, you copied it out of a book, then."

I thought that the best thing to do was to keep talking until I had a chance to run for it.

"It was a real brooch that I found when my dog rescued a sheep from a cliff."

Mr Graham was frowning and standing still. I took a chance and darted sideways, but his arm reached out and he caught me by the wrist, his fingers squeezing hard.

"Found it! You stole it more like, you thieving tinker. *Tinkie, tinkie, tarrie bags, Go to the well and wash your rags.*"

His words exploded inside my head. How dare he insult good people like the Stewarts! Rage gave me the strength of Finn McCoul and I swung the spade, smashing him above the knee. There was a loud crack and Mr Graham lost his balance, toppling over backwards.

"You can't hurt me, wee ruffian. That's my false leg!"

I lashed out then, with my fists, my feet and the spade. I was a creature possessed. After a while he stopped shouting and lay still. That made me come to my senses. Had I killed the man? I knew that I should go and get help, but I would go to prison and how could my poor parents endure the shame of that. But another voice, a devil's voice, told me to clean the spade and put it away in the shed.'

The Second Surge of the Sea

'Is that what you did?' I struggle to keep my voice steady. Pappa is shaking and there are beads of sweat on his brow. It seems to take for ever before he replies.

'Aye. Then I remembered that Mamma had said that she would be out that afternoon, meeting other ladies to knit comforts for the lads at the Front.'

He sees my frown, 'You know – socks, gloves, balaclavas.' He gives a shaky laugh.

'If I was a soldier, I would prefer a nice fruit cake to the rest. Anyway, there would be no-one at home except Bobby. I had to act first before anyone found the body, but I made myself stroll back. Rather than running. I didn't want to draw attention to myself.'

He's stopped dead and is looking out to sea.

'Do you want to sit down, Pappa?' He seems frozen, as if he's reliving that terrible moment. I feel panicky but manage to say, 'It's alright. It's not really happening.'

He looks at me as if I'm a stranger but when I squeeze his hand he seems to thaw and shakes his head.

'I can think better when I'm moving.' He quickens his pace as if he's reliving the story.

'None of the neighbours were about but there was Bobby, waiting for me, his tail wagging so hard as if it would fly off.

"You don't care whether I'm a murderer."

I rubbed my face into his hair and sobbed. Then I crammed a bag with as much food as I could – cheese, oatcakes, scones and some cooked mackerel for Bobby. I put in my penknife, string, fish hooks and wire to make snares. The worst part was leaving a note:

Dear Mamma and Dadda,

I must go away for a while. I'm taking Bobby. Please try not to worry.

I'm sorry that I've not been a better son.

I love you dearly. Pray for me,

Sandy.'

I have to sniff to stop myself sobbing at Pappa's tale.

'I folded the note and left it on the kitchen table. One last look around – everything held memories – the old basket-chair that Bracken the lamb used to sit in, the scuffed stools we children used to sit on, the rag rug Mamma made from scraps of cloth. "It's like Joseph's coat of many colours," she used to say. This was the home where I was born, where I was loved and I was leaving it to become a wanderer and an exile.'

He's sobbing now and I ask him if he wants to carry on. There are so many questions that I want to ask but feel I shouldn't. I wait until his breathing slows down.

'That's the worst part over.'

'Do you want to stop or carry on, Pappa?'

'Let's go back and I'll have a lie down.'

CHAPTER 13

I'm worried that he'll have a funny turn and Granny will blame me for upsetting him, but he surprises me by seeming calm when we sit down and have a cup of tea. I suppose there's a relief in confessing something that has stayed hidden for so long. It's me who feels shaken up, as if we've played some strange game of pass the parcel and I've had something horrible handed to me. Is my gentle Pappa really a murderer? If he is, has it been kept a secret for all these years? If so, am I sworn to secrecy too?

'Aren't you hungry, Margaret?' Granny asks when I say that I don't want any tea. The meals have definitely improved. It's bacon, sausage, and tinned spaghetti today but I can't face it.

'I hope that you and Pappa haven't caught a bug.'

I don't sleep well. It feels like it's the night before some awful exam when I don't know what I'll be faced with.

Pappa, though, looks younger at breakfast, as if he has ironed out his wrinkled cheeks. It reminds me of the "Portrait of Dorian Grey", that we read at school last term. It's not fair. He feels better but I'm in a state of shock. I have to carry the weight of the secret.

When we set out for our walk, he looks hard at me.

'I shouldn't have told you. It's too much of a burden.'

'It's a shock but I asked you to tell me real things and you can't stop half-way.'

'I'll tell you all the rest and you must decide what to do with the knowledge.'

I nod. 'Where did you run to?'

'To find the Stewarts. I was scared that they would already have left but I ran up the road to their camp in Borve, my heart thumping as if it wanted to escape from my chest. As I neared the woods, I heard a horse neigh, so I hurried on. There was Jamie, tethering the horses – the brown one and the valuable white one.

"Hello, Sandy. You've come just in time. We're off tomorrow."

"I'm in terrible trouble, Jamie."

I gasped out my story in a torrent of words and sobs. When I finished, Jamie stroked the brown horse's nose before speaking, "I would be happy if you came with us. You didn't mean to kill that devil. But I don't know what Mamma would say. She wouldn't want to help you run away and cause all that heartache to your family."

"What can I do? I can't go back." I could feel my whole body shaking.

"Wait a moment. I'm trying to think. Have you bruises from where he hit you?"

"Plenty. He always went for places where they wouldn't show."

I lifted my clothes and turned round so that he could see my back. Jamie pursed his lips.

"This is what we'll do. Before the others come back, we'll find somewhere where you can hide. I'll bring you some food. Tomorrow, you follow us but keep your distance. Once we're back on the mainland, I'll tell Mamma and Grandpappy what's happened. By then they will probably agree that you can stay."

So that's what I did. The first night I made a rough shelter of branches and moss, but I barely slept, through cold and fear. In the end I dozed off and dreamed of running through the sea with Bobby. I woke up happy but then a cold wave hit me when I remembered what had happened the day before. Bobby whined and licked my face.

"Well, I have to look after you Bobby, whatever happens."

I gave a start at the sound of twigs snapping but it was only Jamie, with a smile and a bowl of porridge.

The Second Surge of the Sea

"Did you sleep well under the stars, you soft house dweller? Don't look so glum. It's a fine, dry day."

I stayed hidden while the women set off to sell their wares. Jamie and his Grandpappy went off to fish. I couldn't bear being alone with my thoughts so after a while I wandered through the woods with Bobby snuffling at my heels.

"So, there you are, young man."

The voice behind me made me jump. It was Mrs Stewart, "I don't know how you and Jamie thought that you could keep your secret."

I had never heard her sound so stern.

"I was going to tell you once we reached the mainland. Please don't turn me away."

I could hear a sob bubbling in my throat.

"It's odd how folk think that they can run away with us travellers when they're in trouble and how desperate lassies try and give us their fatherless bairns."

"If you don't let me stay, I don't know how I can go on living."

Her voice softened. "There's nothing so bad under the sun that can't be endured. Come and sit down on this tree trunk and tell me your story."

So, the whole tale poured out in a flood while she listened and sucked her clay pipe. Her sunburnt face with its deep-set eyes was so still that I couldn't tell what she was thinking. When I finished, I hung my head, sure that she would send me away. Finally, she sighed, knocked out her pipe and put a finger under my chin to tilt my head up.

"You did a bad thing, but you didn't make excuses. If that wicked man is dead, it's not right that you should be punished. You didn't set out to kill him, only to defend yourself. You can stay but you will have to work hard."

"I don't know how to thank you," I said finally.'

My eyes were moist again as Pappa paused, deep in thought, and I decide to ask a question. 'What was your favourite job when you were with them? I bet that it was looking after the horses.'

He nodded, 'I had to harness them to the cart, feed and tether them when we stopped. I especially liked the white one. He whinnied and nuzzled me when I came up to him. He hadn't a name as they were going to sell him, but I called him *"Gille geal"*.'

'White boy? That wasn't very original!'

'But it's what he was,' he said, pretending to be offended.

'I did all I could to help – snaring rabbits, helping the girls, Jessie and Katie, gather firewood and set up the bow tent by stretching the tarpaulin over the frame of arched sticks. The next day we travelled to Kyleakin and the cart was rowed over on the ferry. I watched, remembering how Iain and I had taken the doctor's car over. That seemed a long time ago but there was no time to feel sad.

"Come on, Sandy. We've got to ride the horses over," said Jamie.

It was a cold, rough ride over the water with no time to dry out on the other side. Jamie laughed when he saw me shivering.

"Have you had enough of travelling yet?"

"No, of course not."

But at night, curled up with Bobby, I felt the ache of homesickness and of guilt. I had been so desperate to leave school but not in this way. It was like in the stories when the fairy folk grant someone a wish and it turns out to be tainted.'

He sighed, 'As we travelled, I got to know, Mr Stewart, Jamie's Grandpappy. I was relieved that he ignored me at first because I found him gruff and frightening but one day, he came up to me as I was brushing the white horse's tail.

"Tell me, lad. Have you got a bad temper?"

"No, Sir. I don't believe I have. I used to argue with my sister when she was bossy. But that's usual, isn't it? We made our peace before she left home."

The old man stared at me, frowning.

"I know that I shouldn't have struck Mr Graham so hard. I won't do that sort of thing again."

He tapped me on my shoulder.

"I believe that the Good Lord gives us a second chance. Would you like to learn tin smithing?"

"Aye, Sir."

"Follow me."

The old man had his own tent. Stacked behind it were sheets of tin, tools and things he had made. There were pails of different sizes, for milking or carrying water. There were baths for babies, tubs for washing clothes, basins, sieves and steamers for clootie puddings. Then there was smaller stuff – jugs, ladles, fish slices.

He pointed to his tools – anvils, hammers, and switches – the pieces of wood for beating the metal on.

"The blacksmith at home has an anvil but it's a bigger one," I said.

"This one's like a three-legged pickaxe. You stake it into the ground. I know of a man who killed someone with one of these – stove his head in. That's why I had to know if you had a temper."

I could feel my face reddening, but Mr Stewart just laughed.

"Then we need a mallet. A matchstick for measuring, solder sticks and resin to hold the tin together."

Next, he picked up a big spatula and turned it over to show me the pattern of a six-petal flower that was punched on the base.

"That's a pea strainer, isn't it? It's beautiful. I would like to make one like that for Mamma."

I felt a stab in my chest as I realised that I didn't know when or if I would see her again.

He smiled, showing yellow, crooked teeth.

"No, lad. You're not ready for that yet. You'll start with one of these."

He rummaged among a pile of old tins behind the pots.

"Folk save their old corned beef tins for us. We burn them for the solder. Wait a moment, that's what we need."

He pulled out a golden syrup tin, you know – coloured gold and green.'

'I used to hate that picture of the dead lion and the flies around it,' I say.

'Out of the strong comes forth sweetness,' Pappa replied.

'Mr Stewart showed me how to hammer out a lip and fit a handle. I was very proud of that wee jug.'

'Have you still got it?'

Pappa scratched his head, 'I've not seen it for a long time. Probably your Granny threw it out when we moved into this house. She doesn't like clutter.'

'That's a shame. I'm so pleased that the Stewarts helped you. Do they still come to Skye?'

He shrugged, 'We best get back home.'

CHAPTER 14

The next day Pappa says, 'I slept well last night.'

'That's good. Have you ever told your story to anyone else?'

'Màiri heard most of it but that was a long time ago. Are you getting weary of it?'

'Not at all. It's made me see how different the world was then.'

'I was thinking about that syrup tin cup. I was very proud of it. It meant that I had passed a test.

"Grandpappy has decided that you're one of us," Jamie had said. "That's why he showed you the tin smithing." He picked up the cup and squinted at it.

"The handle's not level."

"It is so!" I pretended to be offended but inside I was happy at being accepted by the Stewarts.

"He asked me if I had a temper. I suppose that's because of me hitting Mr Graham."

"Aye, but it's not only that. My big brother Angus has a terrible temper on him. Grandpappy told him to curb it and Angus took offence and left."

"Where's he now?"

"He said that he would make his fortune hunting pearls in the Tay."'

'From the oysters?' I interrupted.

Pappa nods, 'Jamie said, "Some travelling families have always done it and that they wouldn't like Angus barging in."

"You sound as if you don't like him very much, Jamie."

"He's a bully. He likes scaring folk with his size."

I felt a stab of sadness as I thought of how I missed my big brother, Iain. So, I asked Jamie more questions to distract myself.

"How big is he? As big as Benadonner, the giant who threw the rocks on the Giant's Causeway?"

Jamie laughed.

"Big enough. His arms are as big as most men's legs. You likely won't meet him. We're going south to Fort William and Kintyre. We may even sail over to Ireland."

My heart sank. That would take me even further away from my family. Jamie must have sensed that I was downcast because he reminded me about the ceilidh we would have that night. It did take me out of myself, right enough. I danced reels with Mrs Stewart and the girls until my feet were throbbing.

"Bring me your new cup, laddie," Mr Stewart said. "You've earned a wee dram."

When he filled it to the brim, I could only smell heather and myrtle in the drink but there must have been whisky too for soon I felt a glow through my body and my head started to spin. Then old Mr Stewart told his tale. It was the strangest tale I've ever heard but I think that I was still in a swoon from the drink.

"This is a story as old as the mists and the tides. I heard it from my Grandpappy who learnt it from his Pappa. Back it goes like a long chain to the beginning of time. It's about a sailor who kept an eye on the weather."

I closed my eyes and let myself be carried on the swell of the tale.

"Long, long ago the High King of Ireland and his wife had a fine son but sadly the Queen died. The king and his whole country were full of grief but in time the king decided that his son needed a mother. He fell in love and married again. The boy grew up into a strong, handsome young man and when he came of age his stepmother told him, 'I have a special present to give you.'

The young man was full of excitement, 'But I've never given you a present.'

The Second Surge of the Sea

'No matter. You shall have something beautiful to mark your coming of age.'"

Mr Stewart paused, and I wondered what this present would be – a bow that could shoot arrows for miles, a horse that could out-gallop any other or a silver whistle that could compose its own tunes.

Everyone seemed to be holding their breath and Mr Stewart went on.

"The present was a beautiful shirt, bright red with gold embroidery worked through it. It was made of silk so fine that the whole garment could pass through a small ring."

I didn't think that much of a present but knew that it must be a magical shirt. So, I kept listening.

"The king's son had never seen a shirt so light and soft. He put it on for the great feast to celebrate his birthday. It fitted him like a second skin and when he looked at himself in the bronze mirror, he couldn't believe how fine he looked. But then the fabric tightened, and he felt something curl up from his waist, creeping over his shoulder and behind his head. It was something alive, something thick and smooth winding over him. He shouted out and put his hand behind his back to grab the creature, but it was stuck fast and hissed when he touched it. It was a huge snake, and he knew at that moment that his stepmother had tricked him.

He locked the door of his chamber and tried to pull off the horrible creature, but it clung on even more tightly. He ran down the corridors of the castle, bent double with the weight of the snake coiled around him, its spitting head swaying from side to side.

'You must go and find the wise woman. She is the only one who can save you,' said his father, the king.

So, he ran to the bothy at the edge of the forest where the wise woman lived.

'Who played this terrible trick on you?' she asked.

'My stepmother the Queen.'

'May she be cursed to Hell and back for her wickedness.'

'Can you cure me and cut off this creature?'

She shook her head, 'Only one wise woman can do that. She lives on the hilltop of the island in Loch Leug.'

'But how am I to get there?'

She stirred the broth in the cauldron hanging over the fire.

'The only man alive who can get you there is the sailor who keeps his eye on the weather.'

The Prince's heart began to leap with hope but then the wise woman said, 'But he's blind and deaf and hasn't risen from his bed for seven years. Finish your broth and go to find him. He lives by the loch in an upturned boat.'

The Prince set out and found the old boat on the shore. He knocked on the hull and bent down to get inside the low door. As he did so he banged the snake on the lintel. It hissed and spat venom but it was the Prince who felt the pain.

'The snake has grown inside me,' he cried out.

It was dark inside the upturned boat, but the Prince could make out an ancient man, the oldest man he had ever seen.

'I'm deaf and blind but the ferry boat lies on the shore. Seven years she has waited for you. If you can move her.'"

I couldn't keep my eyes open. The drink had made me sleepy, and I could hardly bear to listen to the story because I knew that like the poor Prince, I had a monster coiled inside me. The poor Prince didn't deserve his fate. He had done nothing wrong, but I had killed a man and the guilt of that would squeeze my life away. Wherever I ran, I would carry the foul beast with me.

I don't know how long I slept but when I woke up Mr Stewart was still telling the tale and it seemed that the Prince had reached the island and been found by a maiden.

The Second Surge of the Sea

'I'm not afraid of the snake. I shall go and tell my mother that you are here,' the maiden told him. When she brought her mother back, they saw the Prince lying by the spring, tall and handsome, with his plaid covering the hump of the snake. The mother asked him to follow them to the house and her daughter fell in love with him.

So, the Prince got over to the island while I was asleep but now the story was being ruined by all that love stuff. But oddly, I felt more at peace than I had for days.

'I want to marry this Prince,' the daughter said.

'Would you lose an arm for him?'

'I would.'

'And would you lose a breast for him?'

I could feel my face getting red and hot and was glad of the darkness.

'Yes, I would because I love him.'

They killed a sheep for the wedding feast. The mother, her daughter and the Prince sat down while the meat was cooking in a giant frying pan.

'Light the lamp,' the mother told the Prince and she ordered her daughter to bare her right breast.

The cooking meat smelt tasty as it sizzled in the fat and the snake was hungry. Suddenly, it leapt from the Prince's back and straight into the pan where it burnt itself in the fat. It shot out at once but instead of clinging to the young man's neck again it landed on the girl's bare breast. Her mother was ready and with a great swipe of her knife she sliced off the creature's head, but the blade cut through the girl's breast as well. The snake's head and the breast fell to the floor and the mother covered them both with a basin. Then she plunged her knife into the fire until it was red hot and pressed it against the girl's body where her breast had been cut off. The wound was sealed, and the snake was dead while the Prince was straight and true again. When the mother lifted the basin, underneath it was the beautiful red embroidered shirt. She lifted it up on the point of the knife and tossed it into the fire. A huge explosion took down the fireplace and filled the room with black smoke. Once the girl's wound was healed a special gold breast was made to replace the one she had lost and the young couple were married."

The old man fell silent and looked at each person in turn until his gaze fixed on me.

'Is that the end of the story?' I'd asked.

'It is and it isn't, but that is enough for tonight. Do you feel easier in your mind, young man?'

'Aye, Sir, I believe I do.'

Soon after that I fell into a deep well of sleep where no nightmares could reach me but that wasn't the end of my troubles."'

I'm left speechless by the terrible tale and by realising that there is so much I don't know about Pappa.

'I haven't shocked you too much?' he asks.

I just shake my head. I feel beyond words.

CHAPTER 15

'I didn't really understand that strange tale but hearing it gave me some peace. I even began to wonder if I could return home and ask forgiveness but then I thought that real life isn't like a story. I would bring terrible shame on my family if I had killed Mr Graham. Even If he was injured but not dead, it would still be a disgrace.'

'But what you did was in self-defence and you were a child,' I protest.

'The law was harsher in those days, even for a child. And in a small place, people would never forget about it. It would be a stain on the family. Soon after that, I killed again.'

I couldn't stop my mouth hanging open.

'Many people would say that this was different and not my fault, but you will have to decide for yourself.'

I sit in stunned silence and wait.

'The next day, my head was throbbing from that potion I'd swallowed the day before. I decided to take a walk to clear my thoughts. It was misty so I was careful to take my bearings before I set off into the woods. After a few minutes I felt steadier on my feet but suddenly Bobby stopped, sniffed the air and growled. I heard a crashing of branches and a figure, a huge figure, burst out from the trees. I thought I was in a dream because this man was a giant, carrying a stick and beside him was a black dog, bigger than a wolfhound, like a wolf itself.

The giant laughed when he saw Bobby.

"Kill him, Scar!" he shouted.

I felt for the knife in my pocket. I knew that I would only have one chance and as the beast leapt forward to attack Bobby I bent low and stabbed it in the belly, forcing the knife through skin and hair. It howled in surprise and pain as I twisted the blade. I shouted to Bobby to run and the pair of us crashed through the undergrowth. I expected to hear footsteps come after us, but none came. I crouched down and hid behind a thick tree trunk until my heart stopped thumping. I didn't know where Bobby had gone but surely he would find me? I lost all idea of time and kept waiting, my body shaking and my ears straining for any sounds of the giant returning. As my head cleared, I knew that this was no creature from an old tale, but a real man, the brother, Angus Stewart, the pearl fisher, known for his foul temper. And if he found me, he would kill me for stabbing his dog.

That fear made me spring to my feet and run. I lost all track of time. I didn't dare stop in case Angus came after me and I was so cold that I feared I would freeze to death if I tried to sleep. And if I didn't freeze, I would be tormented by terrible dreams. I had hoped that Mr Stewart's story had somehow taken the killer's curse from me but now I knew that the vile creature was still stuck to me. Although Scar was a dog and a vicious one, I didn't blame the poor beast. His master had made him what he was and now I was being punished for the dog's death.

What was I to do? I couldn't go back to the Stewarts and put them in danger from Angus. My eyes prickled with tears when I remembered how kind they had been to me. In the end, I decided to go back to the edge of the thicket and see if Bobby had come back there. Then we could head home, and I would have to face up to whatever punishment awaited me. The cold had locked my legs and I had to rub them back to life. As I got closer to the thicket, I crawled forward on my belly. There was no sign of any living creature, so I risked crouching down and running.

The smell of blood hit my nostrils as I got close to where I had fought the dog. I put my hand down and felt a sticky mess.

The Second Surge of the Sea

I shuddered and wiped my hands on a clump of grass. As I did so, my fingers bumped into something soft. I picked it up. It was a leather drawstring purse that must have hung around Scar's neck and got torn off in the struggle. I loosened the fastening and felt inside – cool, smooth pearls. What should I do with them? I decided to keep them until I could give them to Mrs Stewart.

I stood up, fearing that I would trip over Scar's body but there was no sign of it. I headed downhill, hoping that there would be a village in the valley. If only Bobby was here with his clever nose to help me find the way. But when I scrambled downhill through clumps of bristly heather and whin bushes there was no village, only bleak moorland. Biting rain and bursts of hailstones stung my face. I bent down to scoop up water from the peaty pools, but my empty stomach was churning and worst of all was the panic breathing down my neck. Was Bobby lying bleeding in a ditch? I staggered on, knowing that my strength was ebbing away. Then my shaky legs slipped on the slimy rocks, and I fell. When I staggered to my feet, whimpering in pain, I stumbled against a tumbledown wall. That must mean there were houses at last. I lurched towards a low building but as I got close, my heart sank. It looked abandoned. The thatch had caved in and trees were growing up against the shuttered windows. I groped my way along a sagging wall until I found a door. I pushed my shoulder against the rotting wood. At least I could shelter inside. The door yielded and I peered in, struggling to see in the gloom. There was a glow at the end of the room, and I felt my way towards it.

"Come on dearie, I've been expecting you."

The hairs on the back of my neck stood up in terror. Where was the voice coming from? It didn't sound human. As my eyes became accustomed to the dark, I could make out a heap of rags near the fire. The rags stirred and something rose up. Even if it was a spirit, I knew that I had to risk meeting it if I was to survive.

I crept forward. A face peered out from under a shawl, a face that looked as if its skin was made of bark. The deep-set eyes were milky.

"It's yourself. I knew that you would come back to me."

A skeletal hand grasped my wrist with a grip that was much too strong for any ghost. Maybe it was a witch, but I was too tired to care.

"You must be hungry. I have bannocks and milk that my servants bring me each day."

The figure shuffled away, bent double like a hinge and returned with the food on a metal platter. In her other hand she held a tin cup of milk. Had the Stewarts made the cup, I wondered. I was so hungry that I swallowed the bannock whole.

"You've grown into a big, strong lad," she cackled. "You can have some more and a piece of crowdie too."

I decided that she was just a very old lady, not a witch or a spirit.

"I've been with the travelling people but now I'm heading back to Skye. I would be grateful if I could stay here tonight."

She smiled, showing brown stumps of teeth.

"Now you've come back to me, you must stay."

After she had given me more food, she watched me eat it, crooning to herself,

> *"Hushie, hushie, dinnae fret ye*
> *The black tinker winnae get ye.*

That's what they used to say but in the end I had to let the tinker lady take you. I couldn't keep you any longer."

I was only half listening because I was exhausted. I could feel myself swaying as I crouched down on the floor. She brought me a blanket that smelt sour, but I was past caring. I lay down on the earthen floor close to the fire. There was a hollow space where

Bobby should have been but as Mamma used to say, "The world looks better with a full belly and a good night's sleep."'

Pappa stops to dig out his pipe from his jacket pocket.

'That story sounds like a fairy tale – finding a wicked witch who tries to trap you.'

He shrugs, 'She was a poor soul who had lost a child a long time before.'

'Of course, Mrs Stewart said about women giving away illegitimate children. I suppose that could make you crazy.'

Pappa sucks on his pipe and continues, 'I was too young to understand all that, but I remember waking up the next morning with my heart thumping like a caged bird against my ribs. She was standing over me, her fingers hooked and leathery, the nails yellow and dirty but she was holding a bowl of porridge for me and I was too hungry to care. It was too dark to see if there were mice and cobwebs. She kept staring at me, making me feel uneasy.

"Thank you. You're very kind to a stranger like me."

"But you're no stranger."

I finished the food and gave her back the dish, thinking how horrified Mamma would be at the grime everywhere.

"I have to find my wee dog and then we can go back home to Skye."

She gripped my arm and squeezed hard.

"What do you mean? You're not going anywhere, not when I've just found you again."

The cloudiness had gone from her eyes, and she stared at me with a gannet's fierce blue stare. I shivered.

"But we've never met before, and I must find my family."

"We have met but you were too young to remember."

I was scared now and tried to pull away but she tightened her grip. I didn't want to fight a poor *Cailleach*. I feared that killing strength in my arm, so I pretended to go along with her.

"You're right. I don't remember but I have something in my bag to show you."

She let me go and I forced myself to saunter over to where I had left my bag and jacket. I snatched them up and rushed to the door. But she was quick and almost caught me as I pushed my shoulder against the door. I squeezed out, slammed it shut and leant against it.

"Come back my little one, my son," she wailed.

I had to run away but which way? Through the driving rain I could make out another tumbledown building. Someone was coming out of the door. He shook his fist at me.

"What are you doing?"

"Looking for my way home."

'You're a liar and a thief, preying on that poor soul."

He charged at me, and I ran away but I was weak and he was gaining on me. I remembered watching how hares escaped by suddenly changing direction. I veered to the right and the man stumbled. I kept running without looking round, struggling uphill with no idea where I was. The rain was pouring down and I was more exhausted than I had ever been in my life. I kept looking down at my feet to stop myself tripping over the rocks, but I had to stop to get my breath back. I looked up and saw hills in the distance, hills with jagged spikes like a dragon's back. It was the Cuillin! I fell down on my knees and cried with relief.

I got to my feet and staggered forward. If only I could rest. It was cold and windy, but my body was on fire. I almost missed the bothy, beside the gully. It was empty, dry inside with straw on the floor. I made a rough bed. Sleep came quickly but it was a tormented sleep.

I dreamt that I was on a rocky shore with Mr Graham chasing me. He caught me by my collar so that I fell over. I grabbed one of his ankles and he came crashing down, his head hitting a jagged rock. I knew at once that he was dead and that I must bury him. I scraped out a hollow on the shore and dragged his body to it. Then I piled rocks on top of him.

Then I was back in the old woman's house.

"Eat your fish up," she said, handing me a knife and fork. I turned them over, thinking how strange the handles were. They were made of moving bits of bone.

"They're the fingers of my poor murdered husband. If his killer holds them, they will prove his guilt."

I tried to drop them, but they stuck to my fingers.

"You're the murderer. You will hang!"

I sat bolt upright and screamed. It was a long time before I stopped shaking. It was Iain who had told me the terrible story about the bones. Mamma skelped him for scaring me out of my wits. Now I was too scared to fall asleep again, but my eyelids were heavy and this time I sank into a dreamless pit.'

CHAPTER 16

'I can hardly believe that you had all these adventures.'

Pappa frowned.

'I don't mean that I don't believe you, but I can't imagine that sort of thing happening. Well, not in respectable suburbia where I live.'

'It seems so long ago to you, I suppose, and they were strange times.'

'You were in real danger. You could have died of exposure.'

'Aye, but I was lucky. I don't know – maybe I dreamt some of it. I had a fever. I didn't know what was real and what wasn't.'

He sounds desperate and I don't want him to stop talking.

'It doesn't matter. Please carry on.'

'Well, I woke up to feel a damp nose against my cheek. I thought that I was back home with Bobby and started to cry. I couldn't believe it when I felt a wet tongue licking away my tears.

"Come here, Jock."

I opened my eyes to see bright eyes staring at me. It was a dog! But not Bobby. A sheepdog with one brown eye and one blue one.

"I told you to come." A gruff voice.

Was it the man who had shouted at me earlier? I tried to stand up, but my head was spinning. The man came closer and I saw that he was older than the one I saw before and he was carrying a crook. I tried to speak but all that came out was a croak.

"Who are you? A deserter from the camp?"

I shook my head, and he came closer.

"No, I can see you're too young for a soldier. Well, Jock likes you and he's a good judge of character, so I'll give you the benefit of the doubt."

The Second Surge of the Sea

He reached into his coat pocket and passed me a hip flask. My lips were cracked, and I swallowed the whisky gladly, but it made me splutter.

"So, what are you doing in my bothy? It's rarely I see any living creature, except Jock and the sheep."

He crouched down to fetch a kettle and lit the primus stove. I think I fell asleep before the water boiled and woke again in the darkness to find Jock curled up beside me. I could hear the old shepherd snoring. I sighed with relief and fell asleep again. The following days all slipped together, with me not knowing if it was day or night. Now and then the shepherd woke me for a drink of tea, but I shook my head when he brought food.'

'You must have been really ill, Pappa. I know how you love your food.'

'Aye, that's true but one day I woke up, starving hungry.

"You're back to yourself, laddie," the shepherd said.

"I must be on my way."

"Not yet. You're as weak as water after that lung fever. You were delirious and talking nonsense about killing someone."

"Just nightmares, I suppose."

But I was terrified that I had shouted out Mr Graham's name when I was delirious.

"Go and stretch your legs but nothing more for now."

"Thank you for taking care of me, Mr…?"

"Duncan MacIver. And you're…?"

"Er… Simon, Simon Beaton."

I staggered over to the tiny window and gasped.

"There's thick snow!"

"Aye, it got colder while you were away with the fairies. and I have been getting the ewes out of snowdrifts. So, you can't go anywhere until the snow melts."

I stayed there, getting my strength back. Mr MacIver wasn't

much of a talker but in the evenings, he spoke about his life while Jock curled up round my feet.

"It suits me fine being a shepherd. My father was one before me. He came down from Sutherland after everyone in his village was cleared off the land. Some folk here blamed him for working as a shepherd for the landlord so we kept to ourselves. I carried on. You have to like solitude. I did think of marrying once but my lass, Dolly, died of the consumption."

It sounded a lonely sort of life to me. After a few days, I woke early one morning, and the air felt warmer. I opened the door to see the snow melting and a watery sun.

"I must go now, Mr MacIver. I can only thank you for saving my life."

"You could stay and learn shepherding. You have a way with dogs."

"That's kind of you but I must get back to my family on Skye."

He looked sad but he squeezed my shoulder and smiled.

"Take care of yourself. You don't want to risk getting consumption. It would be best if you head towards the army camp near Fort William and then head north. I'll walk with you to set you in the right direction.'"

CHAPTER 17

'It seems to me that you met the best and the worst of people on your journey, Pappa.'

'Aye, and that wasn't the end of it.

I was both longing to get home and dreading it too. I strode along readily enough for the first few miles but then my legs grew heavy, and my head started to throb. Being ill for so long had weakened me more than I knew. So, I sat down, leaning against a rowan tree at the side of the road, thinking I would rest my eyes for a few minutes. I must have dozed off and I was jolted awake by the sound of voices and tramping feet. I got to my feet and saw soldiers marching towards me. Maybe Iain would be among them.

"Are you Camerons?" I asked one of them.

"No, laddie, we're Lovat Scouts."

I could feel tears pooling in my eyes. I knew that I was being silly. Iain had left for France months earlier. He couldn't be here. I waited while they marched past but then I heard a voice saying,

"Are you alright, laddie? You're swaying on your feet."

The next thing I knew I was on the ground with a strong arm propping me up and someone else holding out a canteen of water.

"You passed out. Do you live near here?" It was the soldier who had spoken before.

"No. I'm on my way back to Skye."

"Just as well. You're too young to join up," he said, laughing.

"Get back in line, Private Ross."

"Aye, Sir, but this lad is ill. I think that we should take him to the doc in the camp."

"He can come if he can walk."

I struggled to my feet.

"Take your time, laddie. Yon pain in the backside officer can wait a wee moment," he whispered and then spoke more loudly, "He's coming, Sir."

So off we went with Private Murdo Ross holding up one of my arms and Private Tom Henderson holding up the other.

"This new recruit's a bit on the small side," the doctor said, peering over his spectacles.

"We found him on the road, Sir. He had fainted."

"Hmm. You look pale, young man. Let me sound your chest."

The doctor had an English voice and was much younger than the doctor at home but he was kind. My eyes welled up again and I had to keep blinking.

"You've had pneumonia but luckily, you're on the mend. Not well enough to go gallivanting around the countryside though. You can stay in the sick bay for a few days where I can keep an eye on you."

I didn't want to stay but I was as weak as a new lamb. I had the sick bay to myself and slept like the dead. I even had to be woken up to eat when my food came. Can you imagine it?'

We both laugh at such an unlikely idea.

'My new friends came to see me and keep my spirits up.

"Are you getting fed properly?" Tom asked.

"Aye. I'm full as an egg," I said, patting my belly.

"We'll look out for your brother when we get to France. How's he doing out there?" Murdo asked.

"I don't know. I've been away from home for a while, so I've not heard." I was getting uneasy about talking about home and closed my eyes.

"He'll be busy killing those damn Huns who wear those funny helmets with the spikes on top. We'll leave you in peace now, laddie."

The Second Surge of the Sea

"Your chest sounds clearer," the doctor said when he came to see me the next day.

"Can I go back home, Sir?"

"Well, I think you need a few more days to recover. What were you doing anyway wandering around the countryside?"

"I...er...it's a long story Sir, but I want to get home."

I could feel the doctor's eyes boring into me but "Hmm" was all he said.

That evening someone else came to see me. He had thinning grey hair and a sparse wee moustache. When he sat down on the edge of the bed, I noticed his clerical collar and felt myself stiffen.

"Hello Simon." I blinked in surprise then remembered my false name and nodded.

"I'm Reverend Sinclair. Doctor Carmichael asked me to look in on you."

"I just want to get home, Sir. I lost my dog and need to find him."

He nodded.

"I see. You're rather young to be away from home."

"It's a long story, Sir."

"Well, I've plenty of time to listen."

His voice was calm and gentle. Suddenly I felt a longing to unburden myself.

"I hit a man but I hurt him more than I meant to."

"What happened?"

"He fell over and banged his head. I was scared and ran away. He was a bully and a tyrant, but I didn't mean to kill him. I only wanted to stop him."

I was sweating and shaking. Saying the words aloud made them come alive.

"Who was this man?"

"A schoolmaster, Sir."

"You hit a schoolmaster?" His voice sharpened.

"Where did this happen?"

Too late I realised my mistake in trusting him.

"Near Inverness."

He rose to his feet and straightened his tunic. His eyes were cold.

"This is a grave matter, Simon. You struck a man who had authority over you. Violence is never justified, even if he treated you unkindly. I'll need to think about this matter."

He stood up and left me all a-tremble. I knew that it was time for me to leave.'

I'm incensed, 'But that's so wrong. He pretended to be your friend, encouraged you to talk and then turned on you without knowing the whole story. And he's telling soldiers that it's their duty to kill Germans. What a hypocrite!'

Pappa shrugged, 'It was a different world then. You had to do what your betters told you.'

'But he wasn't better in any way! He was worse.'

'Anyway, he did me a favour because after running away again I met someone who was very important in my life.'

'Who was that?'

'I'll tell you tomorrow.'

I sigh in frustration. 'You're like Scheherazade, the storyteller in the "Arabian Nights". She feared being killed by her husband if she stopped telling the stories that he enjoyed so much. So, she kept creating cliff hangers.'

'Well, I hope that I'm not in that sort of danger. But I find it tiring, pulling out all these tales from my poor old brain.'

He smiles as he speaks, and I think how much better he looks now and how much happier I feel too. It's as if we escape to another dimension that makes the drab present more bearable.

CHAPTER 18

'Well, I'm waiting for the next instalment,' I say as we set off the next day, giving his hand a squeeze.

'And where were we?' he says, scratching his head.

'You're teasing me! I know that you remember.'

'Ach well. I was thinking about getting away from the army camp before that chaplain brought the police. I dressed quickly although my hands were shaking, and I was putting on my shoes when the door opened. My heart was racing, and I gasped with relief when I saw that it was Murdo.

"What's the matter, lad? Have you seen a ghost?"

I stumbled out the story and he shook his head.

"Well, he's an officer and a chaplain so he sees the world differently from the likes of us. The gentry do, don't they? You were right to hit that bully and it wasn't your fault that he fell and struck his head. That chaplain's always lecturing us about not drinking or mixing with loose women."

I must have looked puzzled, and he hurried on.

"Well, never mind about that. We need to get you on the road. I'll check that the coast is clear and take you out the back way."

We made our way through the fields behind the camp. My legs were still wobbly, but fear spurred me on.

"Do you have to go back to Skye? Why not head for Glasgow until things settle down a bit? Is there anyone there you could stay with? Think about it while I go and get some gear for you."

While I waited, I stamped my feet to stop shivering and thought about Màiri. I knew her address. Would she help me? We argued a lot before she left home, but I remembered how kind she had been in the past. She had clasped my hand when she took me to school when I was wee and told me that it would all be fine.

Murdo was soon back, carrying a kitbag.

"There's some money there from the lads and a Lovat Scout cap. If this war carries on long enough you might be joining us."

"I don't know how to thank you."

"We Highlanders always stick together. Will you go to Glasgow?"

"Aye, I'll go to my sister. Will you get into trouble for helping me escape?"

He tapped the side of his nose and grinned, just like Iain used to do and I felt ill with homesickness.

"How would they know? None of us saw anything. Get along now. Here's a plaid to wrap round yourself at night, like the old Highlanders used to do."

He slapped me on the back and was off. I felt rich. The coins were heavy in my pocket. I soon found a cowshed where I could sleep for the night. The smell of the beasts and their snuffling were a comfort. I slept soundly and when I counted out the coins found that I had over two pounds. It seemed like a fortune. Surely my luck was changing. I would walk to Loch Lomond and then head for the city. I woke to a crisp morning and ate some of the bully beef Murdo had given me. It tasted a bit strange, but I was too hungry to care. I filled my golden syrup tin with clear water from a stream and wondered where the Stewart family were now. If only Bobby was with me. The loss of him squeezed my heart. I kept well back from the road as I didn't want to risk meeting anyone.

I set off before it was fully light and hadn't been walking long when I heard a moaning sound from the undergrowth. I strained my ears. Was it some animal in pain? Fear made me want to keep well away but what if it was Bobby? I crept towards the sound,

The Second Surge of the Sea

ready to run at any moment. I could see some sort of shape right down by the shore. While I hesitated, the mound groaned. As I edged forward it squirmed and tried to move. I dreaded the idea of meeting any more weird or angry people but whoever this was, he looked too helpless to hurt me. As I inched closer the creature let out a sob. The legs were curled up, the head raised. I gasped as I saw the blood on the man's bearded face. Was it the spirit of Mr Graham come back to haunt me? I leapt back in alarm, closing my eyes. When I screwed them open to look again, I realised that this was a younger face, a long, thin one with locks of dark hair curling down the cheeks.

"Can I help you?" I whispered, keeping my distance.

His head wobbled and he seemed to find it hard to focus.

"Wait a moment and I'll bring you some water."

When I came back with cool water from the stream, I found him trying to sit up and feeling his swollen lips. He nodded in thanks and swallowed with heaving gulps. Then he ran his fingers over his face and winced.

"Did someone hit you?"

He licked his lips before croaking, "Two men attacked me before taking my pack."

"Are you able to stand up? Try leaning on me."

"I'll try."

He reached for my arm and lurched to his feet, groaning with the pain, and nearly toppling me over.

"Nothing broken, I think. Just bruised and battered."

When he steadied, I fetched my plaid and wrapped it round his shoulders.

"Do you think they'll come back? If not, I'll make a fire to warm you up."

"No. It must be several hours since they ran off. I think that I blacked out for a while. Now my kind friend, tell me your name."

"Sandy."

"And I'm Samuel Goldstein. I thank you, Sandy, from the bottom of my heart."

"You would have done the same for me. Are you travelling to Glasgow?"

He nodded.

"Well, we can travel together. I've some money so we can pay for a cart."

"I must try to clean myself first," he said.

So, I fetched water from a stream, looking over my shoulder the whole time. What if the robbers came back and took my pearls and money? If only Bobby was there, he would warn us of danger. Samuel cleaned his face and then brushed down his black coat and trousers.

"Do I look a respectable mensch again?"

Then he touched his head. "No, wait a minute, I've lost my hat."

We hunted for it until I noticed something black and crumpled beside a rock.

"Oh dear, it's as battered as its owner," he said as he tried to bend it back into shape before wedging it on his head.

So, we set off, with Samuel leaning heavily on me. I wanted to keep moving so we struggled on slowly along the road.

Some people passed, a few cars, lorries and horses but everyone kept their distance. After a couple of hours, we stopped for a rest, and I offered Samuel some bully beef. But he looked at it suspiciously.

"It's not pork, is it?"

"No, it's called bully beef. It's what soldiers eat. I'll get you some water so that you can wash the rest of the blood away."

Samuel cleaned his face and hands with water from a stream. There was some colour in his cheeks now. So, I felt that I could ask him the question that was pressing on my lips.

The Second Surge of the Sea

"I hope you don't mind me asking but I wondered why you're all dressed in black and your hair is long at the sides."

"You don't know? You've never met a Jew before? That's why the ruffians attacked me. They knew that I'm a travelling pedlar. I've got a German name so that gave them an excuse. And I speak Yiddish which is a sort of German."

"But you sound like a Scot."

"It's complicated, isn't it? My parents came here to escape persecution in their homeland."

"So why do you dress like you do?"

Samuel laughed.

"Why do you Scots wear tartan skirts and play those fiendish bagpipes? It's just different customs. We can talk more about it as we walk along. You can tell me more about yourself.'"

'Did you tell him? You'd given him your real name.'

'I'm glad to see that you've been paying attention. Well, I wasn't going to risk telling him the whole story, but I explained that my sister was working for a family called Cohen.

"Heime Cohen who owns the tailor's shop? Well, I never. He's a good mensch. We'll go and find him."'

'What a coincidence, Pappa!', I say.

'Maybe but Jews and Highlanders are both clannish.'

CHAPTER 19

I think about Pappa's story when I lie in bed. Somehow, I hadn't associated Jewish people with the Highlands. I thought that they only lived in cities although I knew that there were travelling merchants of different nationalities. I remember, too, Granny talking about working as a nursemaid for a Jewish family in Glasgow after she left school. The little boy she cared for came to see her in Skye years later so he must have had fond memories of her, but I hadn't given it any thought beyond that. So, I wanted to talk more about the subject the next day.

'You know Pappa, I've been thinking about Samuel. I don't really know anything about Jewish people at all. There's a girl in my class at school who always seemed a bit separate from the rest of us although she was nice enough. Then someone else told me that she was Jewish and it all made sense. That's why she didn't come to assemblies – Catholics didn't either. I wished that I had known sooner and maybe I could have claimed not to be Church of England and got out of assemblies too.'

'Well, don't tell your Granny that! The only Jews I knew of growing up were men like Samuel who travelled around as salesmen, carrying cases of silks, ribbons, buttons and things like that. I always thought that it must be a lonely sort of life.'

'Anyway, I want to hear what happened next after you met Samuel. You were like the Good Samaritan rescuing him.'

Pappa turns a bit pink, 'I wouldn't say that but he played an important part in the story. We set off on the road to Glasgow. Samuel made light of his injuries, but he was limping badly. Finally, a cart stopped for us, and we climbed on the back among the sacks of potatoes. The rhythm of the horses' hooves lulled us both asleep until I was woken with a jolt by the noises of the city. There was a racket with people shouting, trams rattling along and horns hooting.

"I'll drop you off in the centre," the driver said.

I thanked him and handed over a fistful of coins as Samuel woke up, yawning.

"Isn't the Jew paying? They have pots of money?"

I glared at the man as I helped Samuel climb down.

"Do folk treat you like that all the time?" I asked him as the cart drove off.

Samuel shrugged, "It happens."

"But it's not right."

"Never mind for now. Let's find the Cohens' house. They live near the University."

Màiri would like that, I thought. We had to keep stopping for Samuel to catch his breath.

"I might have cracked a rib or two," he said between gasps.

I noticed that people gave us funny looks as we walked along the streets, full of big houses. I suppose we looked like beggars in our old, dirty clothes.

"Here we are," Samuel said pointing at a big stone house at the corner of two roads. I gawped. It looked nearly as big as the MacDonald mansion at Skeabost. I hung back as Samuel lifted the big lion's head knocker on the front door. It was flung open by a large woman, wearing a shining white apron and a surly expression. I cringed as she looked us up and down before sniffing. Samuel doffed his battered hat.

"I'm a friend of Mr Cohen."

She glowered and started to shut the door, but Samuel put his foot in the way.

"I don't think you should do that. Just go and tell Mr Cohen that his friend Mr Goldstein is here."

She sniffed again and let us into the hallway. Samuel winked at me while we waited. I looked around me at the dark wooden floor, the polished chairs against the wall and the glowing redness of the rug. What would Mamma make of this house? The thought made me tearful, and I had to keep blinking as I looked around me. I heard footsteps and a slight man appeared. He had long curls on his cheeks like Samuel and an embroidered cap on his head.

He stared at us and no wonder. We must have looked a terrible sight.

Samuel laughed, "I've been in the wars, but I'm still your old friend, Sammy."

He held out his arms to Samuel and they hugged, talking in a language I couldn't understand. Then Samuel turned to me.

"This is my saviour, Sandy MacPherson, who rescued me after I was attacked and I believe his sister is working here for you."

"Like the Good Samaritan," Mr Cohen said.

"Our guests look exhausted, Mrs Galbraith. Bring them something to eat."

"I had no idea who they were, sir. They looked like beggars."

"Never mind. Go and find this young man's sister. What's her name?"

A tall, pretty young woman, dressed in a nursemaid's uniform arrived and I realised with a shock that it was my sister. She hugged me tightly against her starched white apron before releasing me and holding me at arm's length. I could feel my face splitting into a huge grin.

"You've grown so tall, but you look a sight in those rags."

"Why don't you take Sandy to the kitchen and catch up with your news," Mr Cohen said.

"We'll go through to the drawing room, Samuel.'"

'The servants were kept in their place, then, even though you had saved Samuel's life,' I snort.

'Well, it's exaggerating to say that I saved his life and times were different then. I didn't feel offended, just happy to see my sister.'

"'Have you heard from Mamma and Dadda? Any news about Iain or any sign of Bobby?" I asked her once we were on our own.

"Hold on a moment. You've not asked me about how I am. And what have you been up to, running off and not telling anyone what you were doing?"

My sister hadn't lost her sharpness.

"Well, I can see how well you look – and happier too. I'll explain later when there's no-one else around but please tell me about the family."

"Aye, but you need to explain yourself. You've caused our parents so much grief." She poked me in the chest before speaking, "Leaving home has turned out better than I expected. Iain is in France now. There was an outbreak of measles in the camp he first went too, in Bedford. He caught it but got better. Some of the lads with him died. Mamma is worried sick about him and especially about you. She doesn't say much about Dadda in her letters. I don't know if his chest is better or if it's that she doesn't want to upset me."

"And what about Bobby?"

She rolled her eyes.

"No sign of him, but dogs can look after themselves."

I could feel my eyes welling up but at that moment a kitchen maid came in with some food – bowls of thin broth with dumplings and shiny bread rolls with a hole in the middle, fish balls and honey cakes. I fell on it all like a wolf. When we finished Mr Cohen came in with Samuel and a woman who was introduced as Mrs Cohen. I tried not to stare. Was she wearing a wig?

"Did you enjoy our Jewish food?" she asked.

"Yes, thank you, especially after that strange bully beef that we had to eat on the way."

"My brother has the appetite of a gannet," my sister said.

Mrs Cohen poured out cups of tea. I looked around for a milk jug until Màiri kicked me under the table. Something else that I didn't understand.

"That attack was a bad business," Mr Cohen said.

"I thought that we had seen the last of the pogroms."

"Those men were just thieves. You find them everywhere," Samuel replied.

"Yes, but they think they will get away with robbing Jews."

Seeing my puzzled expression he added, "The pogroms are attacks on Jewish people in countries like Russia where our people have lived for generations. That's why so many of us emigrated to Britain or America where people are more tolerant."

"I suppose the pogroms are like the Clearances in the Highlands when people were driven out of their homes and forced to emigrate so that the landowners could bring in sheep," Màiri said.

"There's a lot of injustice and cruelty in the world," said Mr Cohen. Then he turned to me, "Well, young Good Samaritan, how did you come to be on the road?"

Everyone turned to look at me and I could feel my sister's eyes boring into me. I had been thinking about what to say and decided that telling part of the truth was better than lying.

"Well, I was unhappy at school, especially with my brother and sister gone away. I couldn't endure the thought of any more school learning. I know it was a foolish thing to do but on the spur of the moment I decided to run away. I knew a family of travelling people and followed them so that they were forced to help me. Then their wild son appeared, and I had to leave in a hurry. I tried to make my way home and stopped at the house of a strange old woman who thought that I was her long-lost son and wanted to keep me with her. I had to run away from there too."

"Poor woman. She must have lost her mind," Mrs Cohen said.'

'You didn't say anything about finding the pearls or about running away from the army camp?' I say.

'Well. Would you? They would either think I was a rogue or someone who made up stories.'

Pappa continued, '"Well, you've had enough adventures to last a lifetime. What will you do now?" Samuel asked.

"Go home and ask my Mamma and Dadda to forgive me for all the heartache I've caused them. I've been punished for it all because I've lost my best friend, my wee dog Bobby."

"That's sad but your parents will be so happy and relieved to know that you're safe. I can't imagine how I would feel if one of my children were lost. Now what about a hot bath and a soft bed?"

"Thank you, Sir."

Now that I was safe, I suddenly felt exhausted.'

CHAPTER 20

The next day I'm ready with my questions.

'Did you make it up with Màiri? I can't imagine what it's like having brothers and sisters.'

'And I can't imagine what it's like not having them. It must be lonely although there were times when I felt I had seen more than enough of my sister. I knew that I would get a tongue lashing about running away as soon as she got me by myself.'

'How did that happen?'

Pappa laughs, 'She caught me in the bath when there was no escape! I was lying down in the warm water, watching it turn black as all the dirt lifted from my skin. She rattled the door and barged in. I shouted out and she threw me a towel.

"What are you shrieking about? I bathed you and changed your nappy often enough."

"But I'm grown up now."

She just laughed. I knew she wouldn't be satisfied until she heard the whole story, so I made her look away while I got out of the bath and wrapped myself in the towel. I had never felt one so big and soft on the skin.

"What did Mamma tell you in her letters?"

"About how upset and worried she was, not knowing where you were and if you were alive or dead. She couldn't understand why you wouldn't tell her about what was worrying you."

"She didn't say anything about Mr Graham, the new teacher?"

Màiri frowned and shook her head.

I took a shuddering breath.

"The weight of it is crushing me. I'll tell you if you promise not to pass it on to anyone else and you mustn't hate and despise me."

She glared at me, "How can I make any promises when I don't know what you're going to say?"

I could feel tears trickling down my cheeks and brushed them away angrily.

"Well, I can see you're very upset and even though you're annoying you're not wicked."

She reached over and wiped my face with her handkerchief. Her unexpected gentleness made me sob all the more.

She listened while I told her the whole story without interrupting me. When I stumbled to a halt, she surprised me by asking, "What do other people know?"

"Mrs Stewart knows but I can't see her going to the police. The travellers don't trust them. I told the army chaplain some of it, but I called myself Simon and said that I lived near Inverness. I tried to tell Murdo the soldier, but he stopped me saying much."

"That's good. You're learning the ways of the world."

"Well, I am older now."

She smiled.

"I know – you're almost a *boduch (old man)*."

"You don't seem shocked."

"When you grow up you realise that things aren't so black and white. It was unpremeditated. You didn't mean to kill Mr Graham and he had provoked you beyond endurance."

"Where did you learn all those long words?"

"The Cohens have a library, and I can borrow what I like. They're good to me. I have to work long hours, but they encourage me to read whatever I want to."

"They've got a library in their house?"

"They have. I've read all of Sir Walter Scott and now I've got interested in the law. I always said that education was a good idea."

"I didn't think that I was strong enough to knock him over. I didn't know that he had a false leg."

She started giggling and suddenly seemed years younger.

"I know it's not really funny, but I can't help laughing."

"But I still killed him, even though I didn't mean to. I'll have to go to court, and I could be hanged. That's what they do to murderers. And Mamma and Dadda will be so ashamed that they will have to go and live somewhere else where no-one knows them."

My voice started to crack and Màiri put her hand up.

"Wait a moment. Children aren't hanged."

She closed her eyes.

"Let me think. Are you sure that he's dead?"

That jolted me.

"No, not for sure but if he isn't he must have been badly hurt and I would still go to prison."

"Not if I can help it. I won't have that bully ruining your life."

She sounded so fierce, and I suddenly remembered how she had punched a bigger lad who was tormenting me in the playground. She had hissed and spat like a wildcat until my attacker backed off.

"Did anyone see you hit him?"

I shook my head.

"Did the other scholars like him?"

"No. Everyone was scared of him."

"So even if anyone saw anything they wouldn't give you away?"

"I suppose not."

"So, it's all circumstantial evidence."

"What?"

"There's nothing to prove you hit him. You stick to your story of him bullying you. You were so miserable and scared that you ran away. You didn't write anything incriminating in the note you left?"

I stared blankly at her and she put on the impatient, superior expression that I remembered so well of old.

"You didn't write anything that could give you away?"

"No."

Màiri smiled.

"It's all circumstantial evidence, then. There's nothing to prove that you hit him. Stick to saying that he bullied you and you couldn't bear it any longer, so you ran away. I'll write home and say that you're safe and will be back soon. When you get back, just stick to your guns – you know nothing about Mr Graham being attacked."

"You should become an advocate. Do they allow women to do that? I'll add a note to your letter. I can write too, you know."

Màiri sniffed.

"I suppose you can. I'll ask the Cohens if you can stay for a few days. I don't think that they'll mind."

"And I've got money for the train home.'"

CHAPTER 21

I notice how Pappa is stronger now. Perhaps telling his story, especially the worst part about killing the teacher – or did he really? Has he purged the poison that was destroying his peace of mind? Or am I kidding myself? Anyway, Granny is not so prickly. She's not criticising me all the time and has started to cook nice food – lamb chops, roast chicken and, especially, pancakes. Both Pappa and I enjoy our food so that's good news. All the other stuff that upset me is sort of at a distance now. It's as if Pappa and I are on a train. The journey is what matters and everything else flashes by as part of the scenery. At the moment, we're relaxing through gentle hills and sunlit valleys.

'Anyway, the Cohens said that I was welcome to stay with them. I tried to help by playing with Benjamin, the elder child who was four. That left my sister free to deal with Miriam, the baby. Màiri explained to me about the family's Jewish customs.

"Married women wear a wig on top of their own hair. It's just a rule like women wear hats in church and men don't. I'm so lucky to work for the Cohens," she said as we walked along to the park, with me carrying Benjamin on my shoulders, his heels drumming into my shoulders and Màiri pushing a pram the size of a small carriage.

"You like working for them, don't you?"

She stopped to think for a moment.

"Aye, I do. I get Sundays off and Wednesday afternoons and two evenings a week."

"Not Saturdays?"

"No, that's the Jewish Sabbath. That's why the family have Christian servants so that we can work on Saturdays when they're not allowed to do anything."

"So, you don't have much time to go courting?"

"That's none of your business, you cheeky monkey," she said, punching my arm. "I'm not interested in any of that. I want to get on and not be a servant for ever."

"You don't want to get married?"

"I do not, at least not until I'm over thirty and really old."

"But lassies always want to get married."

"Not this one!"

She reached into her bag and pulled out a scarf that was coloured green, white and purple.

"Do you know what this is?"

"It looks like a scarf."

"It's a suffragette scarf. Don't look so blank, Sandy. You must have heard of them. There were lots of marches before the War began. They blew up post boxes, threw stones through windows and tied themselves to railings."

"But you could be sent to prison for doing those things!"

"We could go together! Don't look so worried – I'm only teasing you. The Suffragettes have stopped campaigning while the War's going on. Don't worry, Mamma and Pappa won't have to visit either of us in prison."

"It's not funny." I could feel fear tightening its claws.

"I hope that we get a letter back from home soon.'"

The letter arrived the next day, Pappa says, as he rummages in his pocket. He pulls out a yellowed piece of paper, all curled at the edges. He hands it to me.

'You read it. I haven't got my spectacles.'

I open it up carefully and read it aloud.

Dear Màiri,

Thank the Lord that Sandy has arrived safe and sound. We've heard from Iain too. He sent a postcard from the Front saying that he's well. We are blessed that all our children are safe.

Sandy must get home as soon as he can. It's very kind of Mr and Mrs Cohen to let him stay with them. He will want to come back now as Bobby appeared yesterday, looking very thin with his coat all tangled. We didn't recognise him at first. We don't know where he's been. One of the neighbours said that there was talk of some drovers who stopped at the Cluanie Inn with a grey terrier that looked like Bobby. We shall never know the whole story.

Your ever loving parents.

"I can't believe it!" I sobbed, dancing a wild jig and swinging Màiri round with me, "I can face anything now!"

"You deserve some good luck after how you helped me," said Samuel when I told him the news. "I shall get you a new suit of clothes for going home.'"

'You didn't like the suit?', I say, seeing Pappa's mouth turn down.

'I did not. It was a loud tweed with an orange stripe – and knickerbockers! I looked as if I should be on the stage or a grouse moor. "Just stick to your story," Màiri whispered in my ear as I boarded the tram to take me to Queen Street Station.'

CHAPTER 22

'That must have been hard – going home to face the music. I remember last year when a group of us skived off school and hitchhiked up to London but when we went back to class the teacher demanded a letter from our parents about our absence and we got found out.'

'And you weren't alone in your misdeeds, facing the music alone. I remember looking over the rail of the steamer from Kyle, peering into the darkness with my new shiny leather suitcase wedged between my feet. What would Mamma and Dadda say to me? I scanned the pier when we docked. Where were they? Surely, they would come to meet me? I had written to say when I would be arriving. I climbed down the gangplank and stood waiting until all the other passengers had gone. Then I stuffed my fancy tweed cap into my pocket and picked up the case. I hurried away, with my head down and hoping that I wouldn't meet anyone I knew. No such luck!

"Is that yourself, Sandy MacPherson?"

It was Mistress MacQueen, a nosy woman who spent her time scooping up pieces of gossip and offering them to everyone she met. She eyed up my glossy brogues and Harris tweed.

"You look as if you've come into money, young man. Is that why you were away for such a long time? Have you come into an inheritance?"

She tittered as she stared hard at me. I gripped my bag tightly and stretched my lips into a false smile.

"Just my wee joke. Your family haven't come to meet you? Too busy I dare say."

Her eyes were as cold as a seagull's stare. Sweat trickled down my neck. This witch seemed able to read my mind.

"I must hurry. They're expecting me at home."

Her mouth tilted into a sneer. I hurried on, across the cobbles, past the bars, the chandler's and the salmon icehouse. Up the steep climb of Pier Brae, past Macnab's Inn, past the house that used to be a jail, up to the Lump where the Games are held and the path down to the shore and Bayfield. I passed the National Bank where Màiri's friend lived. Like my sister, she loved school. It was lucky that it was the evening and most folk would be inside, eating their teas. But then I heard another voice.

"Is that you, Sandy?"

No chance to hide. It was Anna, a girl in my class.

"Aye, but I can't stop."

"I hardly recognised you. You've grown and is that fluff above your lips?"

I felt my cheeks. My face was getting hot.

"Did you try to join up? Or have you been in prison?"

My blood ran cold, but I tried to laugh.

"What do you think?"

But Anna's joke gave me an idea. I could tell folk that I had tried to join up but was sent away when the army found out my age. At least she hadn't said anything about the business with the teacher. Perhaps he was alive and well, after all. Then another thought struck me, hard as a shove in my back. How had Mamma and Pappa explained me being away? They would hate the idea of people talking about our family, but they were too honest to tell lies.

My heart thudded as I got close to our house, tucked into its curve of the shore. It looked much the same as when I'd left two months before but was it really the same inside? Maybe I would be like someone in a fairy tale who spent a day or two under a

The Second Surge of the Sea

spell with the faeries but returned home to find that many years had passed. That would mean that Mamma and Dadda would be bent and white haired and Bobby would be dead and gone.

I stopped in my tracks, sunk in gloom when I felt something crash into the backs of my legs, making me topple forwards. A ball of shaggy hair, threshing legs and thumping tail. I bent down as Bobby danced round me and licked my face, from top to bottom. I buried my head in his hair and cried for joy. As I stroked him, I could feel he was thinner than before and his coat more tangled than I remembered. We ran together up to the back door, Bobby pressed so close to my legs as if he would never leave me.

Mamma and Dadda were there on the doorstep. Mamma stepped forward, wiping her eyes on the edge of her apron. She opened her arms and I rushed into them. She squeezed me so hard that I couldn't breathe.

"You're back home safely, Sandy, thank the Lord."

"I'm so sorry," I mumbled. I was shocked to see that I was nearly as tall as her.

Dadda came forward and held out his hand.

"Welcome home, Sandy."

"I'm so glad to be home."

I smiled and tried to hide my horror at Dadda's appearance. He had always been a wiry man, wiry but strong. Now he looked frail, as if a sea breeze would knock him over. His cheeks were sunken, his eyes feverishly bright although his grip was as strong as it had always been.

"Come away in," Mamma said.

Once we were all inside, she turned to face me and before I realised what had happened, I felt a heavy slap across my face. I stepped back in shock and put my hand to my throbbing cheek.

"How could you run away! We were almost dead with heartache and worry about you. And what were we supposed to tell people had happened?"

"I don't know. I didn't mean to cause you so much grief."

I was sobbing now.

"Folk gossip. Someone started the story that you were unhappy at school and that was why you ran away."

I sighed with relief. From what Mamma said no-one suspected me of hitting Mr Graham. I wanted to ask questions about the school but remembered in time what Màiri had said about keeping my mouth shut.

"The lad's sorry for what he did. I suppose you ran away without stopping to think?" Dadda's expression was kind but searching.

"Get him something to eat. I'm sure he's still as hungry as ever."

When Mamma went into the kitchen, he whispered.

"She'll get over it. We all do silly things when we're young."

He winked but then a fit of coughing caught him.

"Don't fret. I'll be fine when I throw off this spot of bronchitis. The night air makes it worse."

Dadda looked exhausted but I knew that I shouldn't say anything. It was another secret that mustn't be mentioned.

"Tell Sandy about Bobby coming home," Dadda said when we were all settled down in front of the fire with cups of tea. Bobby was in his favourite spot, curled round my feet but she ignored him.

"I don't understand how you lost him when you two were always glued together," she said.

She kept looking at me sideways, but her voice was warmer now. I could hear my sister's voice in my head, "Keep it simple. Try not to tell lies, just don't tell the whole story."

The Second Surge of the Sea

"I was with the Stewarts in the woods when this huge fierce dog rushed up and attacked Bobby. I managed to beat it away with a stick, but Bobby ran away and I couldn't find him."

"I'm surprised at Mrs Stewart letting you go away with them. She would know that I would be worried sick."

"It wasn't her fault, Mamma. I followed them in secret and when she found out she said it would be better if I stayed with them."

"And did you have some daft idea of going off to be a soldier?"

I hung my head.

"But why? I know you wanted to leave school but you're underage." Mamma's voice was getting sharp again.

"You were going to tell him about Bobby," Dadda said.

She sighed.

"Well, one night, about two weeks ago, wasn't it, John? I woke up with a jolt in the middle of the night. I sat up in bed and listened. There it was again, a sort of whimper. I thought it was a fox and lay back down. Then there was a scraping at the kitchen door. I didn't want to wake your father. He doesn't sleep well with coughing, so I crept downstairs. Then I heard a bark and thought, 'That's Bobby.' I flung the door open because I knew that if Bobby was there, you would be with him."

She gasped, too full for words and I took her hand.

"I'm more sorry than I could ever say."

She sighed and patted my hand.

"He was in a terrible way, very thin and his coat all tangled. He rushed in and made a fuss of me. I found a bit of meat for him, but he wouldn't touch it. He scoured the house from top to bottom looking for you. He's quietened down since but he still spends a lot of time waiting outside for you to come home."

"Just like Greyfriars Bobby," I whispered. I put my face in my hands and sobbed.

"If only he could have told us where he had been," Dadda said. "But then I bumped into old Donald MacPhee a few days afterwards. He told me that he had met some drovers on their way home from near Cluanie. They had found a dog like Bobby and brought him back to Skye with them. When they got to Portree he ran off."

"It's a pity they didn't bother feeding him," Mamma said.

"I thought that it was maybe a good omen, but I didn't say anything. I didn't want to get your mother's hopes up."

I suddenly felt exhausted. My head drooped and my eyelids started to close.

"Time for bed," Mamma said.

Afterwards, when I lay in the darkness, with Bobby at my feet and my new clothes folded on the chair, I dared to relax. No-one had mentioned Mr Graham. Maybe I had got away with it. I just had to hold my nerve and my tongue.'

CHAPTER 23

'The next morning, I had good news. I was having my breakfast when Mamma said, "You don't need to bother about school. It's nearly the holidays. Do you want some more porridge – you're looking thin, especially since you've grown."

It was a great weight off my mind, knowing that I could stay at home and avoid all the questions and funny looks.

"I'm fine, Mamma. Bobby's the one who needs building up. I'll go and help with the nets."

It was a crisp, dry day and they were stretched out ready on poles on the drying green at the end of the road. Looking for holes and repairing them steadied my hands and my mind.'

'I suppose it's like knitting,' I say. 'I would be no good at it.'

'We concentrated on the work and Dadda didn't ask me any questions. Bobby lay down on the grass beside us. Every now and again, he would come and press his nose against my legs. I would bend down and fan out his big bat ears.

"Don't worry, boy. I'm not going to leave you."

"You've done a neat job there," Pappa said when we stopped for a *strupag*. He sat down heavily on a stool while I perched on a wooden crate.

"Fishing's such a fickle business. I think that I should teach you how to be a cooper. It's a useful trade to have. I started to teach Iain but...," he shrugged.

"He'll maybe take it up again when he comes home."

My heart sank. Coopering was the last thing I wanted to do but I didn't want to upset Pappa. Looking at his hollow cheeks and hunched shoulders, I felt guilty.

"That would be grand," I said, forcing a smile.

At that moment, Bobby leapt to his feet, barking. I looked up to see Robbie Stewart, from my class. I stroked the dog and tried to stay calm.

"Good day, Mr MacPherson. You're back then, Sandy. Did the army spit you out?"

I shrugged.

"It's funny how you left without a word to anyone – just when Mr Graham had his accident."

"Oh, when did that happen?"

"After school, when everyone had gone home."

"I was away by then. He was likely the worse for drink and fell over."

I could sense Dadda stiffening while he sat, smoking his pipe.

"We had the police at the school, asking questions."

I willed myself to look him in the eyes. I could feel my heart thudding.

"No-one told them anything. He was a bugger, right enough. No-one's seen hide nor hair of him since."

Dadda looked at Robbie and frowned. I knew that he hated swearing but was he worried, too, about what more he might say?

"I'll see you back at school then, Sandy. It's much better since that devil disappeared. Miss Baxter's an angel compared to him."

"Mamma says I can stay at home until after the holiday."

"Lucky you! Maybe I should try running away."

"Shouldn't you be in school now, Robbie?"

"Aye, I'm on my way, Mr MacPherson, he said, grinning.

"That's a cheeky lad. Keep away from him. He'll get you into trouble," Dadda said after he had gone.

My hands were shaking so much that they stumbled as I worked on the nets. If Robbie was naughty what did that make me? I stabbed a dog to death and hit a teacher. I wondered why Mr Graham had disappeared. If he told them that I had hit him, surely the police would have come to my house to look for me? Even if he didn't speak to them, it must have seemed suspicious that I had run away just afterwards. I wished that I could wind time backwards to before all this had happened.

"Come in for your tea," Mamma called from the kitchen door. I ran inside, Bobby at my heels.

"I've been talking with Mrs MacLean, down the road. She said that she's got a niece coming up from Glasgow. The lassie's not well and she thought that the change of air might help her. She's the same age as you, Sandy, so I said that you would make her welcome and spend some time with her."

My heart sank again. I wanted some peace and quiet to sort out the jumble in my head, but I couldn't say no.'

CHAPTER 24

'The following day I helped Dadda clear out the big shed where he kept his fishing gear. The corrugated iron sides bulged out like the belly of a pregnant cow and the roof sagged. It had been like that for as long as I could remember. Every year he said, "I'll sort that shed out. Maybe rebuild it." And every year Mamma sighed and rolled her eyes. Now, this year every time he tried to move things – bits of old nets, lobster pots or floats it set him off coughing again.

"Dadda, why don't you tell me where you want things put and I'll lift them?"

"Aye, why not, you're a big lad now."

I wanted to howl in pain and had to go and crouch down in the corner to get myself under control while I pretended to hunt for things to move. In the old days Dadda would have laughed off any offers of help. Between us we tidied the neglected heaps and disturbed a lot of spiders.

When we finished there was still some light outside and there had been no sign of the girl from Glasgow. With any luck Mrs MacLean had forgotten about the whole thing. The sky was a cold, clear blue and the tide was coming in gently, the waves in neat rows like pleats on a kilt. Bobby was snuffling among the shingle but suddenly he cocked his ears, his head on one side. Then I heard it too. The sound of a fiddle, playing a beautiful air that soared and plunged like a gull on the wing. Who was it?

I walked along the shore, following the sound. I could see a slight figure down by the shore. Bobby was curious and trotted ahead. The figure bent down to greet him. I ran up to them.

"I'm sorry that my dog disturbed your playing."

The Second Surge of the Sea

I tried not to stare but I was transfixed by the stranger, a slender girl, bundled up in a long coat that was too big for her. The scarf round her head had slipped, revealing hair that was so fair that it was almost white – pale and gleaming like the shells at the Coral Beach where Pappa had taken me once in his boat. I shivered. Was she a real person or some sort of spirit?

Then she laughed, a deep gurgling sound.

"And who are you? I'm Jessie."

"Mrs MacLean's niece?"

"And you must be Sandy, the naughty boy who ran away to join the army."

I blushed to the roots of my hair.

"I think that was an exciting thing to do."

"I wish that my family thought that."

"I'm not allowed to do anything exciting. They keep saying that I'm too delicate. I've been sent to Skye for the fresh air and then they tell me that the wind is too cold for me to be outside. I better go back or my auntie will be fretting. You can walk along with me if you like."

I couldn't take my eyes off her. She was so pretty and delicate with her green eyes and pale skin. The silence hung heavy between us while I wrestled my brain for something to say.

"I liked the tune you were playing but I didn't recognise it."

"It's an Irish air my Mamma taught me, called, 'The lark in the clear air'."

I nodded and wondered what to say next. I felt like a clumsy bullock beside this girl who seemed to float, rather than walk.

"Aren't you going to ask me why I'm playing down on the shore?"

"Well, I did wonder."

"I'm playing to get the seals to come close. They're drawn to music."

Then I understood why Jessie seemed so strange. She was like a selkie herself, as if she had hidden her sealskin while appearing to be a human being.

"Jessie, where are you?"

We both turned as we heard the voice. Jessie sighed.

"You see what I mean about my auntie. I'd better go now but I'll see you tomorrow at the same time."

She disappeared and I began to wonder if I had imagined her.'

'I think that you had fallen in love with her, Pappa.'

'I was much too young for that nonsense,' he says, blushing a little, 'but she was like a spirit, not a flesh and blood girl. Anyway, I ran home to find Mamma waiting for me at the kitchen door.

"You were away a long time."

I told her about Jessie, and she looked relieved. Would it always be like this, with her not trusting me? Did she think that I would run away again? I longed to lay down my burden and tell Mamma the whole story, but the truth was like a horrible kind of leprosy that I mustn't pass on. Màiri was right. It was better to leave them wondering.

The next day I ran down to the shore, half expecting Jessie to have melted away in the mist, but she was there, playing her fiddle.

"Do you know 'Màiri's Wedding'? You could sing while I play."

"No, I would spoil it."

But she insisted we sing together, her voice like herself, delicate and pure, my voice cracking on the high notes and Bobby howling like a wolf.

> *Step we gaily, on we go,*
> *Heel for heel and toe for toe,*
> *Arm in arm and row on row'*

The Second Surge of the Sea

Now Pappa starts singing the words and I join in, humming.

> *All for Màiri's wedding*
> *Over hillways up and down,*
> *Myrtle green and bracken brown*
> *Past the shielings, through the town*

'Then she suddenly stopped singing and was doubled over in a fit of coughing. It scared the life out of me.

"Is there anything I can do? Dadda coughs like that sometimes. He says that it's bronchitis."

She shook her head and pulled a handkerchief from her coat pocket. She held it to her mouth, and I could see the dark red splash and smell the rusty scent of blood.

"I think that your Dadda might have the same thing as me – consumption, TB, whatever you want to call it. I'm not supposed to know but I overheard the doctor talking."

I rocked back on my heels with shock. TB was something people whispered about, a terrible illness that killed you.

Then Jessie grabbed my arm and pointed out to sea. Two, no three, sleek heads were bobbing above the waves, their faces smooth with big, moist eyes, doglike muzzles and whiskers sprouting around their mouths. I whispered to Bobby to sit down, and we all stayed still to watch them. I couldn't say how long we sat quietly looking before first one and then the others in turn, dived underwater and slipped away, with hardly a ripple. Jessie and I turned away too, holding our silence on the way home, not wanting to break the spell.

That night I had a strange dream. I was in the sea, swimming with the seals. They kept nudging me, pushing me along and jostling me out to sea while Jessie was standing on the rocks, playing her fiddle faster and faster. Suddenly the biggest seal rolled over in the water and shot upwards, almost standing on its tail. It shook its flippers, made an eerie howling sound, and sped away, with the others following it. The dream stayed with me because it seemed to hold some sort of warning.

"I'm pleased that you're spending some time with Jessie," Mamma said at breakfast, and I tried not to blush. I was relieved that Màiri wasn't there to tease me. I noticed that Dadda looked livelier this morning. Jessie must be wrong about his illness. He stood up.

"Some of the men are going after the seals this evening. We've seen them close to the shore."

I jumped to my feet, my stool clattering over behind me.

"You can't do that. They come close to the shore to hear Jessie playing her fiddle."

"But they bite through our nets and steal our fish."

"There's enough fish in the sea for them and for us. You can't kill them when they've learnt to trust us."

"What's the matter with you, lad? It's the way of the world."

He spoke to my back because I was already out of the door and running to the MacLean's house. Jessie saw me coming and came outside.

"The men are going after the seals," I blurted out.

"Keep your voice down. My uncle's one of them."

"What can we do?"

"We can warn them."

"What do you mean?"

"Well, I can draw them in again with my fiddle before the men get there and somehow scare them away."

"How can we do that?"

Jessie bent down to pat Bobby.

"What about the wee dog? He could bark and scare them away."

"Maybe but he couldn't do it on his own and the seals might turn on him."

The Second Surge of the Sea

We walked past the houses by the shore, deep in thought. I glanced at the rowing boats, drawn up out of the water.

"That's it! You lure them in with your playing while I row over in a boat and scare them away."

"You're so clever!"

My heart swelled with pride. So, later on, Jessie walked towards Scorrybreac while I rowed round the point. I saw that she had clambered along the rocks to the Black Rock. She pointed over towards Camus Ban and I could see ripples in the water, close to the beach. I rowed closer to them. Then the seals dived under water. That could be dangerous if they swam under the boat and tipped us over. I stopped rowing and held my breath. She pointed again to show where they had surfaced, further out in the bay. I turned in that direction, keeping my distance but making a racket – shouting and splashing the oars, getting Bobby to bark. They had dived again and we waited to make sure that they had gone, before I turned back to get Jessie. She eased herself into the boat, making it rock and knocking a surprised Bobby off his feet. I laughed, thinking to myself that she didn't seem like a faerie creature at all.

It was getting dark by the time we moored the boat and walked home. Mrs MacLean met us, hopping from foot to foot.

"I've been worried sick about you. And you're wet, Jessie. Look at your shoes and the hem of your skirt. Getting soaked won't help your chest."

Then she turned her rage on me.

"I would have thought better of you Sandy. I don't know what's come over you – running away and now this. You used to be such a nice, sensible lad."

"Don't blame him, Auntie. It was my idea."

Mrs MacLean pushed Jessie towards the door and glowered at me.

When I got home Mamma said, "Come in and have your tea. You must be hungry. Your father's out still."

She wouldn't be so kind once Mrs MacLean spoke to her but I was too worn out to care.

The next morning when I came downstairs, I could see smoke through the kitchen window and when I opened the backdoor there was a terrible smell. I rushed down to the shore to find Pappa stirring a big pot over a fire of driftwood. There was a sickening fatty, fishy stink that made me hold my nose.

"What are you doing?" I shouted.

"What does it look like? Boiling up seal meat. I saved this for you."

He bent down and picked up something folded on the ground. He opened it out. It was a beautiful silver-grey sealskin, mottled with darker patches.

"You killed one of the seal pups!" I suddenly wanted to hit Dadda. The feeling scared me so much that I ran away, back inside the house.

"What on earth's the matter?" Mamma asked.

"Dadda's killed one of the young seals that listened to Jessie playing the fiddle," I shouted, trying not to cry.

"And how big was this skin?"

"Huge."

"Too big for a young one, then. The men didn't catch any young seals last night. They had disappeared."

"Where did this one come from?"

"They found a dead, grown seal, washed up on the shore. Too good to waste. The oil will do for our lamps and I dare say that Bobby will eat some of the meat."

Later that day there was a knock on the door. I opened it to find Jessie.

"Come away in", Mamma called.

The Second Surge of the Sea

"I've come to say Goodbye, Mrs MacPherson. I'm away down to Glasgow tomorrow. And please don't be cross with Sandy. It was my idea to go out in the boat."

"It was a silly thing to do."

"I know." She hung her head and I saw Mamma's face soften.

"It was odd how the seals suddenly left," she said. "Never mind. Why don't you two go out for a last walk as it's a nice day."

"Our plan worked," Jessie said as she skipped along. She reached out and squeezed my hand. I nearly leapt in the air with surprise. Then I curled my fingers around her hand, as delicate as a mouse's paw.

"Do you feel better for your holiday?"

"Aye, it made a change."

"Will you come again?"

Her eyes clouded.

"I don't know."

My heart sank at the thought of not seeing her again.

"You should meet my sister, Màiri. She works in Glasgow."

"And where does she stay?"

"Near the University."

"That's a bit different from where I am in Govan. I don't think that our paths would cross."

"Will you write to me?"

I was trying not to sound too desperate.

"Will you reply? I don't see you as much of a letter writer. Don't look so down. My auntie will give you my address if she's forgiven you for leading me astray."

She reached up on tiptoe and kissed me on the lips. It was like the touch of a falling autumn leaf and afterwards I wondered if I had imagined it. Then she bent down to stroke Bobby's ears and was off.'

'What a lovely story!' I say. 'She was your first love, Pappa. Did you write to her or see her again?'

'No. I did write to her, but she never replied. I heard later that she had died but by then so many other things were going on.'

He's silent and I wish that I hadn't asked. Talking about her seems to have brought all the sadness back. So, I change the subject.

'I don't like the killing of seals. It's done in Canada too. They kill the baby ones before they can swim.'

'It's sad but people who have a hard life don't want to lose their livelihood.'

'I read *Ring of Bright Water* and one of Gavin Maxwell's pet otters was killed by a crofter with his spade. I don't think it's right to kill animals just because they need to eat the same food as us.'

'Maybe when your generation runs the world things will be different. We better hurry home or your Granny will think that we've run away.'

CHAPTER 25

'Did you begin to relax more when you didn't hear any more about Mr Graham's disappearance?' I ask the next day.

'Aye, I suppose so, but if anything out of the ordinary happened I would be all on edge again.

I was still missing Jessie when one day I came home and Bobby stopped at the back door, cocking his head on one side and lifting a paw. That made my heart beat faster and I tiptoed round to the front door to see what I could hear. Voices were coming from the parlour. That meant important visitors. Friends and family sat in the kitchen. I couldn't hear what was being said but I recognised the voice of Miss Baxter, my teacher. She must be there to say that I had to go back to school. I crept closer, pressing my ear to the edge of the door. She had a booming voice to keep everyone in order and I could make out most of her words.

"Of course, he's well short of his fourteenth birthday and should be in school but in the circumstances, I think that we can stretch the rules."

I listened hard, holding my breath.

"And there's the question of his influence over the other pupils. He set a bad example running away like he did."

I crouched low and made my way to under the window. Mamma's voice was softer than Miss Baxter's but when I pressed my ear to a gap between the windowsill and the bottom pane I could hear her.

"I'm so grieved at him running away, even if he was unhappy. What became of Mr Graham?"

"Er... I'm sure that you heard that he went away rather suddenly. Sergeant Galbraith came to the school to ask everyone, staff and scholars, if they had seen anything unusual."

My heart was thrashing now, like a fish caught on a line.

"And did anyone see anything out of the ordinary?"

"No. At least no-one admitted to knowing anything."

"I've heard that Mr Graham was known to be quick to use his fists on the boys."

"Maybe so."

Miss Baxter had the brisk edge to her voice that she used when she was getting tetchy.

"That's all done with now and there's still the question of Sandy being a bad influence. We don't want him to encourage other boys to run away. This is what I propose. I shall bring work each week for your son to do at home. He will have to bring it to me, properly completed after school each Friday evening. I want him to continue with his painting as he has a talent for it."

There was a shuffling as Miss Baxter stood up.

"He did an excellent study of a Viking brooch for the art competition. Of course, in the circumstances he couldn't be given a prize, but I would be interested to see the brooch."

"What brooch?" Mamma's voice was shrill. "I'll see if he's on the way home."

I tiptoed round to the kitchen. Bobby jumped about, thinking that I was playing some sort of a game. Then I stopped, stamped around as if I had just come in, and walked into the kitchen.

"What have you done now? Are you a thief?" Mamma hissed, grabbing my wrist. "Go and get this brooch."

I ran upstairs, tears of rage and pain spurting out of my eyes. How could she think that I had stolen the brooch? Would everyone always expect the worst of me? I crawled under my bed and eased up the loose floorboard. I reached inside for the wooden box. I felt inside with trembling fingers, pushing aside the lucky rabbit's foot and the scuffed leather bag full of pearls that had fallen from Scar's neck. The pearls made me wince. They were tainted but I would look after them until I could give them to Mrs Stewart. I unwrapped the soft piece of cloth that covered the brooch. It gleamed as if it was new. The streaming tail, galloping legs and arched neck made the horse look as if it would leap into life. I tucked it into my pocket and went downstairs, drawing myself up to my full height.

"Bobby found the brooch when we were out rounding up some sheep near the top of the croft. I was keeping it safe, Mamma, to give it to you at Christmas. I could see that it was beautiful, but I had no idea that it was Viking treasure."

I gave it to Mamma. She gasped when she opened up the package, then handed it to Miss Baxter. The teacher's eyes widened, and she cleared her throat.

"If I'm right it's very valuable and should be in a museum for everyone to admire it. I know one of the curators in the museum in Edinburgh and I would like to show it to him."

Mamma was holding the brooch and she reached out to hand it to the teacher, but I stretched out my hand and took it, wrapped it up again and put it in my pocket.

"I should like to speak to the museum gentleman myself about it. I shall keep it safe, and you have the picture to show him, Miss Baxter."

Before either of them could speak I walked out of the room, head held high with Bobby at my heels.'

'Good for you, Pappa,' I say.

'I don't know where my boldness came from. Maybe my adventures had made me stronger, or I already had an idea about how to use the money. Anyway, when Màiri came home not long after that she was impressed by me, maybe for the first time ever.

"I can't believe that my wee brother spoke like that to Miss Baxter. I would never have dared. She can be very fierce."

"But you care about her having a good opinion of you. I'm not so troubled about what she thinks of me."

"You must ask this curator for a fair price for the brooch. I'll ask Mr Cohen what he thinks it's worth when I get back. He's always asking after you. He thinks you're a hero."

"I'm glad that someone does. How is it that you're allowed a holiday at Christmas?"

"Jews don't celebrate Christmas, remember. But they're happy to let me have a few days off."

"I want as much money for the brooch as possible, to help Mamma and Dadda. They need the money, especially now Dadda is ill."

Màiri frowned, "Iain doesn't earn much from the Army and I don't get a lot either."

"I can earn too, now I don't have to go to school. And there's still the money from the eggs."

"But you will only get boys' wages and the birds don't lay so much in winter. Listen, Sandy. I've important news. Let's go for a walk and I'll tell you."

What on earth could it be? She looked very serious. Was she courting someone down in Glasgow?

She started striding along the shore so that I had nearly to run to keep up. Bobby was busy, sniffing among the mussel shells dropped by the seagulls.

"I'm going to stop working for the Cohens."

My jaw dropped.

"Why? They've been so good to you."

"I can make much more money in a munitions factory – almost a man's wage."

Her voice was eager but her grey eyes looked sad.

"Munitions – shells for the Army? Isn't that dangerous?"

"It can be. That's why you mustn't breathe a word. Mamma has enough on her mind already."

The Second Surge of the Sea

I was pleased that she had confided in me, but sad too. So much about growing up seemed to be about keeping secrets. Still, I was excited about Christmas – bringing in a tree, making paper chains, breathing in all the spicy smells of Mamma's cooking. I had bought the presents – a bar of lavender soap each for Mamma and Màiri, baccy for Dadda and a butcher's bone for Bobby. Iain wasn't forgotten either. Mamma sent him a parcel with tinned ham, cigarettes, a fruit cake and new socks and a muffler. We had a good lunch too – one of the old hens boiled up with neeps and tatties, followed by a pudding that had steamed in a cloth for hours. Then we sat down, our stomachs straining at our buttons, and opened our presents. Mamma gave me new gloves and a bag of sweeties. Then Dadda surprised us by handing out presents wrapped in newspaper. Mamma opened hers first. It was a white polished brooch of a seagull, carved in wood. "It's beautiful, John. More beautiful than that heathen Viking horse that Sandy found. It reminds me of that eagle you carved for me when we were first married."

She blew her nose and busied herself pinning the brooch to her blouse.

"Aye, I was still in the Merchant Navy in those days and had more time for carving. It was whalebone in those days."

Màiri opened her parcel to find a brooch too. Hers was a wren, with an upright tail and a bright eye. When I opened mine, I found two models of seals, curled up in a U shape as they do when they're lying on a submerged rock. I stroked them, too overcome to speak.

"I know how keen you both are on the beasts."

"Well, I think that I'll just go and put the kettle on," Mamma said, blowing her nose.

"I've some good news," Màiri said. "I'll be earning more money when I go back to Glasgow."

"That's good to hear. Are the Cohens giving you a better job? Cooking maybe?"

"No, not the cooking. That would be hard when they have all that special food. Do you remember that, Sandy? They have all sorts of special festivals, like Hanukah, the Festival of Lights, when we have Christmas. It's to do with when the Jews recaptured the temple in Jerusalem and the light that was only enough to last for one day burned for eight whole days instead."

"I think I'll stick with Christmas," Dadda said with a laugh. "Now I think there's enough whisky left to have a wee dram.'"

'Your sister was smart!' I say. 'She knew how to dodge difficult questions. Have you still got the carvings?'

'I don't think so. They must have got lost when we moved house.'

'And did you hear anything more about the mystery of what happened to Mr Graham?'

'I'll tell you some more tomorrow. All this remembering is tiring, you know.'

CHAPTER 26

'After Hogmanay I looked for work. One of the fishermen in Bayfield said that I could help him paint the hull of his boat. First though, I had to scrape off all the rust and old paint, with wire wool and a blade. It was rough work that made the joints of my fingers crack and bleed. Bobby lay down watching me and licking the salt water off his paws.

"I wish that I was a dog like you, taking my ease."

I was happy to be earning and things seemed to have settled down. I didn't feel that folk were whispering about me and I was back playing shinty and football again with the boys I used to go to school with. At first, they had kept tripping me up and aiming the ball at my head, angry that I had escaped school but they forgot their anger after a while.

One day when I was walking home, blowing on my cold hands, I could hear a stranger's voice. There was someone going in the back door with Pappa behind him. When I stepped into the kitchen, I saw a stranger sitting by the table, a stranger in a policeman's uniform. His helmet was on the table, and he was holding a notebook. I felt like running straight out again. Bobby stood beside me, ears back and growling.

"There you are, Sandy. Sergeant Henderson wants to ask you a few questions."

"Aye, you can leave us to it, Mr MacPherson."

He had an accent like Jessie's. Although he smiled, showing big brownish teeth, the smile didn't reach his eyes that flickered over me, like a snake's tongue.

"No, I'll stay. You can see that my son isn't of age yet."

Pappa's voice was quiet but firm and my legs stopped trembling. I sat down and remembered what Màiri said about watching what I said.

"Mr Graham taught you?"

I nodded.

"What do you know about what happened to him?"

I paused while I decided what to say.

"I think the sergeant means what do you know about Mr Graham's accident. But you had already run away when it happened. You had that daft notion of joining up, like your big brother."

"I would like the lad to speak for himself."

"What Dadda's just said is right." I licked my dry lips.

"What was Mr Graham like?"

"Come on, why do you ask? Everyone knew that he was a bully. All the children will have told you that."

Sergeant Henderson glared at Dadda.

"I've read the report but there are some unanswered questions. Strangely enough, there were no witnesses. No-one saw anything."

"Because there was nothing to see. The man was a drinker. He fell over and hit his head."

The policeman opened his notebook.

"When the doctor treated him, he kept muttering, 'It was that boy'."

"And how many boys are in the school?" Pappa asked. "Is that all the evidence you have?"

"Unfortunately, we didn't speak to Mr Graham again. He left the area suddenly."

"I wonder why? Did he have something to hide?"

The policeman frowned but didn't reply.

"He lived in Glasgow before he came up here. So, the Skye police sent me their report. I don't like unsolved mysteries, and something smelt bad about this business – a conspiracy of silence."

He stared hard at me, and I forced myself to look him in the eye.

"And why would you imagine that Sandy, who is only a child, would know anything about him?"

I could hear the anger in Dadda's voice. The talking brought on his coughing. He took out his handkerchief to muffle it. Sergeant Henderson took no notice and questioned me again.

"You were one of the last people to see him, Sandy. Why did you run away so suddenly? Did Mr Graham pick on you more than the others?"

He leant forward and stared at me.

"Because I wanted to join up, like my brother."

I made my voice ring out, like Màiri had said I should.

Dadda stopped coughing and leapt to his feet, banging his fist down on the table and making the dishes rattle.

"That's enough! Has this man or anyone accused my son of wrongdoing?"

"No."

"So that's the end of it! It seems to me that this Graham man is the one who you should be investigating."

Sergeant Henderson stood up and closed his notebook.

"You must understand that my job is to tie up loose ends."

"There are no loose ends here. We won't keep you. I'm sure that there are plenty of crimes in Glasgow awaiting your attention."

Sergeant Henderson put his notebook away in his pocket, before gathering up his helmet and his dignity. Bobby stood up too and stiff legged, watched the policeman leave. After he had gone, Dadda sat down, white faced.

"Well, I'm glad to see the back of him. He should find something better to do than persecuting an innocent boy. I always knew that you were innocent Sandy.'"

I had to hold myself from letting out a huge sigh.

'What did you feel, Pappa?' I ask him.

'Proud of my Dadda, relieved but sick with guilt too. It was me who had brought all this trouble on my family.'

I keep quiet because I can see that I won't convince him differently. His guilt is a deep, indelible stain. I just squeeze his hand and suggest a cup of tea.

CHAPTER 27

When we start talking the next day Pappa looks tired but calm. I give him his cup of tea, black and stewed as he likes it and wait. I'm learning patience.

'Well, the next visitors to the house were an improvement on the policeman. At least they were expected – Miss Baxter and the curator from Edinburgh. This time it was Mamma who was there when they arrived. Mr Campbell was tall and had a sweep of grey hair. He sat down, stretching his long legs in front of him and steepling his fingers. Miss Baxter as always sat up very straight, with her feet in their shiny boots neatly crossed at the ankle.

"Before we start talking, I should like to give you these, Sandy."

I must have looked horrified at the large bundle wrapped in newspaper. Surely it couldn't all be homework?

Miss Baxter smiled, reading my thoughts.

"There is some homework, but you'll find that there are art materials as well and something else too."

I gasped when I found the picture I had done of the brooch but now it was framed in dark wood so that it looked like a proper painting.

"Thank you. I don't know what to say. This is for you, Mamma."

"Well, we couldn't award you the prize, so this is instead. Why don't you go and fetch the original?"

I brought it from its hiding place and looked at it again, probably for the last time. It was beautiful but the money it could bring was more important. I wrapped it up again in the cloth and took it downstairs. When I handed it to the curator, he opened the cloth with soft, white fingers and his eyes gleamed when he saw it.

"Just as you described it, Miss Baxter. Almost certainly Viking and well executed."

He peered at me.

"Well, young man, I am empowered to pay you something for this find."

I stiffened. I didn't trust this man, with his clipped voice and superior manner.

"Well, it was my dog Bobby who found it when we were rounding up sheep."

"Really? He doesn't look much like a sheepdog with those stumpy legs. But you can buy him a bone as a reward."

Mr Campbell opened his wallet and took out a note.

"I don't suppose that you have seen any of these before? They're Bank of Scotland notes. I'll give you £20."

But I had seen his greedy eyes when he set eyes on the brooch.

"It's worth more than that."

Mamma gasped and I waited, feeling light-headed that I had spoken so boldly. But after the interview with the policeman I felt bolder.

"What about £100?" I asked.

"Very well, but I will have to give you a cheque. Do you have a bank account?"

The mocking tone angered me.

"I can arrange that," I said, thinking I could talk to Màiri's schoolfriend whose father was manager of the National Bank.

Mr Campbell made a great play of writing a cheque, sighed and gave it to me. I made a great play of reading it slowly and turning it over until I saw Mamma frowning.

After Miss Baxter and Mr Campbell left, Mamma shook her head.

The Second Surge of the Sea

"I don't know what to make of you, Sandy. You've changed so much since you came back. That's more money than your Dadda would make in a year."

"But the brooch is valuable, and he was greedy to get his hands on it. That money will mean that Dadda can see a chest doctor."

She hugged me tightly.

"I just hope that he agrees to that.'"

CHAPTER 28

'Did your Dadda see a doctor?'

'He did. I was surprised that he agreed to it but I think he was impressed by my success in getting the money from the curator.'

Pappa hesitates and fiddles with his pipe. I'm learning not to rush him when he does that. I've been thinking about this TB business. I had imagined that it was a Victorian disease, not something that lasted into the 20th century. I remember being told in English lessons that most of the Bronte sisters died from it and John Keats too. I hadn't realised that it was so common in the Highlands. I suppose that the damp climate and people being stuck inside in the wet winters made it worse.

'He went with Mamma to see a chest doctor in Inverness, but he told him that the best thing that Dadda could do was to go to a sanatorium somewhere warm, down on the south coast of England. He said that the Isle of Wight would be the best. That's as far south as you can get, isn't it? Pappa said that he wouldn't go all that way and that we needed to keep the money for a rainy day.

"Well, we've got a downpour now", Mamma shouted, "Use the money!"

I heard them arguing in whispers about it during the night. How could we change his mind? He was a stubborn man. Then a postcard arrived from Iain which cheered us all up. He said that he was coming home for a few days' leave. It felt as if Spring had arrived early. Mamma was in a flurry of baking, Dadda looked brighter than he had for a long time, and I whistled as I scraped and painted the boat.

It was Bobby who knew he was coming, hearing his footsteps and smelling him. And did he stink! As he stood at the back door,

The Second Surge of the Sea

he gave off a horrible musty smell that made you want to throw up. I couldn't take in anything else about his appearance as I tried not to retch. Iain stood back from the doorstep.

"I know that I stink to high heaven. I'm lousy. I'm glad that it's you who saw me first, Sandy. Will you fill the bath for me while I take off these stinking rags and find me something to wear? I'll wait outside."

"Did I hear Iain's voice?" Mamma called out from the kitchen.

"He says that he's lousy and he's waiting outside while I run a bath for him."

"Hurry up then or he'll freeze to death. I'll get him some clean things."

When I told him that the bath was ready, I found him standing bare-chested, with just his kilt on.

"Burn it all, apart from the tunic. That can be washed but I don't know what to do with the kilt."

Mamma moved closer to him, but he put up a hand to stop her. "Don't touch me."

"Make a fire outside, Sandy. I know what to do with the kilt."

While Iain had a bath in the kitchen, I made a fire with a flat stone at its edge. She went to find her iron and while it heated on the stone, she spread the kilt out on the washing line, wrinkling her nose, When the iron was hot she ran it lightly down each of the pleats in turn. The foul smell got worse, and I could hear popping sounds.

"That will finish off the wee devils!" she said, laughing.

Once Iain was dressed in his old trousers and gansey, we could sit down for a *strupag* and a cup of tea.

"It's so good to see you again, son, but you look thin. How did you get so lousy?"

"We were living in trenches, Mamma. You can't keep clean. There's mud and worse everywhere."

"I don't understand why you were left in that state."

I could see Iain clenching and unclenching his fists. He looked away.

"Don't keep asking the lad questions. He needs to rest," Dadda said.

"You can tell us in your own time, son."

But he didn't. He slept for hours and when he was awake, he just sat, gazing into space. He didn't answer if anyone spoke to him but just grunted. A sudden noise, like Bobby barking, made him jump up and cower in a corner. It was as if some crazed beast had taken over his body. The only living creature he responded to was Bobby. The dog never left his side. He sat by his chair, curled up beside him in bed and padded alongside him if Iain walked away. The tremble in his hands only stopped when he stroked the dog.

"I don't know what to do," Mamma said when Iain was outside, pacing up and down the shore as if he was on sentry duty.

"He doesn't seem to hear me when I speak to him and sometimes he looks so angry that he scares me. Maybe he would talk to you, Sandy, if you walk over Scorrybreac with him and the dog?"

I nodded but I felt scared too. My big brother had become a bad-tempered stranger. When I asked him about the walk, he laughed and for a moment it seemed as if my brother had returned to his old self.

"Don't look so scared. I won't bite you. I was so looking forward to coming home but now…."

"It must be very different in France."

Again, the harsh bark of a laugh.

"I can't begin to tell you."

"You don't need to. We can just walk."

The Second Surge of the Sea

Suddenly he leapt forward and grabbed my shoulders, shaking me so hard that I nearly fell over.

"You ran away to be a soldier, didn't you? Don't ever do that again. Swear that you won't."

"No, I won't. Let go of me, Iain. You're hurting me."

He pushed me away.

"It's hell on earth out there."

We walked on in silence, Iain striding along so that I had to trot beside him. When we reached the shore, he started to pick up stones and hurled them, one after the other, like cannonballs, into the sea. Bobby and I stood stock still, waiting for the barrage to end.

"I can't find the words to tell you what it's like. You live in fear the whole time. Fear of being hit by a shell, fear of seeing your friends blown to pieces, fear of gas that chokes you to death. But the worst is the waiting, waiting in the dirt and the cold and the roar of shells for the next attack to come."

"I didn't think it would be like that," I said, as he crouched down, with his head in his hands.'

CHAPTER 29

'Soon, Iain had to leave. We all went down to wave him off on the steamer.

"I wish that he had spoken to us properly. I've never seen him like that before, so silent and sullen," Mamma said.

"Well, he's never been off to fight in a war before. Did he talk to you at all?" Dadda asked me.

"Er… not much. He said that no-one who had not been there could understand what it's like in the trenches."

"I just hope and pray that it soon ends. I shall worry about him more than ever. At least your sister is safe working for the Cohens and surely the war will be over before Sandy is old enough to fight."

I felt guilty about Mamma not knowing that Màiri had left the Cohens, so I squeezed her hand.

"Don't worry. Iain made me swear that I wouldn't join up."

Iain's visit seemed to have sucked the life out of both of them. Dadda looked even more haggard but kept saying that he was fine while Mamma rushed around even more than usual as if keeping herself busy would stop her having to think. The atmosphere at home was heavy, like when a thunderstorm is coming. I stayed out as much as I could. When I wasn't helping the fishermen mend their nets I was out walking with Bobby.

It was late one murky afternoon when I first saw the stranger. Bobby and I were heading for home when the dog barked softly and looked up the hill towards Torvaig. I could just make out a dark figure against the slate grey sky. Whoever it was stood still, a dark shadow looking out to sea. When I got home, Mamma and Dadda seemed sad and distracted as they so often were. For something to say, I told them about the figure on the hill.

The Second Surge of the Sea

"Mrs MacLean saw someone like that, a figure wearing a big hat that hid his face," Mamma said.

"Could it be a German spy?" I wondered.

Dadda laughed.

"Well, he's not much of a spy, acting suspiciously like that so everyone notices him. Anyway, what is there that's worth spying on?"

"He could be looking out for naval ships," I said.

"More likely to be a deserter," Mamma said.

"But I suppose that a deserter would want to keep out of sight too. Unless it's a poor soul driven mad by the fighting?"

The next day I saw the stranger again when I was walking to Fingal's Seat. I tapped Bobby on the muzzle to warn him not to bark. We followed at a distance, and I crouched down so the tall, thin stranger wouldn't see me. He kept marching uphill, without looking round, then suddenly disappeared. I pointed to the ground and Bobby started sniffing, following the trail over stones and grass until he stopped dead in front of a clump of whin bushes and small rowans. There was a dip in the ground and some tumbled stones that looked as if they had fallen from a wall. I remembered hearing about there being a ruined house here, the remains of a black house, long since deserted, an old black house that was haunted. Bobby was still sniffing and wagging his tail. Surely ghosts didn't have a scent? If Bobby wasn't scared, I wouldn't be either. So, I climbed over the crumbling wall and pulled the branches apart to see what was there.

"Oh, no!" I shrieked as I came face to face with a pair of piercing blue eyes glaring at me through the branches. I stumbled back over the wall and took to my heels, crashing through the undergrowth.

"Come back!" It was a low, squeaky voice.

Bobby cocked his head and raised a front paw while I stood frozen until the owner of the voice climbed out. A stranger all in black who looked smaller close to. Bobby sniffed his hand, and he rubbed the dog's ears. Then he beckoned me to follow while he scrambled back over the wall, and I followed.'

'Weren't you scared, Pappa?'

'A wee bit but Bobby trusted him. On the other side of the wall, birch branches were bent over what was left of the house walls, making a living roof, with moss and heather pushed into the gaps.'

'It sounds a bit like the Stewarts' caravan.'

'Aye. I hadn't thought of that. That's maybe why I felt so at home. But then a sudden flapping sound made me duck. It was a jackdaw, flying over my head and brushing my hair with its wings. It landed on the stranger's shoulder. He was standing at the far gable end of the house where a pot hung on a chain over a fire. Suddenly I felt scared again, remembering the strange old woman who had tried to make me stay with her. I froze but Bobby trotted happily up to the stranger. He filled a wooden bowl with liquid from the pot and handed it to me. it was a greenish colour and I waited until the stranger drank first before I took a sip.'

'You've heard too many old folk tales,' I say.

'Aye maybe. And I had been living in a tale myself before I came home. The liquid tasted strange, like a mixture of heather and seaweed. I tried not to make a face. Bobby was sniffing around, and he poked his nose into a pile of dried heather in the corner. Suddenly, he yelped and jumped backwards. I rushed over and a pair of gleaming eyes stared at me.

"That's an orphan otter cub," the stranger laughed in a light, strange, rasping voice. "Its mother was killed."

"My Dadda says that otters and seals are pests that kill our fish, but I think there's enough fish for them and us."

He nodded and I realised that I wasn't scared, just curious about the stranger. I lowered myself onto the floor while he sat down on an upturned box and took off his hat. A waterfall of white hair fell down.

"You're a lady!"

"I am indeed. You must have seen ladies before now."

"People think you're a spy or a deserter from the army."

"This terrible war makes people suspicious. When I first started walking, people used to shout 'Witch' after me so I disguised myself as a man, but I couldn't bear to cut off my hair."

"Where are you from?"

"I'm a lady from Wales, a long way from my home."

I stood up.

"I'd better get to my home."

"Come again, if you would like to."

And I did go back. There was something calming about the stranger. Bobby had sensed that at once. I took food with me because she looked thin – tea, bannocks and crowdie.

"You don't like my herbal tea?" she said with a smile.

I never found out her name, but she told me how her son had gone to be a soldier and died in France. She was widowed and there was nothing to keep her, so one day she closed the front door behind her and never looked back. She kept walking northwards and stopped in Skye because she liked it here. It reminded her of home and even the language sounded like Welsh although she couldn't understand it.'

Pappa stops talking and looks deep in thought.

'I found that I could talk to her. I told her all about my adventures and poured out my worries – about Iain being so strange and Màiri's dangerous new job in munitions. When I had finished, she said, "Is there something that you've left out?"

That was when the tears started to splatter down into my cup and on to the floor.

"It's about your Dadda, isn't it?"

Again, she listened as I sobbed and stumbled through saying how scared I was because I was sure that Dadda was dying. When I fell silent, she rocked me in her bony arms and smoothed back my hair.

"You're a good, brave boy," she said and then sang a beautiful song. I couldn't understand the words, but it comforted me.

When I went the next time, the otter cub had gone.

"He decided to fend for himself in the big, bad world."

We were sitting drinking our tea when Bobby leapt to his feet, growling. The jackdaw squawked and flew outside. I could hear shouting and trampling feet. The stranger pulled back some pieces of driftwood covering the gap in the back wall that once led through to the byre. We squeezed through just as two men forced their way in through the front.

"This is the place! We'll beat the living daylights out of the German spy!"

One of them knocked over the pot and doused the fire while the other one kicked over the seat. I recognised one of the voices. It was Finlay Morrison who was in Iain's class at school but hadn't gone off to fight. I was furious at them tearing the place apart.

"Go and chase them out," I whispered, opening enough space for Bobby to get through the gap. He squeezed into the darkened ruin and ran silently up to the first man, sinking his teeth into his ankle. He shrieked in pain, hopping around on one leg and barging into the other man.

"What the hell was that?" the second man yelled as Bobby sank his teeth into his ankle too. He fell over and lay groaning. Bobby struck again, tearing his trouser leg. Then he rushed back to the first man who kicked out at him.

"I'm off before that beast gets me again," he yelled.

They hobbled over to the branches and hurled themselves at the wall, cursing as they pulled themselves over it. Once they were gone, we laughed so much that our ribs ached.

The Second Surge of the Sea

"You can't stay here now. They could be back and with more of them."

"Where can I go?"

"Come back to our house."

"But I don't ever stay in houses."

"Well, stay in our shed. I helped Dadda clear it out."

She agreed and gathered up her few belongings in a sack. I carried it and the jackdaw perched on her shoulder, with Bobby leading the way.

"Where have you been?" Mamma asked sharply. But when I explained she welcomed the Welsh lady and found an old mattress and some blankets for her to sleep in the shed. She wouldn't eat with us, so Mamma gave her some food to have outside.

"Will she stay with us, do you think?" I asked Mamma.

She shrugged.

"She's a poor wandering soul."

The next morning, I took out a bowl of porridge for her. I tapped on the shed door and when there was no answer I peered inside. No sign of her or of the jackdaw. Her sack was gone but beside the folded mattress there was a small cloth bag. I opened it and found a beautiful carved spoon, with a pattern like a tree, its branches curling around the handle.

"What a beautiful thing," said Mamma when I showed it to her.

I traced the pattern with my fingers and then took it upstairs and put it in my special box where the Viking brooch used to rest. Bobby stood in the doorway, watching me.

"Come on boy, I think you deserve a big bone.'"

CHAPTER 30

'The days were getting longer. It started with a few minutes more of daylight in January and by February, when it was Iain's birthday, the days were noticeably longer.

"I was pleased my first born arrived as winter was losing its grip," Mamma said every year, making my brother roll his eyes. But this year there was no word from him. All we could do was send a parcel of cake and cigarettes and hope that it reached him.

I noticed that Mamma's eyes were red when I came home on the evening of his birthday. I didn't know what to say so I crept upstairs.

"I hear that those Stewarts are back," she said when we sat down for tea. "I don't want you to have anything to do with them."

"Why not?"

"Because they took you away with them, of course."

"They didn't. Jamie let me come along but didn't tell Mrs Stewart and when she found out she wasn't well pleased."

"I won't have you going near them," Mamma shouted.

"But I won't run away again. Why won't you believe me?"

"I don't know what to believe anymore but I forbid you to see them."

"That's so unfair! It's not their fault and they were kind to me. Why won't you trust me?"

I thudded upstairs and flung myself on my bed. Bobby jumped up and nuzzled my face while I pounded the bed covers. I had been desperate to grow up and finish school but even though I was earning money I was treated like a child. All I had gained were the miserable parts of being older like having to keep secrets to stop Mamma from worrying. And she probably sensed that I was doing that. Should I have told her about the bag of pearls? But that would have meant explaining about the fight with Angus and his hell hound. How could I risk upsetting her more when she was already so worried about Dadda and Iain? Whatever I did, I would be in the wrong. As I stroked Bobby's soft, batwing ears I wished that I could go back in time, before the war started, to the day when Bobby swam home. Everything was much simpler then.

First though, I had to make my peace with Mamma, bite my tongue and say that I was sorry for answering her back. Then after a day or two I could slip away and see the Stewarts. In the end it was easy. I just set off in the morning as usual as if I was off to work on the boats.

"See you later," Mamma called out, without looking up from the bannocks she was kneading.

I prodded the bag of pearls to make sure that it was buried in my trouser pocket before setting off on the road to Borve where the Stewarts liked to camp. When I reached the woods, I sent Bobby off ahead so that he would warn me if there was any sign of Angus. I kept my own ears pricked and looked all around me as I tiptoed through the undergrowth.

"Aahh!" I bellowed as I felt a hand on my shoulder. I swivelled round, heart thumping and fists raised.

"Hold on! It's only me," Jamie laughed.

"How did you get past Bobby?"

"I stayed downwind of you," he said as he stroked my dog.

"I was worried that your nasty big brother would be here."

"We haven't seen hide nor hair of him. We didn't know what had happened to you either."

"I need to see your Mamma and explain everything."

"Come along then and tell us your tale."

Mrs Stewart wrapped me in her arms.

"Thank the Lord that you're alive and well. We thought that Angus had harmed you. He never came back that night and we've not seen him since. We looked for you but all we found was Scar's body."

I sat down with them and told them of my adventures. I remembered how *Seannair* Stewart made his stories exciting by building up the suspense and I tried to follow his example. So, when I got to where I left the army camp and was heading for Glasgow, I said, "When I reached the shores of Loch Lomond and was trying to get to sleep I could hear snuffling and rustling and a fox barking but what terrified me was another sound, a terrible moaning."

I was pleased to see them hanging on every word as I told them about finding Mr Goldstein.

"It's like the Good Samaritan story," Mrs Stewart said.

"But I've saved the best for last," I told them as I reached into my pocket and handed over the drawstring bag.

"It must have come off Scar's neck during the fight. I've kept it safe and not told a soul."

She eased the bag open and rolled the pearls into her open palm where they gleamed like tiny, pale moons.

"These are fine pearls. They will fetch a good price and you should have a share."

"No, they're yours. I just found them. But I don't understand why Angus fights the whole world as he does. He's so big and strong that he doesn't need to threaten other people."

She sighed, "I think that he finds it a terrible burden being different from everyone else. Giants are taunted, like crows mobbing an eagle. And folk think that giants are slow witted. Look at the tales where giants are tricked."

"Like Finn McCoul deceiving the giant Benandonner," I said.

The Second Surge of the Sea

Jamie's wee sister, Grace, piped up, "I know that tale. Finn's wife Oonagh had a huge cradle made that was big enough for Finn to lie in. Then she dressed him in baby clothes. When the giant came roaring into the room looking for Finn she said that he wasn't there, only his baby son. Benandonner peered into the cradle and was scared out of his wits when he saw the size of the baby. He ran back over the causeway as fast as his legs would carry him and as he ran, he threw the rocks into the sea so that Finn couldn't follow him."

"All the world and his son want to get the better of a giant," said *seannair* Stewart. "Did you ever hear of Charles Byrne, Sandy? No? He was a giant who lived over one hundred years ago. They said that he was more than eight feet tall. He was born in Ireland, over in County Tyrone. He decided to leave home and make his fortune abroad. So, he travelled to Edinburgh and it's said that the nightwatchmen in the city were amazed when he reached up to light his pipe from a streetlamp. They had to use a long pole, but he could reach up without even going on tiptoe."

"Did he make his fortune?"

"Aye, Sandy. He did. Crowds of people came to see him, and they wrote about him in the newspapers. He was a good-humoured young man and folk took to him. He did so well in Edinburgh that he travelled through the north of England, all the way down to London. He was a great success there too. There was even a stage show about him. They called it 'The Giant's Causeway'. He was in and out of alehouses, being toasted by strangers, his pockets bulging with banknotes."

He sucked on his pipe while I waited with bated breath. It's no use badgering a storyteller.

"It couldn't last. The poor lad sickened. Giants are too tall for their own good."

"That's the trouble with Angus," Mrs Stewart said.

"He gets terrible headaches when he feels as if his head will split open like a dropped egg."

Mr Stewart continued, "Charles Byrne was in 'The Black Horse' one day with all his money on him when a pickpocket lifted the whole lot. He went into a decline after that. He knew that he was dying and told his friends that they must seal his body in a lead coffin and bury him at sea."

"Why did he not want a burial on land?" I asked.

"Because a doctor called John Hunter was after him. He paid men to follow Charles, waiting for him to drop dead."

"But surely a doctor would try to help him, not torment him like that?"

"Not this doctor. He liked to collect freak things, like cows with two heads, and he didn't care if they were Christian souls – bearded women, dwarves or giants. They were just curiosities to him. Charles' friends did the best they could to follow his wishes when he died. They took his coffin to the coast ready to go on a boat."

He stopped again to fill his pipe.

"But Hunter's men plied the friends with drink and while they were sleeping it off the rogues opened the coffin, took out the giant's body and weighted the empty coffin down with stones."

"What a terrible thing to do!"

"Worse was to come. That devil Hunter boiled up the body in a huge cauldron for a day and a night until all the flesh came away from the bones. Then he hid the bones away for many years. Maybe he felt some shame at treating a Christian soul like that, but it didn't stop him from displaying the skeleton in his museum."

I was shocked into silence. Then a thought struck me.

"Has Angus heard this story?"

"Not from me but someone took pleasure in telling him."

"So, he fears for his life, but I dread him killing someone in one of his terrible rages and ending up on the gallows," said Mrs Stewart with a sob.

And I believed that he would kill me if he got a chance. He wouldn't forgive me for killing Scar and losing the pearls, I thought, but I kept my fear to myself.'

CHAPTER 31

'I turned down Mrs Stewart's offer of rabbit stew.

"I need to get home."

"Does your Mamma blame me for you running away?"

"She does, even though I told her that you didn't know that I was following you."

"Hmm, I shall come and speak with her tomorrow. I've something to tell her."

"I hope that she listens. She forbade me to see you."

"Well, for once I approve of you disobeying her." She tapped her nose with the stem of her clay pipe.

"We'll talk woman to woman."

I hurried home and was relieved that Mamma didn't question me. She was busy plucking two of our hens.

"They're too old to lay now, just hungry mouths. I'll boil them up and strip the meat from their bones to make soup."

I felt sick and put my hand over my mouth.

"Why are you turning up your nose? Collect up the feathers and put them in this pillowcase."

Mrs Stewart came the next day. Bobby barked when he heard the tin pans she was carrying, jingling and bumping together. Mamma looked out of the window and stepped outside, shutting the door behind her. That meant that she wouldn't be inviting Mrs Stewart inside for a cup of tea.

"I won't be needing anything," Mamma's voice was cold.

"I've not come to sell you anything. We need to talk about Sandy."

"I've nothing to say."

"You will have when you hear what good fortune he has brought us – and you. I can tell you the whole story on the doorstep if you like."

"Very well. You'd better come in the house."'

'I bet that you had your ear pressed to the crack of the door, again!' I say.

'Of course! But I couldn't catch all that Mrs Stewart said. She was softly spoken. If only my hearing had been as sharp as Bobby's.

"……… in a terrible state when I found him following us, shaking like a creature caught in a trap, half out of his wits."

It sounded like Mamma was letting Mrs Stewart do most of the talking.

"……… must come and claim his share."

"Sandy, come here," Mamma shouted.

Mrs Stewart smiled at me, looking composed while Mamma's face was pale and her hands were clasped together.

"I had no idea that you were keeping Mrs Stewart's pearls safe all this time. She says that you're a brave lad and as straight as a pine tree. And she's right. I've told her that you may ride down to Dingwall with her and Jamie, to see the man who buys the pearls."

"And you shall have a third share of the money," Mrs Stewart added, "I shall have a third and keep the rest for Angus."

I was overjoyed to be travelling with them but not so sure about riding all the way.

"Bruach will be best for you, Sandy. He's a steady beast. Jamie and I will ride the horses we mean to sell, nice white horses that the gentry like and the *seannair* and the girls will stay at the camp."

The journey took three days, in the saddle from first light until dusk. Then we fed the horses oats from a nose bag and let them graze. Bobby trotted alongside, tail waving and tongue hanging out in a grin. We followed the drovers' trails that doodled and looped over the moors and the saddles of the hills. The heather and grass on either side was trampled from the scores of cattle that had marched that way. There were few other travellers as we plodded along, letting the horses find their footing. After all the worries of the last months I felt at peace, letting my thoughts wander free, like the ragged-winged buzzards that circled overhead.

We met a shepherd whose face was hardened to leather by the elements. He stopped to greet us while his dog lay panting and alert at his feet. He warned us of coming rain but had little else to say. It was as if the long days without human company had made him forget how to talk. I remembered that other shepherd who had taken me in when I was lost and offered to teach me shepherding. I knew that I could never bear the loneliness of that life. It was strange to think that I could choose what I wanted to do with my life. For years I had seen the course of my life flowing ahead. I would be a fisherman with Dadda. But now the river was splitting as it stretched its fingers towards the sea.

"I don't think that I'll ever get on a horse again," I groaned as I half slid, half fell of Bruach's back.

"I don't think I will ever sit down again without my backside being on fire."

"It gets easier," Jamie said, laughing.

"Go and sit in a stream to ease the pain."

Late on the third day we passed a scattering of houses near Dingwall. I looked around, wondering where the merchant's house would be. Surely it would be a big solid, stone mansion with a high roof. So, I was surprised when Mrs Stewart stopped outside a rough, low cottage.

"He hides his wealth. Lives like a pauper to fool the thieves," she said.

As we tied up the horses, I could hear fierce barking from inside the house and I recoiled, remembering Scar's crazed eyes

The Second Surge of the Sea

and rows of spit-flecked teeth. I was relieved when Mrs Stewart told me to wait with the horses. I sat down with my back against a bank and Bobby flopped down beside me. The horses tugged at the grass while I closed my eyes and stretched out my legs.

Bobby's sudden barking woke me with a jolt. I rubbed my eyes and blinked at the sight of a group of horses trotting towards me. The leading horse was ridden by a man in khaki uniform, a smart officer's uniform. Behind him were two other mounted soldiers, leading several more beasts behind them. I leapt to my feet as the group halted sharply beside me. The officer jumped off his horse and walked up to our animals, slapping one of the white ones on its rump.

"These will do."

"What do you mean?" I asked in alarm.

"I'm requisitioning them for the army, of course. We need hundreds of horses at the Front. We pay for them," he drawled.

"But they're not mine and my friends might not want to sell them,"

"It's military orders." The officer gestured the other soldiers to come over.

Bobby moved in front of their horses and started snarling and snapping at their ankles.

"Call that animal off!" The officer was reaching for his gun belt.

"Come here! There's trouble!" I yelled at the top of my voice. Jamie and Mrs Stewart rushed out of the house. While the soldiers turned towards them, I darted forward, untied the horses and yelled at them.

"Chase them away, Bobby!"

The animals kicked up their heels and charged down the road, with Bobby snapping at their heels. The officer was red in the face with fury.

"I can arrest you for obstructing His Majesty's forces."

"Just try it," Mrs Stewart shouted.

The two dismounted soldiers were grinning at each other. They weren't rushing to help the officer. At that moment the front door of the hovel opened and another man appeared. He wasn't tall but he had the shoulders of an ox and a hard face.

"Off with you!" he said without raising his voice, but it was the sort of voice no-one would want to argue with.

"You've not heard the end of this matter," the officer said, straightening his tunic and trying to look dignified, but his voice was squeaky.

Bobby re-appeared, lathered with sweat, and headed for the officer, who stepped sideways and vaulted onto his horse as if a pack of wolves was behind him. The riderless horses were stamping their hooves and straining against their leashes as the soldiers struggled to control them. The rest of us slipped back into the house and watched through the small smoky window, laughing as the officer shrieked at his men, making the horses prance around even more. Finally, they got them under control and trotted off, away from Dingwall.

"Will they come back?" I asked.

The tough looking man shook his head and spat.

"Yon's not proper soldiers. Let's have a dram for settling the deal and making the bastards run."

He gripped my shoulder so hard that my arm went numb.

"Now, laddie, can that wee dog round up horses as well as he can scare fools in uniform?"

"Aye, Sir. He's a dog who can turn his paw to anything." My heart swelled with pride.

"And his master's smart, too," Mrs Stewart said.

I bent down to rub Bobby's ears and hide my embarrassment.'

CHAPTER 32

'We found the horses two miles back, peacefully cropping the grass as if nothing had happened. Old Bruach seemed pleased to see us and bent his shaggy head to accept the halter. The two white horses were friskier but were calmed down by a handful of oats each.

"I think that Bobby should sit up on the saddle for a rest. He saved our skins," Mrs Stewart said.

"We should tie the purse round his neck, like the drovers do when they've had a dram or two after the market. They send the wee dog ahead with the money."

The journey back seemed shorter. My bottom still hurt but my heart was lighter. My share after selling the pearls was £70. With all that treasure in the National Bank surely Pappa would agree to go to a sanatorium? When we reached Kyle Mrs Stewart found a boatman to take us over and the horses swam alongside.

"Please don't tell Mamma about the soldiers. She would only worry. She's scared stiff of me getting into more trouble."

She tapped her nose and smiled.

"Trouble seems to stick to you like a burr. Don't worry, I shall stay as quiet as a mouse avoiding the owl. A young man needs to keep out of his mother's skirts. Just watch that you don't run into that officer again. He had a mean look."

I sighed. I seemed to have so many enemies now. Angus was the most frightening but now there was the officer as well as Mr Graham who might come back to haunt me.

"What will you do with the horses now?"

"Sell the white ones and keep Bruach hidden."

"I hate the thought of horses going to war. Iain said it's terrible out there."

Mamma was waiting at the front door for us. Once we were all crammed into the front room around the fire, I announced my good news.

"Well, you have no excuse now not to go to the sanatorium," she said to Dadda.

I knew that she was pressing him to change his mind in front of witnesses.

"I'm thinking hard about it."

"Is that a 'Yes' or a 'Maybe'?" Mamma had an edge to her voice.

"Let it be. I'll decide soon."

Mamma's hands were crushed together in her lap as she bit her lip. Dadda sat as still as a standing stone. His eyes were sunken and his hair had turned as white as hoar frost.

A few days later I arrived home to find Miss Baxter sitting with my parents.

"No long face, Sandy. I've not brought more long division for you. Did you enjoy 'Treasure Island'?"

"Aye. It's a grand adventure."

"Well, I've brought you 'Kidnapped'. Have you done any painting since I saw you last?"

"Not much, I'm afraid Miss Baxter. I've done a sketch or two of Bobby. I saw some beautiful views when I went to Dingwall but it's hard to remember them afterwards to draw them."

"You could do with a camera to record what you see."

"Yes, Miss." Inwardly I was thinking what a daft idea that was. A camera was far too expensive.

When she left, Dadda put down his cup.

"I've made up my mind. I'll go to the sanatorium."

Mamma cried out with joy, but he put up his hand.

"But there are two things to do first. Sandy must go to Glasgow and buy a good camera. Then I have a notion to sail to St Kilda. After that, I'll go."

The Second Surge of the Sea

"But why…?"

"Sandy deserves a reward, and he can see how Màiri is doing. You've been saying how worried you are about her. I'm sure that the Cohens will let you stay in their house."

I nodded and kept my face blank.

"Miss Baxter had news about that Mr Graham," Dadda said.

I felt my head begin to spin and was relieved to be sitting down.

"You know how he disappeared after banging his head? Well, that policeman who came here has tracked him down. His real name was Ross, not Graham."

My heart was thudding, and I could hardly breathe but Pappa looked calm so he can't have said anything – what was that word Màiri had used? – incriminating?

"He told a pack of lies. He was in the Army right enough, but he didn't lose his leg fighting for King and Country. He was thrown out for stealing and lost his leg later in an accident. It was very wrong of that policeman to come here and treat Sandy like a suspect."

Dadda started coughing violently and held his handkerchief up to his mouth.

"Don't fret, John. We can put that scunner out of our minds now," Mamma said.

One less enemy to worry about, I thought, as I closed my eyes that night. I slept deeply except for a strange dream. I was aboard the "Hispaniola" from "Treasure Island", sailing on a blue green sea. Tropical birds flew overhead, their colours bright as a spilled paintbox. A boat was lowered over the ship's side and I caught a glimpse of the man rowing it. It looked like Long John Silver but when he turned his head it was Mr Graham.'

CHAPTER 33

'The next week, I found myself on the train to Glasgow. Mamma made me wear the clothes that the Cohens had given me, even though I complained that they were too small. They made me feel as if I was on the stage pretending to be a laird.

Màiri was waiting for me at Buchanan Street Station as the train pulled in. I almost didn't recognise her because she seemed taller. She wasn't still growing, was she? No, she looked taller because she was thinner and her face looked different – pale, sallow even.

"Stop gawping at me, like a daftie," she said in the sharp way I remembered so well. She took my arm, and we jostled through the crowds.

"I've got you a room in a lodging house, near the hostel where we factory girls stay."

"Mamma thinks I'm staying at the Cohens. That's why she made me dress up. But I've put my old breeks in my bag."

"Good lad. You would get fleas and be picked on wearing that garb."

"And Mamma said that I had to make sure that you were not working too hard."

"What? My wee brother is going to look after me?"

But this time she laughed and punched my arm.

"I suppose mothers have a sixth sense. I don't write such long letters home now as there's not much I can say. I work long hours and I don't see the Cohens."

She was striding along but then stopped suddenly so that I crashed into her.

"We can stop here and have a cup of tea," she said, pointing at a teashop. The windows were steamed up from the smoky air.

"Why don't you see them, now? They're good people."

"Aye, but they weren't pleased about me leaving them. It's hard to keep servants when the factories pay much better wages. Now tell me about how things are at home."

"Well, as you know Dadda has agreed to go to the sanatorium. He made me put all the money in my name in the Bank. Your friend Isobel's Dadda arranged it all, or maybe one of his clerks, as he's off fighting himself."

"School seems so long ago."

"Do you miss it? I don't at all."

"Well, you were longing to escape. I loved studying and then I had the run of the Cohens' library."

She looked wistful but shrugged.

"It's more important to have the money. I'm putting most of my wages in the Savings Bank. I can go back to evening classes when this war's over. Did you know that I'm a supervisor now? The youngest one in the factory."

"That's good. When I get this camera, I'll take some photos of you to give to Mamma."

"It's lucky that they'll be in black and white so that she can't see my yellow skin. It happens to most of the girls filling shells. They call us 'canaries' because the powder stains our faces. Now tell me properly how Dadda is doing. I don't think that Mamma tells me the whole story."

It was the question I was dreading.

"He's very thin and he can't work much now. Some days he's a wee bit brighter, especially since he's talked about going to St Kilda. it's a mystery why he wants to go."

We sat drinking our tea and I thought how Dadda was like a brittle, dried leaf tossed by the wind. Màiri caught my eye.

"Do you think that…?"

"He's going to die? I don't know."

I brushed the tears away. It was terrible to say the words out loud but a sort of relief as well. I could see the bleakness in my sister's face.

"We mustn't lose hope. The sanatorium will give him a chance, thanks to you. Now, sup up your tea and we'll go to the camera shop. It's just off George Square."

I followed her as she swept through the crowds.

"Don't show me up by greeting everyone like an old friend. You're not on Skye."

She clanged the bell outside a cramped shop, its windows filled with cameras of every kind.

"How do you do, Mr Fraser. I've brought my wee brother to buy a camera. He's an artist."

There she was taking charge again. The shopkeeper smoothed down his grey moustache.

"So, you'll want a portable one."

"The only cameras I've seen are big ones on a tripod."

"They're fine to use in a studio but heavy to carry. A Kodak Box Brownie is a good wee model but maybe you want something more advanced?"

"A Box Brownie sounds fine to…"

"Show us your best ones. This is a special gift from our father," she interrupted, sounding grand.

He went to a glass display cabinet and unlocked it. He lifted something out, hiding it in his bear paw of a hand. Then he uncurled his fingers.

"It looks like a vesta case, doesn't it?"

"I don't know."

"Five inches long, less than three wide and not even an inch in thickness. Made of aluminium so that it's light. They call it, 'The Vest Pocket Folding Camera'."

"Have a proper look at it, Sandy," Màiri said.

"But who has a pocket in their vest?" I asked.

Mr Fraser laughed, "That's what Americans call a waistcoat. This camera is so neat that it can fit in the pocket where a gentleman keeps his watch chain. It's a bargain at thirty-five shillings."

I had been reaching out to touch it but now I drew my fingers back as if the metal case was on fire. Who did I know who wore a watch chain apart from the doctor and the bank manager? My sister's grand manner was misleading the shopkeeper.

"Come on Sandy, let Mr Fraser show you how it works. Our parents want him to have a really good camera."

"I'll show you some pictures I took using it."

By now, I was clenching my teeth with rage, but I forced myself to look at the pictures of Glasgow he had taken. I was amazed at the clarity of them.

"That's Kelvingrove Park, the University and a shipyard."

I couldn't help but be excited.

"Now when I open it up you can see the shutter. It works very smoothly because of the ball bearing inside. There's four different shutter speeds so that you can take a picture in poor light." Mr Fraser said.

"Isn't that neat?" Màiri said.

"And so small that it would fit in the pocket of an army tunic. Wouldn't it be grand if Iain could take some pictures at the Front?"

Mr Fraser said, "Only officers are allowed to take photographs, not ordinary soldiers."

I was pleased to see my sister look affronted, after putting on a pretence of being wealthy. I stroked the case gently with a forefinger.

"Well, it's this brother who shall have the camera and I want him to have the best there is," she said in her best hoity-toity, Highland lady voice.

So, I handed over the money and put the wee folding camera into my inside jacket pocket, as gently as if it was a newborn chick.'

CHAPTER 34

'I was so pleased with the camera that I forgot how much Mr Fraser and my sister had annoyed me by treating me as a child.'

'That happens, Pappa, doesn't it? Teachers, especially, and parents. Patronising is the word for it, thinking that young people know nothing.'

'Aye, but to be fair Màiri was better than she used to be – for some of the time anyway. I started with photographing her. I wondered if Mamma would notice her hollowed out cheeks. Then she had to rush to do a late shift at the factory.

"Off you go. I'll find my own way to the lodgings."

"Take good care of that camera. There's thieves around."

"As if I wouldn't guard it with my life!"

I walked out of the centre towards gloomy streets near the river where rows of tenements blocked out the light. The thick, smoky air meant that I had to adjust the setting as Mr Fraser had shown me. There were some ragged bairns playing hopscotch and I offered them a few pence in exchange for taking photos of them. They frowned at my accent but once they understood, they went to line themselves up against a wall.

"No, I want pictures of you playing."

They nodded and did as I asked. As I walked around the dingy streets, I thought how much worse it was to be poor in a big city. On Skye you could cheer yourself by gazing at the hills and the sea. Down at the shipyards I could see men scurrying antlike over the hull of a ship that loomed above the street like a giant Noah's Ark. Màiri had told me that the riveters made good money but I could never do their job, even if I were paid a fortune.

She came to see me onto the train the next day.

"You must persuade Dadda to go to the sanatorium." Her face was screwed up with worry.

"I'll do my best but first he must go to St Kilda."

"He can't be sailing his own boat?"

"No. The Captain will take him there."

When I boarded the train I settled down and took my copy of "Kidnapped" out of my bag and held it up to the window for Màiri to see.

She laughed, "Well, I never thought that I would see the day when my wee brother read a book."

I looked up as I heard shuffling and saw a soldier with crutches trying to back himself into the opposite seat. I tried not to gawp at his empty, pinned up trouser leg.

"Don't you recognise me, then? It's Sandy, isn't it?"

"Aye, but…"

"I daresay I've changed. I'm Jimmie. I was at school with your brother."

"I don't suppose you've seen him? Mamma gets worried because she gets so few letters."

"No. Out in France is not like being in Portree, you know. You don't just bump into folk. You've done well for yourself," he sneered, looking me up and down.

I blushed.

"When Iain was home on leave, he said how hard it was over there."

"Is that so?" His voice dripped sarcasm. He prodded his empty trouser leg with his crutch.

"Well, I'm out of it for good now. The doctors said that I'm lucky to be alive. I could have bled to death. Easy for them to say. I'm a cripple now. How can I earn a living now and what lassie would want me?"

The Second Surge of the Sea

I didn't know what to say and felt relieved when Jimmie closed his eyes and started to snore. His face looked softer then, more like the boy he used to be not so long ago. I wiped my own tears on my sleeve, but I wasn't sure who I was crying for.

When I arrived in Kyle, there was no sign of the steamer that should have been waiting for the train.

"Where's the boat?" I asked a *bodach* who was standing on the pier, smoking his pipe.

"Who knows? You can't rely on anything, nowadays. Blame this dratted war."

The boat finally arrived, two hours late. When I came ashore, my feet dragged me up the road home. It was a feeling of dread that slowed me. The thought of Dadda looking so thin and gaunt and Mamma smiling and pretending that everything was fine. I adjusted my jacket collar and my smile as I opened the back door. Bobby shot out and danced around me, followed by Dadda with a grin on his face.

"Come away in and show me how it works."

"It's the pictures of Màiri I want to see, more than the camera, but you won't have those yet," said Mamma.

"I have, Mamma. Mr Fraser sold me the camera and developed these."

"Oh, aren't they clear. She looks so bonny but thinner. She must be working too hard."

"Well, we must take the camera with us. George MacKinnon has said we can go in a couple of days, Sandy."

"It's not on his usual run, is it?"

Mamma said, "No, but he's taking supplies for the folk there and he'll bring back tweed that they want to sell. It's hard for them now that so few ships call while the war's on."

Dadda seemed so happy that I dared to ask him a question that had been puzzling me.

"So, why do you especially want to go there?"

A slow smile played over his lips, "Auld Lang Syne you might say. I went there for the first time when I was not much older than you."

"And it was on the boat that you first met Captain George, wasn't it?" Mamma said.

"Aye. He was just a deckhand in those days. He sailed round the world after that. Then he bought the puffer. But I didn't want to be away for months at a time after I met your mother. So, I took up fishing instead."

He reached over to squeeze her hand. She smiled and for an instant she looked as young and bonny as Màiri did in the photograph. Then she frowned.

"I hope that he has some crew. It can't just be you and Sandy doing the unloading."

"Don't fret. He has two strong lads to help who haven't gone off to fight yet."

Mamma sighed, "And we've still not heard from Iain. I worry about him being safe."

"There's no use worrying about things we can do nothing about," Dadda said gruffly.

Mamma's light-heartedness had disappeared like the sun behind a storm cloud. Even when people didn't speak of it, the war was always in the back of their minds. The first news of deaths had come after the fighting at Neuve-Chapelle. Telegrams arrived with news of deaths of a son, brother, husband or father. Before the War, telegrams were like rare migrating birds, bringing exciting news like a prize and only wealthy people sent them. Now they carried the taint of death. Every day Mamma waited for the postie, scrunching up her apron in frightened hands. Would he bring a letter or a telegram? When nothing came, she would straighten up and get on with the day's tasks. Safe for another day, until the next morning.

Finally, a letter came. With trembling fingers, she tore it open. I've got all her letters. She kept them tucked inside her Bible.'

Pappa gently unfolded a paper from his jacket pocket.

'Dear Mamma, Dadda and Sandy,

I enjoyed the mealie pudding and fruit cake. I shared it with the lads. That's what we do when one of us gets a parcel. The socks and gloves I kept to myself. No sharing those or the cake of soap. We've been busy but we're resting now. I think of Skye when I hear the birds singing. I was always the first to hear the cuckoo. Do you remember?

With all my heart, Iain

Mamma was crying and laughing at the same time. She tucked the letter away in her apron pocket and for the rest of the day she sang softly to herself as she worked. I remembered with a jolt how she used always to be singing. When did that stop? Was it when I ran away, when Iain joined up, or when Dadda became ill?

Two mornings later Captain George arrived with his big seaboots and booming voice.

"Are you both ready – and the wee ship's dog?"

Mamma walked with us to the end of the road, with a spring in her step which, like her singing, had disappeared for so long. This was going to be a good trip, I decided as I tapped my camera, wrapped up snugly in a piece of oilskin in the bag slung over my shoulder.'

CHAPTER 35

'Of course, I took pictures of everything. There was plenty of time as we chugged around North Skye and over to Harris. Then we left the land behind as the boat pointed her snout to the wide ocean. As a boy who had hardly left Skye it amazed me to see that endless sea and to think that beyond St Kilda there was no land until the New World. Captain George stood at the wheel with his pipe clenched between his teeth, Dadda leaning over the rail and the gannets plunging straight as needles into the foaming sea. The two deckhands, Colin and Rab, were small, dark-haired twins who muttered to each other but ignored the rest of us.

"We're lucky with the weather, just like we were all those years ago," the Captain said as we watched the jagged coastline of Harris fall away behind us.

"If I remember rightly, you took a fancy to a girl on St Kilda. Is that why you've come back?"

"Nonsense! I'm an old married man and I barely spoke to her. She'll have turned fat and grumpy."

But Dadda's face reddened.

"But you never forget your first love. She stays forever in your memory," the Captain teased. "You'll find out yourself soon enough, Sandy."

I felt a pang as I remembered pale Jessie from Glasgow. I felt sad both about her dying and about forgetting her so quickly. Getting no response from either of us, the Captain changed the subject.

"St Kilda's a long way from anywhere else. I couldn't live there. Next stop, America. I suppose the people here are bred to it."

The Second Surge of the Sea

I gasped as huge cliffs came into view with flocks of seabirds swirling around them like a flurry of snow.

"I've never seen so many birds!"

"That's how people came to live here. The birds and their eggs and feathers are like sheep and cattle are to us."

As we drew closer, we could see the grey cliffs rising sheer above the churning waves. There were steep slopes with grassy meadows that looked impossible for any sheep to reach. As we sailed closer the outlines of the different islands became clearer.

"There's Soay. It's green and flat while Boreray to the northwest has the highest cliffs. That's where the men go every summer to catch the gugas on Stac Lee and Stac an Armin. I don't know how they do it, risking their lives at the end of a thin rope."

"I don't think that I could do that."

"Better to stick to boats, Sandy. They're safer. Folk say that St Kildans have stronger feet and ankles than most of us to make it easier for climbing."

I knew that my wee camera could never capture the scale of what I could see. So, I stood and gazed around me before taking out my pocket sketchbook.

"I've just realised what's missing. There are no trees, anywhere."

As we headed towards the mouth of Village Bay, I saw several rowing boats heading towards us.

"This is the only place where bigger vessels can land," the Captain said, "And if storms whip up you can't land at all."

Bearded men and bare-footed boys helped us unload. We manhandled lengths of wood, baskets of nails and sacks of coal. Bags of potatoes, boxes of kippers and crates of groceries followed, then flour, sugar, apples and tins of treacle. I thought of the Stewart family turning the tins into cups and wondered if the people here did the same.

"I thought you lived off seabirds, rather than all this shop bought stuff," I said as I handed over a box to a ruddy-faced boy of about my age.

He laughed, "Not these days. We've got used to having supplies from visiting ships and since the War started the Navy brings us stuff. We've a taste for luxuries now."

He spoke Gaelic with a strange lilting accent, and I wondered if I had heard him right. How could sugar and treacle be luxuries?

"My name's Niall. What's yours? I think that you're staying in our house."

We walked up Main Street – the only one – and Bobby trotted along behind, nose to ground, breathing in the new, strange smells. Here was another surprise. I had expected to see old-fashioned black houses where people lived alongside their animals. There were still plenty of those on Skye and I knew that the St Kildans were poor. But to my surprise nearly all the houses were newer white ones with gables and zinc roofs. Dogs came out to greet us. They looked like a mixture of terrier and collie.

"We need the dogs to hunt puffins as well as rounding up sheep," Niall said. "Yours is a funny looking dog. What use is he?"

"He's not a funny dog. He's the smartest dog that ever lived."

Niall smiled.

"Don't take offence. I'm sure he is. Shall I show you the island?"

I decided not to take offence. Niall was friendly, even though he had a funny way of speaking and looked odd in his rough homespun clothes and bare feet.

"I think that Skye is the best place on earth. I bet that you think the same about here."

I was surprised when he just grunted.

"I'll show you the radio masts. That's where the sailors stay to look out for Germans coming."

"Are there any guns there?"

"No and no Germans have come either. The most exciting thing was one day when a fishing boat came in for supplies, only it wasn't a real fishing boat. It was a naval boat in disguise looking for submarines."

"Did you speak to the sailors?"

"No, the only person who talked to them was one of the *cailleachs*. They asked her where they could get water."

"And don't you find it hard living here?" the sailor asked her.

"I wouldn't want to live anywhere except in this beautiful place."

Niall made a face.

"Don't you like living here?"

"I do not. I want to escape. It's no use living here if you don't like climbing up cliffs after birds."

"Why don't you leave and go to Harris?"

"My mother won't hear of it. I'm the only boy in the family and she says if all the young men leave the island will die."

I couldn't think of anything to say to that so I changed the subject.

"I would like to climb higher up so that I can take a picture of the ship in the harbour. Can we do that?"

Bobby ran ahead with his tail aloft as we climbed the hill.

"The boat looks like a toy, and I can see another ship out at sea."

Niall seemed to have cheered up.

"There's an old song about a boat out at sea, looking like a dimple in the ocean. My Granny used to sing it to me even though our minister doesn't approve of songs."

"Not at any time? We can't sing on Sundays but it's fine the rest of the week."

"Not here. Maybe you can see now why I want to get away."

I looked out at the endless ocean.

"You're right about the boat looking like a dimple. It makes a sort of dent in the sea."

Niall's mood changed again.

"I can tell you a rude story if you like."

"Go on, then."

"Well, we always welcome strangers here. Once, many years ago in the egg collecting season, six men set out to Kittiwakes' Gully to collect eggs. While they were there, they saw a fine-looking vessel heading for Village Bay and put down its anchor there. The strangers stood on deck looking through binoculars but they didn't come ashore. That was odd but the men thought nothing more about it. They didn't find any eggs so they climbed over Gob na Muice where they hoped for better luck. They expected to find thousands of kittiwakes sitting on their nests on the rocks but the birds had flown. What do you think they found instead, Sandy?"

I could guess but I knew better than to interrupt a story-teller so I just shook my head.

"It was three of the strangers. One sat down in a wee boat while the second one was stealing the eggs. And the third one…"

"What was he doing?"

"Standing down on the shore, bending down and putting the eggs into a pair of breeks. His bare backside was gleaming like a pair of moons. Our men picked up rocks and threw them down as hard as they could. He got the shock of his life, dropped the breeks, and ran to the boat. I bet that he had never rowed so hard in his life. Those sailors never returned. Our men clambered down and put all the eggs into sheepskin sacks. Those thieves had saved them a lot of work."

"I like to hear about wrongdoers getting their just desserts," I said.

"Aye. We'll go back to the house now. They'll be wondering where we are."

My stomach was rumbling by the time I reached Niall's house. I tried to ignore it because I was dreading what they might give me to eat. Birds' eggs would be fine but what if it was something that stank of rotting fish, like the oily grey flesh of a cormorant?'

'When on earth did you taste that, Pappa?' I ask, looking disgusted.

'At my Granny's. She wouldn't waste anything.'

'Well, to my great relief a tasty, meaty smell wafted through the door. Neil's mother and a girl who must have been his sister, were already sitting at the table.

"Your Dadda's out on watch duty," his mother said.

"You wouldn't be any good at that, having to stand on a hilltop and running down if there's a message."

"Sandy, this is my sister, Rachel," he said through gritted teeth. She was a tall lass and sturdy looking.

"I bet you're not scared of heights, Sandy," she said.

"We've hills on Skye, right enough, but I don't know what it would be like to climb the cliffs you have here."

Niall flashed a smile at me. I took an instant dislike to his sister. Even when we fell out, my sister would never show me up in front of strangers like that.

"I've made mutton stew," his mother said as she passed us plates and I stuck my fork straight in. Niall kicked me under the table as Mrs MacKinnon started to speak.

"First we must give thanks to the Lord for providing us with food, from land and sea."

The prayer went on forever as the stew got colder and colder. At last, we could tuck in.

"It's a shame that you're not staying longer, Sandy," Rachel said, "You could have helped us to catch the fulmars. We use their oil. When you catch one you have to break its neck and twist the head round so that the oil doesn't pour out of the nostrils. Am I upsetting you, dear brother? You're fidgeting like a hen on a hot griddle."

Mrs MacKinnon sighed.

"Rachel should have been born a boy. She would love to climb the cliffs. You're allowed to catch the puffins in their burrows. Be content with that."

Rachel scowled.

"Any fool can do that. The dogs make it easy by digging the birds out. Your dog could do that Sandy."

Suddenly the stew didn't taste so good. I could kill fish and rabbits, but I liked the cheerful puffins with their rainbow beaks. Surely there wasn't enough flesh on their wee bodies to be worth eating? I was glad that I wasn't born on this bleak, treeless place where the wind bent you double all the time and you had to risk your life on those cliffs to get enough to eat. No wonder Niall wanted to leave.

That night I slept in blankets in front of the fire with Dadda and the Captain snoring on either side. When I woke up, I realised that I hadn't heard Dadda coughing. The trip must have done him good. The next morning, we loaded up a cart with bales of cloth, knitted goods and baskets of eggs. Mrs MacKinnon pressed a sack of seabirds into the Captain's hands.

"Niall will help you load up," she said.

"You don't need a head for heights to do that," Rachel sneered.

There was the same excitement as when we arrived. Small boats clustered round the puffer and the boys jostled each other to pass the loads to the twins who had stayed on the boat overnight. Everything was ready when Niall appeared on deck.

"You forgot this," he said, holding out a sack of seabirds.

"We have some already," I replied.

The Second Surge of the Sea

"Oh, I'll just put it in the hold for you," he said and hurried away.

Soon we were under steam, and I waved to the people on shore, relieved to be leaving. Bobby though was unsettled. He kept padding up and down the deck.

"Are you after that stinky old sack of seabirds?" I asked him as he started to scratch at the trapdoor down to the hold. The dog became more insistent, and I decided to listen to him. After all, Bobby's instincts had often been useful. I lifted the hatch and climbed down the ladder into the darkness. I nearly called out in shock as my arm was grasped.

"Don't give me away. I can't bear to go back."

"What on earth are you doing, Niall?"

"What's it look like? I'm a stowaway. Don't give me away, Sandy."

"Let me think."

I climbed down and sat on the bales of cloth, my head in my hands. What would Dadda say if he knew that I had helped Niall run away? He had never been as angry as Mamma about my running away. Would he blame me for egging Niall on? But I knew that my new friend was desperate to escape, and I could understand that too.

"Here's what we do. I'll go back on deck and say nothing. You stay hidden until we reach Portree and don't let on that I knew. Will you swear to do that?"

"Aye, I do. Thank you, Sandy. Have we passed Harris yet?"

I nodded.

"That's good, then. They won't land me there."

"The Captain could just throw you into the sea. He's got a temper."

Niall gasped.

"I'm joking, you fool. We're not pirates from 'Treasure Island.'"

Niall frowned.

"It's a grand book about adventures at sea."

I climbed up again and opened the hatch gently. No sign of anyone. I walked over to the engine house, whistling with my hands in my pockets.

"Any chance of anything to eat, please?"

"I swear that you've got hollow legs, lad," the Captain said. "Go and ask the twins."

I walked over to the crew's quarters where one of the twins was stirring a pot on the stove that nearly filled the narrow space while his brother was lying down on a bunk beside the water tank.

"What's got into your wee dog? He's got the fidgets."

"He can smell those dead seabirds down in the hold."

I could feel sweat trickling down my neck. The cook frowned and stopped his stirring to dish me up a tin plate, piled up with bacon, bread and eggs.

"You can have some bacon if you keep still," I told Bobby.

After we had eaten, I relaxed a little. It wouldn't be too long before we were in Portree. I closed my eyes, glad of my full stomach. I don't know how long I slept but a shout woke me up.

"Who the Hell are you?"

It was the Captain's voice. He strode along the deck, hauling Niall behind him. "Look who I found coming out of the hold."

"I'm sorry, Sir."

"The twins saw the wee dog sniffing around there."

"Did you know what was going on, Sandy?"

"I thought Bobby was just after those stinking birds."

"I took my chance when no-one was looking. Just let me ashore, Sir, and I'll find work. I just had to get away and see the world and…"

"Stop babbling." The Captain's voice was quieter now.

The Second Surge of the Sea

"I could join the Navy or the Army soon."

"Don't do that, lad, until you're old enough," Dadda said, looking hard at me.

"We won't tell your Mamma about Niall being a stowaway. You didn't encourage him to come to Skye, did you?"

"No, Dadda. But he told me how unhappy he was. That sister of his was always tormenting him."

"Please, Sir, would you let me stay on the boat and work for you?"

"I'll give you a trial, but you must write to your Mamma and tell her."

So, I breathed a sigh of relief. My Mamma, of course, was pleased to see us back, safe and sound.

"You look so much better, John. You must see the doctor tomorrow about going to the sanatorium."

"Now let me in the door before you start ordering me around."

Miss Baxter came round the next day. She reminded me that once I reached my next birthday, I could officially leave school. I tried not to look too excited.

"We've been doing a lot at school for the troops. The girls have been knitting gloves and mufflers."

"What about the boys, Miss?"

"Well, they've not been idle. They've been collecting sphagnum moss to put on wounds and raising money for cigarettes."

"Let me give some money towards that."

Mamma nodded her approval.

"Now, have you been doing any drawing, Sandy?"

I showed her sketches I had done of the cliffs and some of the people going about their work.

"Well done, Sandy. What an incredible place it is. You've captured something of the spirit and endurance of the people. And have you been reading too?"

"Aye, I enjoyed 'Kidnapped' but not as much as 'Treasure Island'."

"And why was that?'"

'That's the way with teachers, isn't it Margaret? Always quick on the draw with questions?'

I laughed in agreement.

"'I liked 'Treasure Island' because it was about pirates and the sea. I told Niall, a boy on St Kilda, about pirates but he hadn't heard of them."

"I'm not surprised," she said with a sniff. "They're so far from civilisation there."

She fished inside her bag.

"I've another book for you. It's not about the sea but I think that you will enjoy the subject matter."

She smiled as I craned my neck to see the title, "It's called, 'The Call of the Wild'. It's about a man and his dog in the wilds of Canada."

That night, I lay in bed, reading the book. Bobby lay asleep at my feet, his paws twitching. Maybe he was imagining chasing the puffins. I shuddered at the thought of eating the comical wee birds. I must have dozed off because voices woke me. There were fierce whispers coming from my parents' room.

"But you promised that you would go."

"And I will. I'm just not going all the way to the Isle of Wight."

"But it's mild weather there. You'll get better more quickly, and we have the money to pay for it."

"But it's a terrible long way to travel. I want to stay in Scotland."

"But Aberdeen! The east coast is so cold."

"Bracing they call it. It will be good for my lungs. Why else would they build a sanatorium there?"

"You're an awkward, stubborn man who won't listen to reason."

Mamma stifled a sob and the bed creaked as she got out of it. In the morning she looked puffy eyed and there was no sign of Dadda.

"Your Dadda is off out. Did he tell you that he's decided to go to a sanatorium in Aberdeen?"

I shook my head.

"Well, he told the Captain all about it and he's taking him down there in that rusty old bucket."

"He will prefer that to the train."

"Well, Sandy. It's just you and me who will be left at home. I wish that Iain would get some leave." Her face drooped.

"At least he'll have some time to enjoy his leave when it comes. When I was over in St Kilda I heard a story about two soldiers from there who were given leave but by the time they finally sailed over from Harris and waved to their family in Village Bay they had to turn round and go straight back again."

"What a thing to happen!"

I was pleased to see Mamma smile, even though it was a pale ghost of one.'

CHAPTER 36

'The Captain came for Dadda two days later. Niall was with him, grinning broadly.

"Do you like it on the old puffer?" I asked him.

"It's grand. He's forgiven me for being a stowaway and I think that Mamma will get used to the idea, in the end. He says that I'm a blether but the twins never say a word, so I have to make up for them."

"You'll soon be wanting to be on a clipper ship – you know, the tall ships where you have to climb the masts."

A look of horror swept across his face.

"I'm only teasing you! You can stick to steamships."

When I got home, Mamma was swirling around spring cleaning.

"Off out you go, Sandy. You and Bobby are getting under my feet."

I felt at a loose end or like a hen on a hot griddle, as Neil's Mamma would have said. Bobby kept circling my legs and looking up at me.

"Now, you're getting under my feet. You look hot. You could do with a swim."

I remembered that day that seemed to be part of an earlier life, when I had met the Canadian lady who bought Bobby.

I decided to take the boat over to Camus Ban. It's always been one of my favourite places, that wee sandy pocket of land, tucked into the hills across the bay. I would make a fire and find some whelks to eat and prise limpets off the rocks for Bobby. The sea was calm, with tiny crinkly waves. I was tempted to dive in, alongside the dog but the chill took my breath away and I was soon out again. While I was drying myself with my shirt, I sensed that there was someone else there. Bobby stood erect, his nose twitching as he looked up the slope of Ben Tianavaig above us. There was someone there, crouching down in the heather.

The figure stood up, a boy rather than a grown man. I waved but he didn't respond so I started to gather pieces of wood to make a fire. When I stood up and looked again the figure had come down to the beach. He was wearing a fancy tweed jacket, like the one that the Cohens had given me, the one that made the other lads sneer and say, "Here comes his Lordship in his stalking jacket."

His jacket was strained across his plump belly and the sun gleamed off his spectacles. I stared at this apparition, but Bobby trotted up to him, his tail wagging.

"I say, is your dog friendly?"

"Aye."

"I'm Henry. What's your name?" he asked, stretching out his hand.

I stared at his hand and then shook it.

"Sandy."

"I'm here for the hols, staying up at the Lodge." He pointed up the hill towards Penifiler.

"At the big house? Have you come for a swim? It's a bit chilly."

"I'm not dressed for swimming."

"Well, help me make a fire, then."

When I got the fire alight, I dug down in the sand for razor fish.

"Look, there's an old tin plate, hidden in the grass," I said. "We can put the shellfish on it to cook."

"Isn't this jolly," he said as we tucked in. "I wish we had a dog, but we live in a town."

"Do you like being here for your holidays?"

"I do but it's lonely with only Mater and Pater for company."

What language was he talking? I wondered.

"Will you be here tomorrow? Maybe we could go out in your boat?"

I nodded. Henry was odd and not someone I would choose for a friend, but we were both adrift, so why not?

"I'll bring my swimming costume."

I smiled. Who on earth wore a costume? You just stripped down to your drawers. When I got home, Mamma had turned the house upside down. All the floors were swept and the rugs spread over the rocks to dry. I told her about meeting Henry.

"He was friendly enough, but he kept talking about Mater and Pater."

"That's the upper classes for you. They don't say 'Mamma and Dadda' like normal folk."

The next day I went back to Camus Ban. Mamma had given me a basket of bannocks, crowdie, scones and jam.

"I don't want this Henry to think that we're savages who live off shellfish."

He was waiting for me, wearing a lighter jacket this time and carrying a rolled-up towel.

"Shall we go for a swim first?" I asked.

"I can't swim properly. Pater says that I'm a cissy because I'm scared of the water."

"My big brother Iain taught me to swim, and I can teach you if you like."

I stripped off quickly but then I had to wait for Henry to take off his jacket and shirt, fold them neatly and balance his spectacles on top. Then he wrapped the towel round his middle and wiggled into his costume. His skin was very white, and he squinted anxiously without his glasses. We waded into the sea up to our chests.

The Second Surge of the Sea

"I'll support you around your middle while you do breaststroke."

Henry tried to stretch out his limbs, but he was stiff with fear and clung to me in a panic.

"I can't do it. I'm terrified of drowning. Pater threw me into a swimming pool, but I sank and had to be pulled out."

"That was a harsh thing to do. Never mind. Just look at Bobby there. No-one taught him how to do doggy paddle."

He smiled at the dog's short legs paddling along and his tail stretched out behind him.

"This time lie on your back, and I'll support you while you float."

He stretched out, his limbs shaking. I waited until he had relaxed a little.

"By Jove, it's easier than I thought."

Afterwards we ate all the food and then I showed Henry how to row.

"It's hard going backwards," he said as he sprayed water everywhere.

"Give it a few days and we'll make a sailor of you yet."

"I don't know about that. I'm very clumsy."

But gradually Henry became more confident. He learnt to row in a straight line and managed to swim without stiffening up. Afterwards while we rested he told me more about his life.

"I'm the youngest. My Pater calls me 'the scrapings', you know – the scrapings of the barrel, what's left at the bottom. I've two older brothers, Edward and Albert, only one now, I suppose. Edward was killed at the Front. He was a captain and mentioned in despatches for bravery. Albert is fighting out there now."

"And is he alright?"

"I hope so. We don't get much news. I suppose that he's too busy to write."

"We don't hear much from Iain either. I suppose they can't say what it's really like. He was strange when he came home on leave. Jumping at shadows and hardly saying anything. I worried that he was losing his mind."

"Albert was the same! He wouldn't stay inside. Spent all his time pounding the streets. My, these scones are tasty. I must ask Cook to make some."

We carried on munching happily.

"Do you go to school here, Sandy?"

"Aye, I did. I'm finished now."

Henry's mouth hung open in amazement.

"Well, I never! I've only been at my school for a year. I'm stuck there until I'm eighteen. Then Oxford afterwards. Do you think that the War will be over by then?"

I shrugged.

"Do you like school?"

His eyes glittered.

"To be honest with you, I hate it. Cold dormitories, greasy food, playing Games on muddy fields. But home isn't much fun either with Mater being so miserable."

I chewed slowly while I digested what Henry had said.

"I hated school because I wanted to be away working on the boats and then we had a new teacher who was a tyrant but at least I could go home at the end of the day. Your school sounds like a prison."

"It is! and it's worse because my brothers did so well there. Edward was a sportsman. His name's on the Honour Board for rugby, cricket and boxing. Albert won prizes. He loved Latin but it's all Greek to me."

I frowned.

"Just my silly joke, old chap. 'It's all Greek' just means when you don't understand something. I'm hopeless at both Latin and Greek."

"Albert sounds like my sister, Màiri. She loved school and wanted to stay on. All I heard from the teachers was 'You're not a scholar like your sister.' She even went to night school down in Glasgow. Cheer up. You can nearly swim now. You'll soon be swimming over to Harris."

Henry gave a wobbly smile, "Well maybe Pater will be pleased with me for once."

When I was walking home, I thought about Henry. I had never talked with anyone like him before. Mamma always said that money didn't always make you happy and I could see now that she was right.

"You're very quiet tonight. Did you fall out with Henry?" Mamma asked.

"When we talked together, he seemed so unhappy, and his Dadda calls him 'the scrapings'."

Mamma looked shocked.

"Well, of course we have nicknames for people, like 'Tatoe MacKay' because he eats so many of them but that sounds like an unkind name, as if no-one cares about the poor lad."

I put my arms around her waist.

"It makes me see how lucky I am with my family.'"

CHAPTER 37

'The next day, I met Henry staggering down to the beach, hauling a heavy hamper.

"We had better swim first. If we eat what's in that hamper now, we'll sink like stones," I said.

Henry could swim properly now without me supporting him. He kept grinning and humming as he dried himself afterwards.

"Come on then," I said, "Open the hamper. I've a huge hole in my belly."

He lifted the lid and swept off the cloth to reveal a king's banquet of cold ham and beef, venison pies, sausage rolls, hard boiled eggs, chicken legs and shop bought cheese. And that was just to start with. There was lemonade, slabs of sponge cake filled with cream and raspberry jam, grapes and oranges. After eating my fill, I lay back with a sigh of contentment. Bobby, full of chicken, was snoring gently.

"You must take home anything that's left, Sandy, or Cook will be offended."

"Who made that nice sponge?" Mamma said as she licked her lips.

"It's good but not as light as yours," I replied. Mamma laughed, something she rarely did.

"You're very loyal, Sandy."

Overnight, it turned windy. It was a bit rough for swimming, but I thought that Henry might like to fish instead. I showed him how to cast out from the rocks. He shouted with excitement when he felt a tug on his line and lifted out a glistening mackerel.

"I wish that I could stay on this island for ever," he said.

The Second Surge of the Sea

I thought how strange it was how some people wanted to live somewhere else. Henry wanted to leave his home in England, Niall wanted to leave St Kilda and Iain wanted to leave Skye. But I was like Dadda. I wanted to stay at home.

"We're going home tomorrow, worst luck, but I want to show you something first," Henry said as we scrambled ashore. I followed him up the hill and across the moor to the big house where Henry was staying. I hung back when we got close.

"I shouldn't come in with my wet clothes."

"We're not going inside. Come this way," he said.

He walked towards old stables round the back of the house. Then he opened the door and came back wheeling a bicycle.

"Of course, I can't ride it properly, but I thought that you might like a go on it."

"Aye, but I've not ridden one before so hold onto the saddle while I have a go."

I wobbled and nearly fell off at first but then found my balance.

"You can let go now!"

"I already have."

I turned back to look and wobbled sideways in surprise, making Bobby jump out of the way as I fell into a clump of heather.

After that we took turns in riding it.

"Can I have a last go before I leave?"

I rode down the path at the back of the house before sweeping round all the out-buildings.

"Time me with your watch and then you have a go and see if you can beat me."

I had my head down, concentrating on pushing hard on the pedals when I heard a shout. Someone stepped in front of me and I had to swerve and brake. Thwack! I felt a hard blow across my shoulders. I dropped the handlebars and skidded off the bike. A red-faced man was wielding the walking stick to hit me again.

"Thief! That's my son's bicycle."

Then Henry cried out. "No, Pater! It's my friend."

I dropped the bike and called out.

"Cha do ghoid mi an rothair, idir!"

Shock had made me shout out in my mother tongue.

"Don't speak gibberish. And get that cur off me!"

Bobby had sunk his teeth into the man's ankle.

I said that, "I didn't steal the bicycle at all!"

My hands were shaking with longing to hit this man's sneering face with his own stick. Henry came and stood beside me.

"This is my friend Sandy who has taught me how to swim, fish, row a boat and ride my bicycle."

"He must be a miracle worker, then. Come to the house, boy."

I was tempted to run away but I felt sorry for Henry who looked terrified. So, I took my time picking up the bicycle and whistled to Bobby to follow. As we reached the back of the house, the door opened and a woman appeared, wiping her floury hands on her apron.

"Do you know this boy?"

"Of course, I do, Sir. It's Sandy MacPherson."

"I told you, Pater."

"Silence!"

"I shall go home, now. My mother will be expecting me."

I couldn't bear to stay a moment longer.

"What's going on?" A lady in a dark dress appeared.

"Don't fret, Agnes. Our son has been wasting his time with this local fellow."

"Mater, Sandy here has taught me how to swim, row a boat and ride a bicycle and his brother is fighting in France."

Henry's mother swallowed hard.

The Second Surge of the Sea

"That must be difficult for your mother. This terrible war is putting such a burden on families."

"And my sister is working in a munitions factory in Glasgow."

"And what does your father do?"

"He's a fisherman. At least, he was. He's in a sanatorium."

"I'm sorry to hear that."

Suddenly, I felt tears smarting.

"Mater and Pater, I want to thank Sandy for being my friend. I want him to have my bicycle."

Henry's father frowned but his mother spoke.

"An excellent idea," she said, staring hard at her husband.

"Thank... thank you. I could get a job as a telegraph boy."

"Very well. Off with you now." Henry's father turned on his heel and strode away, his wife following him. The cook beckoned us into the kitchen for a glass of milk.

"I could ride it back home!"

"What about the boat? When we've had tea, I'll help you put it in the boat. It's a pity you can't ride it across the water," Henry said.

"Will you write to me when I'm back at school? It would cheer me up no end to hear about Skye."

My heart sank but I didn't want to disappoint him.

"Why don't you write to me first? – Sandy MacPherson, Bayfield, Portree, Isle of Skye, will find me."

Henry kept waving until I was half-way across the bay. I was tired when I got home and to my surprise there was no sign of Mamma. I called out. Where was she? Then I saw the piece of flimsy paper on the table.'

CHAPTER 38

'I steeled myself to pick it up. I hadn't seen one before, but I somehow knew what it was.'

'A telegram?' I ask. I hold my breath. Who was it about? I reach for Pappa's hand and squeeze it.

'"COME AT ONCE. YOUR HUSBAND GRAVELY ILL." I whispered the words.

I bent down and buried my face in Bobby's hair. I had been sure that the telegram would be about Iain being killed. Dadda had seemed so much better the last time I'd seen him.

"Is that yourself, Sandy?"

It was one of our neighbours, Mrs Murray, hovering in the doorway.

"Your Mamma's gone to the sanatorium."

"She didn't wait for me!" I wailed.

"There wasn't time to waste, son. The telegram arrived just after you left the house. The Minister borrowed the doctor's car to take her to Aberdeen. The doctor, bless him, said that he would use his pony and trap for his calls, like he used to do."

"Does it mean that…?"

"I don't know what it means. Come next door and have something to eat. There's nothing you can do at the moment."

I let her take my hand and lead me next door, but for the first time in my life I had no appetite. She gave me tea laced with whisky and when I dozed in the chair, she helped me upstairs. I stumbled through the following days in a living nightmare, my mind numb. Then Mamma came home, her face stiff with pain.

"Dadda?"

"He died yesterday. Thank the Lord that he was still conscious when I got there."

"I didn't have a chance to say goodbye to him."

"I know son. I'm sorry that it couldn't be, but he spoke about you with such love before he slipped away."

She wiped away her tears and put her arms around me.

"We had to bury him there, but the Minister will have a service for him here."

"Do you think that he knew that he would never come home again? That was why he wouldn't go down to England. He wanted to be buried in Scotland, even if it wasn't in Skye?"

"I think so. I was wrong to accuse him of being stubborn."'

'Did you think that Dadda would die?' I whisper.

'No, at least not for a long time. He had been ill for so long and he did seem better when he came back from St Kilda. I heard afterwards that people with TB can seem to rally just before they die. For a long time I couldn't believe that he had gone. I would lie awake at night, waiting to hear him coughing, the coughing that never came.

The most heart-breaking part was how Bobby kept looking for him, padding from room to room and waiting outside the back door, peering up the path. He seemed to think that his job was to console us. Whenever Mamma was overcome with tears he stayed pressed to her side and every night he stayed on my bed, instead of wandering off as he used to.

A stream of visitors came to pay their respects.

"I'm so glad that we made that trip to St Kilda," the Captain said. "The thought of the journey kept him going for longer."

Màiri came home and I was surprised how pleased I was to see her. I had found it hard to go out and leave Mamma on her own and knew that my sister would cheer her up. The minute she arrived, Mamma stared hard at her and said, "You look very pale, lass. And why are your hands so yellow?"

She sighed, "I've been working in the munitions factory to earn more money. The powder stains your skin."

"And you never thought to tell me that you had left those nice Cohens?"

"I didn't want to worry you."

"Worry me? I worry more when you keep secrets. I knew there was something going on. Sandy's as bad. Iain's the only truthful one."

She swept out of the room, leaving Màiri tearful.

"She doesn't mean it," I said.

"Will you go back to Glasgow?"

"Aye. We need the money more than ever now, but I'll stay a week longer."

I showed her the bicycle and told her about my plan to work as a telegraph boy.

"It will be hard delivering terrible news."

"I won't be doing the Portree ones, only further afield where I'm less likely to know the people.'"

'And was it hard?' I interrupt Pappa.

'Aye but I managed. It was a release riding at breakneck speed. I found an old basket to take Bobby with me. When Màiri left she suggested that Mamma go down to stay with her for a while.

"Maybe," she said with a shrug.

Meanwhile, I kept going. Sometimes when I was busy, I would forget about Dadda dying but then the grief would rush in like a black tide. Mamma didn't say much but she spent a lot of her time knitting for the troops.

"If only Iain would come home," she kept saying.'

CHAPTER 39

'So did you carry on as a telegraph boy?'

'The burden grew heavier until it felt as if it was growing into my back, like that terrible story I heard when I was with the Summer Walkers. People recognised my Post Office uniform and before I knocked on the door there would usually be a woman standing there, her hand held up to her throat and her eyes anguished. One day the Postmaster gave me four at once to deliver.

"There must have been a big battle," he said.

My heart lurched, thinking about Iain. But my big brother had always been lucky. Mamma told the story of how he fell down the stairs from top to bottom when he was a baby but somehow bounced all the way, howling with shock but unhurt. He had cracked his head many times playing shinty and fallen out of boats but never been badly hurt. Iain had lived as many lives as a cat. Still, I felt dread hovering like a sea fog. But one day, I felt it very strongly. I couldn't shake it off and it grew as I walked into the kitchen, my stomach clenched and my heart thudding. There was another flimsy telegram, fluttering in the draught as I shut the door. This time Mamma was at home, rushing up to me.

"He's only missing," she said, terror and hope battling in her face.

I read the message:

"PRIVATE IAIN MACPHERSON stop MISSING IN ACTION stop"

"I would know if he was dead. I would feel it in my bones. I heard about a lad from Kyle who was missing and then turned up."

I didn't know what to think. The hope that Iain was alive was a fluttering spark in the darkness. I couldn't bear to deliver telegrams any more after that. I got a job working at the icehouse instead, down at the pier. I had to climb up to stack rows of salmon on top of a layer of ice, then add more ice, followed by a layer of fish until the space was full up. My fingers tingled painfully until they went numb, but the worst part was when I finished, and the blood throbbed back into my aching fingers.

Màiri wrote to me and voiced the thoughts I couldn't put into words to Mamma:

But what if we don't hear for months or never hear at all, even when the War is over?

One evening when I was restless, I went out late for a walk. I listened to the waves lapping the shore and thought about the time before the War began when all I wanted was to grow up and leave school. Bobby was pottering around when suddenly he ran towards me and cowered behind my legs.

"What's the matter, Bobby?" I said as I bent down to stroke him. I looked up to see someone approaching us, a figure whose gait seemed familiar. Who was it? With a jolt I remembered and bent down to pick him up, ready to run for my life but I was too late.

"Is that you, Sandy MacPherson?"

They say that bad luck comes in threes. Dadda had died, Iain was missing and now it was Bobby's turn. I was rooted to the spot as the figure drew close. She seemed older and shrunken. Her black gown was very different from the vivid blue one that she was wearing when I saw her before.

"You'll be wondering why I'm here."

I was braced for her to demand that I hand over Bobby. I closed my eyes and held him tight.

The Second Surge of the Sea

"My son is fighting in France, and he's been reported missing."

I opened my eyes.

"So is my brother. And my Dadda has died."

"I'm sorry to hear that you've had such grief. I came back here because I couldn't settle at home in Canada and I thought that at least I would be nearer to France if there was any news about him." She shook her head.

"Did you say that your brother is missing too?"

I nodded, unable to speak. She stared at me, deep in thought. Then she seemed to make up her mind.

"May I come and speak to your mother? I've an idea I want to put to her."

Without waiting for an answer, she strode towards my home. I stumbled after her, dread in my heart. Mamma's eyes opened wide in surprise.

"You remember me, Mrs MacPherson? Dora Gillespie from Canada. I'm so sad to hear of your loss. I remember meeting your husband when I came here before."

"Will you come inside, Mrs Gillespie?"

I could see how bewildered Mamma was feeling. She hadn't wanted to see her again. Nor did Bobby who slunk away outside. After Mamma brought tea and scones there was an uneasy silence.

"My son Hector is missing in action, as I believe your son is too."

Mamma nodded, her eyes glistening.

"I didn't know what to do with myself when I heard the news. Like you, I'm a widow and in the end, I decided that there was nothing to keep me at home. Hector's my only child and I felt that I needed to be nearer where he is in France so I came back to Scotland. I didn't know why I returned to where his great-grandfather was born but now I do know."

She took a sip of tea before going on.

"I don't believe that he is dead. I would feel it in my bones if he was."

"I understand. I feel the same about my son, Iain."

"I have to do something so I'm going over there to find him. He must be lying injured in a hospital and I shall bring him home."

"How will you do that?"

"I shall get an ambulance and drive it to the Front."

Mamma's hand shook so that her cup clattered in the saucer.

"You seem surprised, but it can be done. The only difficulty is that I need someone else to come and do some of the driving. I was pondering that problem when I met your son. He could come and look for his brother."

"No! Sandy is tall for his age but he's too young."

But my heart was beating fast.

"Listen, Mamma. Màiri could come too. We'll never have another chance like this!"

"But girls don't drive!"

"But they do, Mrs MacPherson. This terrible war has changed so many things."

"She already works in a munitions factory – and she's a Suffragette."

"I like a girl with spirit. We women already have the vote in Canada. Well, what do you think, Mrs MacPherson? Will you lend me your children?"

Mamma sighed.

"How can I say no if here is a chance of finding our lads?"

Bobby trotted back inside. He sat down by my feet, watching Mrs Gillespie closely.

"He reminds me of that puppy I lost, the one who jumped ship."

My face was afire as Mamma said, "It's the same dog."

"I was sure that he had drowned!"

"No, he swam back home, and we had no way of telling you what had happened. Of course, he's your dog if you want him."

I put my arms around him, unable to breathe.

"He's turned into a fine dog and I'm so glad that he didn't drown."

She came over to stroke him and Bobby cowered.

"Don't look so stricken, Sandy! Do you imagine that I would be so heartless as to take him away? And I don't want my payment back either."

My tears of relief splattered down on Bobby's head. I let go of him and he wagged his tail.

"May I stroke him now that you know I won't kidnap him?"

"Of course. Could he come to France with us? He's a very handy dog."

"But that would mean leaving your poor mother completely on her own."

"He should go too. He's a very clever dog. It was thanks to him that Sandy found hidden treasure. Will you have more tea, Mrs Gillespie."

"Yes, please. And I should like to hear these stories about Bobby.'"

CHAPTER 40

'A flurry of activity followed. Mrs Gillespie went to Glasgow to find an ambulance and get passports. Mamma wrote to Màiri who was thrilled to be going abroad. A frenzy of washing and mending followed.

"You've grown again, Sandy. I'll have to let down the sleeves on your good jacket that the Cohens gave you," she said through a mouthful of pins."'

'I bet you were glad, Pappa, when you finally outgrew it,' I say. 'I remember a horrible frilly party dress that I was forced to wear and it seemed to fit me for years.' He nodded in agreement and chuckled.

'Bobby was lucky. He just needed a good wash, but he ran away when he heard the word "bath". He loved swimming in the sea but he hated getting soap in his eyes.

In the end we were ready and I left, loaded up with extra socks and two big fruit cakes.

"Iain can share them with the other lads in hospital," Mamma said.

My sister met me off the train in Glasgow and we set off to join Mrs Gillespie.

"Do you think we have a good chance of finding Iain and Hector?" I asked her.

"I don't know. I suppose soldiers must get lost in the heat of battle and we've got to try."

We found Mrs Gillespie, sitting at the wheel of a smart black ambulance, with a big red cross painted on its side.

"Jump up into the cab. I've a hamper of food for the journey and the back is full of bandages and medical supplies. We'll drive down to Dover to catch the boat. Then we go to the hospitals and work our way inland. Have you a photograph of Iain?"

"Aye. It was taken when he was training in Bedford. They didn't have enough tunics and kilts to go round so they had to take it in turns to borrow what they had for the photographs."

"Well, he looks very soldierly. Here's my picture of Hector."

It showed a tall, dark-haired man with a moustache and a serious expression.

"He's in a kilt too. He looks like an officer," I said.

"He's a second lieutenant."

"Will we see the Isle of Wight? Dadda was meant to go to a sanatorium there," I asked.

"It's quite close, I think."

As we neared Dover, I stared wide-eyed at all the marching men, horse-drawn vehicles and lorries that were surging towards the ships. The docks were like a city, full of wooden warehouses, heaped-up crates and railway tracks. A soldier checked our papers before directing us to join a line of lorries heading for a ramp into a ship. Bobby was hidden under a pile of blankets in the back of the ambulance.

"It's best to keep quiet about him. If the authorities don't know about him there won't be questions about quarantine later," Mrs Gillespie said.

Although we were travelling for a serious reason, I couldn't help feeling excited. I took as many photographs as I could, taking care not to be noticed in case I was accused of spying. On the crossing Mrs Gillespie explained her plan of action.

"Wounded soldiers are taken first to a dressing station near the Front where they receive emergency treatment and then on to a casualty clearing station until they've recovered enough to go on a train to a base station. They're not kept too long at the clearing stations so I think we should try the base hospitals first, starting at Le Havre and working our way northwards."

She opened out a map, showing a necklace of towns and villages, strung along the coast.

"If we don't find them there, we'll need to travel inland to Rouen and maybe Abbeville. Do either of you speak French? I've forgotten what I learnt at school."

I shook my head and said, "Màiri can speak it."

My sister glared at me for speaking out of turn, "C'est vrai," she said.

Le Havre was even busier than Dover had been. We ground to a halt as a lorry tried to squeeze past a cart. A soldier jumped down from the lorry to coax the horses through. As he did so, a car nosed out from behind and the driver hooted his horn.

"Make way for the officers!"

And so our search began. We visited hospital after hospital, Mrs Gillespie striding ahead, brandishing the photographs, and asking to speak to the doctor in charge. We followed behind her, carrying bundles of bandages and blankets. The hospitals were all crammed full. We weren't allowed in the wards where the sickest patients were housed but caught a glimpse of long lines of beds, pushed close together. Each time our hopes were raised as a nurse or orderly looked at a photo but each time they were dashed as the medical staff shook their heads.

"It's unusual for a soldier to arrive without any identification, whether he's alive or dead," an orderly told us at the first hospital we visited. "I suggest that you check the cemeteries too."

So, Màiri and I read the wooden crosses to spare Mrs Gillespie that grim task.'

'How could you keep going, Pappa?'

'I don't know. I suppose you get used to anything in time. What upset me most were the crosses that read, "An unknown soldier."

The Second Surge of the Sea

"At least we'll know that we've done our best," Mrs Gillespie said.

Sometimes we could stay overnight at a hospital but other times we had to sleep in the ambulance, Mrs Gillespie and Màiri in camp beds in the back, while Bobby and I curled up in the front. We were all exhausted but one rainy afternoon Mrs Gillespie said, "Let's try one more hospital before we stop for the night. It's not far."

I groaned at the thought of more bone-jarring knocks through potholes. As we walked into the last hospital of the day, a doctor with splatters of blood on his white coat, rushed out of the door, nearly knocking us over.

"What are you doing here?"

"Looking for two missing soldiers," Mrs Gillespie said.

"We have more important things to do than attend to you. We're waiting for hundreds of new casualties to arrive. They don't have rich relatives waiting for them."

He rushed off, leaving us shaken.

"I wish there were more private ambulances available for the wounded soldiers," Mrs Gillespie said, dabbing her eyes.

"But we haven't come empty handed," Màiri said, squeezing her hand.

"Look at all the supplies you've brought."

We stood together, feeling dis-spirited when an orderly spoke to us.

"Don't take any notice of Doctor Barnes. He's been operating day and night. Can I help you?"

Again, we went through the routine of handing over the photos. Again, the shake of the head and the murmured regrets. We returned to the ambulance, our shoulders slumped. We were about to climb wearily aboard when the kind orderly rushed up to us.

"A Canadian and a Highlander, you say? I think that they might have been in the last big push. Have you tried the Casualty Clearing Stations?"

"We were told that wounded men were moved on from them very quickly," Mrs Gillespie said.

"Not always. It's worth a try," he said.

He gave us directions and patted Bobby before wishing us good luck.

"I never imagined that it would be like this," she said.

"There must be thousands upon thousands of casualties. But we must keep going and not give up hope. If we can just find two missing soldiers."

But the unspoken thought was, "What if we can't?"'

CHAPTER 41

'No-one slept well that night. Even Bobby stayed awake, bolt upright in the cab. After a rushed breakfast of stale French bread and strong tea we set off to the casualty clearing station. The ambulance juddered along through woods. Each time it hit a rut we were thrown together.

We all jumped as a terrible booming and thumping filled the air. Bobby leapt onto my lap and lay there, quivering. It felt as if the whole world was about to explode.

"We're much nearer the guns here," Mrs Gillespie shouted.

"I can see a flash of white ahead. It looks like a line of washing from here, but the orderly said that we would see tents around the old farm buildings, didn't he?"

"Well spotted, Sandy," said Mrs Gillespie as she hauled the steering wheel hard round to avoid a pothole. We reached the clearing station, and she climbed stiffly down. For the first time, I realised how old she was, much older than Mamma.

"Shall I go and ask?" Màiri said, "You have a wee rest."

I whistled to Bobby, and we walked around the graveyard. Many of the graves were freshly dug, waiting for new bodies. The fields beyond were waterlogged marshes where rain had filled the craters made by shells. It was deserted now. The Front had moved forward. Stumps of blackened walls poked through the rubble, and I found a bell that had crashed down from a bombed church. The only sound was the harsh cawing of crows. I felt in my pocket for my camera. It seemed right to capture this grim landscape, to show the destruction.

When I returned, I found Mrs Gillespie slumped forward with her head resting on the steering wheel. There was no sign of Màiri yet, so I opened the provision box in the back and took out a biscuit. I shared it with Bobby and then I must have dozed off because the next thing that I remember is my sister shaking me awake. She had a strange expression in her eyes – hope and something I couldn't read.

"I've found Hector."

Mrs Gillespie sprang awake, and I scrambled down from the cab.

"He's alive but in a coma. He hasn't stirred since they brought him in, weeks ago."

"Alive!" Mrs Gillespie flung the door back on its hinges and hurled herself down from the cab. She fell forwards, pushed herself upright and charged towards the tents. I went to follow her but Màiri held me back, shaking her head. We followed more slowly through the rooms of the farmhouse, all crammed with beds until we reached the side door that led to the tents.

"He's in the last one."

I nodded, holding my breath, and struggling not to retch. There was a smell of decay that caught the back of my throat.

"He's in the moribund ward. That's where they put the men who are beyond helping."

I shook my head. Outside I could hear birdsong but inside it was deathly quiet.

Mrs Gillespie came out, followed by a young nurse.

"You just left him here to die! Why did no-one write to tell me where he was?"

"I'll go and fetch Sister, Mrs Gillespie."

Màiri and I stood back as the young nurse who had spoken ran past. Tears glittered in her eyes. We followed her and found Mrs Gillespie was beside a bed near the entrance, holding the limp hand of what looked like a corpse. I tried not to shudder.

"He feels warm but look at how gaunt he is. And he's grown a beard. No-one would recognise him from that photograph."

"But it was that nurse who realised who he was," my sister said, but Mrs Gillespie didn't hear her.

"You've never been so hairy in your life. Even I didn't recognise you," she said, sobbing.

An older woman in nursing uniform pushed back the flap of the tent and glided towards them.

"He came in with a lot of other injured men. I understand that he had fallen into a crater. The others were crying out and he was nearly missed but luckily a stretcher bearer spotted him and found a faint pulse. He's not regained consciousness, I'm afraid."

"Why did no-one write to me?"

"Because we didn't know who he was. His identity tag must have been ripped off by the explosion. He's Canadian, is he?"

"Yes. Lieutenant Hector MacKenzie."

"Ahh. He could be moved to the officers' tent, if you wish."

Mrs Gillespie was cradling his head.

"I don't care a fig about that. I want to know how to help him recover."

The Sister sighed, "There's little we can do for coma cases except wait and see. At least he's stable and not in pain, unlike these other poor men who are dying."

All the colour drained from Mrs Gillespie's face and the Sister spoke in a gentler tone.

"There's always hope. Sometimes unconscious patients respond to the voice of a loved one. Keep talking to him."

"Thank you. That's what I shall do."'

CHAPTER 42

'And did she?' I ask.

'For hours at a time. She squeezed his hand and talked, hummed and sang lullabies until her voice was hoarse. She didn't want to leave him at all, but she allowed the young nurse, Emily, to stay and keep watch at night.'

'What did you and Màiri do?'

'We tried to help in the hospital. There was a constant tide of injured soldiers. No sooner were some sent off on the hospital train to the coast than more came in from the dressing stations at the Front. I joined the orderlies who unloaded the injured from the ambulances. Some could walk with help, but others lay groaning on blood-stained stretchers. I lit cigarettes for them and tried to cheer them up. Bobby was a big help.

"That's a nice wee dog. We had a terrier in our trench. Earned his keep, killing rats. Rats are the only creatures growing fat in this war. Can we take him back with us?"

I shook my head and laughed, trying not to look at the soldier's leg with its mangled flesh.

"This is a dog that jumped off a steamer and swam home when he was only a puppy," I told him.'

'But you must have been wondering if you would ever find Iain?' I say.

'I was, but then I thought, What if he's badly injured? Would that be even worse?

I tried to keep busy by sketching what I saw around me – the old farmhouse, the recovering soldiers as they hobbled in the fresh air, the shattered woods and fields. One evening I was so absorbed that I didn't see Mrs Gillespie until her shadow blocked the light.

"You have a real talent, Sandy. You should study Art properly."

"I'm sure there are plenty better than me and I'll have to earn a living."

"Well, you keep practising. You never know what might happen."'

'What about Màiri? What was she doing?' I ask Pappa.

'She was being useful – making beds, bringing water and food to patients, teasing them when they asked to marry her when the War was over. She hardly seemed to notice the horrible sights and smells. She gathered up lousy uniforms, bedpans and blood-stained bandages without flinching. Her clothes soon became stained and the Sister gave her a spare nurse's uniform to wear. When patients arrived, she cleaned off as much mud as possible from them and surrounded them with hot water bottles. Once they could sit up, she gave them spoonfuls of hot coffee. The other nurses treated her as one of them and showed her how to change dressings. One evening when I came to say goodnight I saw her poring over an anatomy book.

"Would you like to train as a nurse?"

"No. I want to be a doctor. Not much chance of that but this is so much better work than making shells in a factory. I just wish that Hector would wake up."

"And then we could look for Iain. We can't drive the ambulance on our own. No-one would take any notice of us."

"Sometimes it's so hard to be young!"

The next day, I brought Mrs Gillespie a bowl of soup to eat at her son's bedside when I got a shock.

"Look!" I said so loudly that she nearly dropped soup into her lap. "I saw him move a finger."

We both stared, hardly daring to breathe.

"And his eyelids flickered!" She leapt to her feet.

"I'll fetch a doctor," I called over my shoulder as I ran out.

A doctor arrived, white coat flapping open over his Army tunic, and we all stared at Hector. He lay there unmoving.

"I hope that this isn't a false alarm." The doctor started to tap his foot.

"No. We both saw him move," Mrs Gillespie said.

A sneeze erupted from the bed, and we all gasped in shock.

"What's that goddam smell?" Hector croaked and his eyes snapped open.

"That's my chicken soup, son."

He tried to turn his head.

"Or is it the lavender bag you can smell? All you boys have one on your pillow. Maybe you've never smelt lavender before. Oh dear, I'm babbling! What should I do, doctor? I don't want to alarm him."

"Just keep talking calmly. We must let him recover at his own pace."

Hector sighed, closed his eyes and fell asleep again but an hour later he raised a trembling hand and rubbed his chin.

"What's this on my face?"

"You've grown a fine old beard, son. It's all black and bushy like a pirate's."

Hector came back to life over the next few days. It seemed like a miracle. Dr Russell declared him to be recovered but undernourished. His mother spooned food into him as if he was a baby again.

"This beard makes me itch," he complained, so an orderly shaved if off. Then he was allowed up and tottered around on his wasted legs learning how to move again.

"I can't remember anything about that last battle at all. Waking up here was like being born again but I'm sure as Hell glad to be alive."

"Watch your language, son. You've learnt to swear since joining the Army", his mother scolded but her eyes were full of pride.

The Second Surge of the Sea

He wanted to re-join his regiment, but the doctor insisted that he build up his strength first, "You can't take miracles for granted."

So, like us, he became a useful pair of hands. He acted as a scribe for soldiers wanting to write home, sat with depressed patients and made it his mission to look after the irritable Doctor Russell. Like a loyal dog, he followed him on his rounds, brandishing a plate or a cup of coffee until the doctor gave in and accepted it. But I fretted about wanting to look for Iain.

Then one day when we were eating stew after another exhausting day, Sister Humphries bore down on us. She was a large woman, but she had the knack of gliding along, like a ship in full sail.

"Mrs Gillespie and I have decided that she will take you to hunt for your brother."

"What about me?" Màiri asked.

"You will stay here to keep an eye on Hector. He would never admit to it, but he needs watching in case he relapses."

After the Sister had gone, Màiri said, "I wish that Mrs Gillespie had spoken to us first before arranging everything."

"But it'll all work out well, won't it?"

"I suppose so. But it's strange, isn't it? One minute we're treated as grown-up people and then we're told what to do as if we are children.'"

CHAPTER 43

The next day Pappa surprises me by saying, 'So, it's Màiri's turn to tell the story for a while now.'

'So how does that work, Pappa?'

'I have to get into the loft to find her diary. I want you to write down what I've told you so far and give it to your Granny. Then maybe she will stop worrying about me.'

I've been so wrapped up in Pappa's tale that I've not thought about Granny's opinion about it at all. He does look much more relaxed, now he's talked about what happened and it's lucky that I kept notes to jog my memory. Maybe I'll even get some credit from Granny and from Mum for doing something useful. It's a sunny day so I decide to go out for a walk and live in the present again rather than in the bubble of Pappa's past.

I hear the blare of an ambulance as I walk back and get a shock when I see that it's parked outside our house. Two ambulance men are carrying out a stretcher and I see to my horror that it's Pappa lying there, his face as white as his hair and scrunched up with pain.

"What happened?" I croak.

"I slipped on the ladder and hurt my bad leg. They're taking me to Inverness, but I found the diaries. Read them."

Granny is going down with him but before she does, she pulls me into the kitchen.

"This is all your fault. He only went into the loft because you told him to."

I'm too taken aback to say anything. So much for thanking me for cheering him up! But I know how upset she is, so I bite my lip.

"Stay here and don't do anything else stupid."

The Second Surge of the Sea

After she's gone, I slam a few doors to release my rage and then decide to find these diaries. They're on the little table in the hall. The loft door is hanging loose, and the ladder is half propped up against the wall and half fallen on the stairs. I suppose Pappa fell when he was trying to shut the loft up again. I prop up the ladder and reach up to shut the trapdoor. Then I make a drink with the jar of instant coffee that I persuaded Granny to let me buy, take it into the sitting room with the diaries and settle down to read. I want to know more about Grandad's sister who sounds like a girl with a mind of her own. I bet my Granny would have disapproved of her.

I blow the dust off the cover. It looks like an old exercise book with lined paper. Her writing is that old-fashioned sort of copperplate, done with an ink nib:

10 October, 1916

I waved goodbye to Mrs Gillespie and Sandy, my thoughts a turmoil of hope and fear. We had been so lucky to find Hector. Could we expect that sort of luck again and find Iain? Meanwhile, I had a chance to learn more about medicine and hospitals. I spoke to Dr Russell.

"Would I be able to assist in operations?"

He scowled. "You're too young. I spend much of my time amputating shattered limbs. It's a gruesome business."

"It can't be much worse than dressing stinking, gangrenous wounds and I help with that."

"I prefer to have orderlies assisting in operations. They're soldiers and more resilient than women."

"But there aren't enough orderlies and some of the nurses assist. Surely women can cope with blood. Midwives do all the time."

My knees started to tremble. Maybe I had said too much.

He let out a barking laugh. "What is it about you Highlanders? You never give up."

He agreed to give me a trial. I was allowed to boil the instruments and set them out ready for the operations.

"You've done well. You're alert and calm," he said after a long, gruelling day of endless amputations.

I glowed with pride, "I think of operations as a job to be done and don't dwell on it being a living person."

"That's the right approach. We always aim to save a life and even if we fail, we might learn something new that benefits the next patient."

"It's the infection that is the worst thing. The patient survives the operation but dies afterwards."

"There's no solution to that. The wounded are left too long with open wounds in a morass of mud and dirt."

Later, I went to find Hector. Now he feels better he complains of boredom.

"The Gorgon – I mean Sister Humphries – has said I can go for short walks as long as you come as my guard."

We started to go for strolls in the woods, kicking through the autumn leaves.

"It's hard to believe that the War is so close," he said.

"How long will it go on?"

"Who knows? It's already lasted longer than anyone thought possible. What will you do when it's over? Marry some lucky man, no doubt."

"Marry? I'm barely eighteen. I'm in no rush to marry, now or maybe ever. This war has made me see that there are different things I could do with my life."

"But we get on well, don't we? I was hoping that you would write to me when I'm back at the Front. And who knows? After the War we might…"

"I'll gladly write to you but that's all."

"Well, I'll settle for that, but you can't stop me hoping."

Meanwhile, Mrs Gillespie wrote to say that they were having no luck in their search for Iain.

"What else could have happened to him?" I asked Hector. "Could he have been wounded and taken somewhere else?"

He inhaled his cigarette while he thought. "It's possible, I suppose."

"But not likely?"

"So many soldiers have told me about their comrades disappearing into the mud. Is that what happened to Iain?"

He squeezed my hand. "It could be but don't give up hope. After all, I turned up when mother was losing hope."

"Aye, turned up like a bad penny." I grinned and wiped away my tears.

"You heartless hussy. You'll miss me when I'm gone."

15 October

Hector is declared fit for duty and leaves for the Front.

I sigh and put the journal down. Like Pappa, Màiri expresses herself so well. Better than me, if I'm honest, and they both left school early. But they had to grow up quickly. I do hope that Pappa will get better. I can't concentrate while I'm worrying about Pappa.

It's so difficult when there's no phone but I decide to go and contact the hospital from the phone box. I wait in a queue before I can get inside the stuffy telephone box and use up most of my change just getting through to the right ward.

"He's comfortable," is all I'm told. Should I phone home? I decide not to as I don't want to get blamed again for Pappa's fall.

I decide to read more of Màiri's diary:

1 November

I've been too tired after my shifts to write anything. I'm missing Hector, more than I expected. His easy-going nature made the strain of hospital life easier. I miss all of them, even that daft wee dog although I would never admit that to Sandy. I'm determined to impress Dr Russell who never shows any signs of flagging and expects everyone else to be the same. I strive for his approval, usually in vain. He doesn't believe in praise and encouragement.

"The nurses have done well but when the War is over, you will all return home, and all that hard-won knowledge will go to waste."

"Why is that?" I asked, although I could guess his answer.

"Surely that's obvious? You will all get married and raise families instead. That's why there's no point in allowing women to train as doctors."

I knew that I risked a tongue lashing but I had to respond.

"Maybe there won't be enough young men left for them all to get married. And there are lady doctors. What about Elizabeth Garrett Anderson who set up the hospital for women patients treated by women doctors?"

I waited for an explosion but instead he laughed, "You've clearly had a sound education young lady and learnt how to debate."

I smiled to myself, silently thanking both the Cohens for giving me the run of their library and the Suffragettes for writing all those pamphlets I had devoured. No-one would guess that I had left school when I was fourteen.

I was unsure what to expect when several ambulances of wounded Germans were brought in. I had heard those terrible stories of Germans impaling babies on their bayonets when they invaded Belgium. But when they came in on stretchers, ashen-faced and scared, they looked no different from our Tommies. They calmed down when they found that they were treated with kindness. I asked Sister Humphries what would happen to them when they recovered.

The Second Surge of the Sea

"They'll be sent to a Prisoner of War camp. The fighting is over for them."

They would be glad to escape the fighting. I've heard our lads talk about wanting a 'blighty wound,' bad enough to be sent home but not bad enough to be crippling.

A concert party arrived yesterday to entertain the patients. They put on a show with popular songs and extracts from plays. I had never heard some of the songs before, like, 'If you were the only girl in the world and I were the only boy'. I thought that the words were silly. If there was only one boy left it would be very boring having no choice of sweetheart. I preferred the acting although some of the soldiers weren't impressed. They groaned when they heard that scenes from Shakespeare would be performed. First was the balcony scene from 'Romeo and Juliet'.

> *But soft! What light from yonder window breaks?*
> *It is the east and Juliet is the sun.*

There were cat-calls from the audience.

"What a load of baloney."
"Stop talking and kiss her."
"Yes, grab her and give her a bit of how's your father!"

Sister Humphries stood up and turned round from her seat in the front row to glare at them.

Then, another actor strode on to declaim from 'Henry V':

> *Once more unto the breach dear friends, once more;*
> *Or close the wall up with our English dead!*
> *In peace there's nothing so becomes a man*
> *As modest stillness and humility:*
> *But when the blast of war blows in our ears*
> *Then imitate the action of the tiger.*

He tensed as he sensed the strained atmosphere, realising too late that this was too close to home for men who had been in real battles. The audience cheered up when it came to the witches' scene from 'Macbeth'.

> *When shall we three meet again*
> *In thunder, lightning or in rain?*

"Sounds like our trenches!"
"You could meet us anytime if you were younger and prettier."

I had enjoyed reading the play at school, but those days seemed to belong to a different lifetime. I wrote to Hector, telling him about the concert although I didn't include the rude cat-calls.

There were no more entries until nearly Christmas:

10 December

I was upset by Hector's letter.

He wrote that he didn't want to waste his second chance at life. He didn't want to study Law anymore but do something practical like farming, whether in Canada or Scotland. He could see me as a rosy cheeked farmer's wife!

No thank you! I shall write back, ignoring that comment and saying that I'm busy reading anatomy books and watching operations. Maybe then he will see that I have plans for the future too.

It's been quieter than usual, and I had been helping the recovering patients to make decorations until Sister Humphries asked me if I would transfer to a larger hospital where a lot of the nurses had been laid low with illness. My heart sank but how could I refuse?

So, the next day I found myself jolting along in an ambulance on a muddy road to St Omer. This hospital is in a building that had once been a convent. The sister in charge there told me that I would be working with the shell shock cases.

The Second Surge of the Sea

"I've not heard of them."

"You'll soon learn. Here you can give them this cotton wool."

"Is it for cleaning wounds?"

"No. It's for them to stick in their ears. Sudden noises startle them."

I was directed to a ward very different from what I was used to. Several patients were curled up in their beds with their heads hidden under the blankets. Others wandered up and down the ward. They didn't seem to be injured but as I got closer, I noticed the shaking hands and the vacant expressions. I walked up to a nurse who was trying to persuade a man to get back into bed. He was muttering to himself but suddenly started shouting and throwing his arms around.

"Gas attack, lads. Get your masks on. Where's mine? I've lost it!"

He was scrabbling in his pockets as he pushed the nurse away. I went up to him and took one of his arms.

"I've come to tell you that the attack has ended."

"Are you sure?"

"I am certain. You can rest now."

Suddenly he sagged and almost fell. I helped the nurse steer him back to bed.

"You can sleep now. You're on leave," I said.

"I'm overjoyed that you've come, whoever you are. I'm Sophie Randall," the nurse said.

She was tall and had a clipped, upper-class voice.

"I'm Màiri MacPherson. Are you in charge of these patients?"

"I try to be." She bent down and whispered, "No-one bothers with these poor fellows. The doctors ignore them, and Sister Thompson thinks that they're malingerers."

"Is she the one who gave me the cotton wool?"

Sophie rolled her eyes, "She has no understanding. She thinks wounds are only on the body. These poor fellows have been gassed, buried alive in mud or watched comrades blown up next to them. It's no wonder they've gone mad. Wouldn't you?"

I shuddered when I remembered what Sandy had said about Iain being so strange when he came home on leave. Had he been suffering from shell shock too?

"What treatment do they get?"

"Only morphine to help them sleep but some of them are too terrified to close their eyes because they have such terrible dreams and relive their torments."

I fell silent because I felt so helpless.

15 December

I couldn't sleep after what I saw yesterday. Those poor men with their stumbling walk, staring eyes and trembling hands. I remembered a terrified horse that I had seen many years earlier, owned by a brutal man who beat the poor beast until it stood shivering, its sides heaving and not even trying to avoid the blows. I had been out with Dadda who was helping to cut peats on a neighbour's croft. He had watched for a while and then walked up to the man, grasping his wrist so hard that he had to drop the stick.

"If you can't treat the beast properly, I will buy it from you."

"You'll have to pay a good price."

"I'll pay a fair one," *he said still squeezing his arm.*

In the end they agreed, and we took the horse home and spoke to one of Dadda's friends.

"I'm a fisherman. I don't need a horse, but I'll own half of him If you'll keep the other half."

So 'Half horse' he was called. At first, he wouldn't allow anyone near him but after a while he stopped trembling and would come over for a carrot or lump of sugar, scooping it up with his soft, hairy lips.

"It's not magic," *Dadda said,* "Just time and kindness."

I told Sophie the story of "Half horse" and she clapped her hands and laughed.

"Well, people are more complicated of course. We would need more than carrots. What about choral singing? Or games – draughts and dominoes maybe?"

"We could start by making Christmas decorations, and knitting?"

So, we brought in evergreen branches and asked local people for donations for a Christmas party. Sophie didn't seem to notice how they screwed up their faces, trying to understand her strange upper class accent.

"I hope they give us some of the drink they make round here?" one of the orderlies said.

"You mean Armagnac" replied Sophie, "it's a kind of brandy made from apples."

The orderly rolled his eyes at me behind Sophie's back. We explained our idea to the patients but some of them weren't too keen.

"I'm not doing any knitting – that's women's work."

"So, what happens when a button comes off your tunic? You all carry a housewife kit in your packs," said Sophie.

"And my Dadda mended his nets – and knitted too," I added.

"Come on Harry. We've not got a chance against these two. Just do what you're told. I'll give it a go, Miss."

"Hark at you, Stan," the first soldier laughed. "How are you going to thread a needle with your shaky mitts?"

23 December

We've sent out invitations for a carol service to all the doctors and nurses and most of them came tonight, even Nurse Thompson. At the end a skinny young soldier who has been silent for days, got to his feet and sang in a strong, pure tenor voice.

'Stille nacht, heilige nacht'

"What a beautiful song," I whispered to Sophie.
"It's a German carol. Some of our fellows learnt it from the Bosch."

I felt a sob rising in my throat and bit my lip to stop it bursting out. The horror of this war! For the first time, I accepted that Iain is almost certainly dead. Maybe it is time to give up the search and go home? I was blinking away my tears when Sister Thompson spoke to me.

"Well, what a difference you have made to those shell shock cases. It means that they can be sent back to the Front more quickly. I'll ask Major Fortescue to examine them tomorrow and see if some of them can be discharged."

My heart sank. To think that helping these men would only speed up their return to Hell! It was like fattening up cattle so that they would get a higher price at slaughter. All the joy from the concert leaked away. Exhausted and downhearted, I escaped and collapsed onto my camp bed. Tomorrow I will ask Sister Thompson if I may go back to the tented hospital. Sandy and Mrs Gillespie should have returned from their searches further north. If they have found no sign of Iain, we should face the truth and return home.

24 December

I cried myself to sleep – tears of pity and frustration but sometime in the middle of the night I felt someone shaking me.

"What is it?" *I groaned. I felt as if I was being dragged up from deep underwater caves.*

"I'm so sorry to wake you but I didn't know what else to do."

I rubbed my bleary eyes and peered at the face of the middle-aged nurse who slept in the room off the shell-shocked soldiers' ward.

"We've had a new admission. We fixed his dislocated shoulder but he's running amok, shouting and screaming. Two of the orderlies pinned him down while I came to find you."

"Why me?"

"He's not shouting in English, you see. Someone said it could be Welsh so they asked me to come but I can't understand a word of it. Then someone said that he's from one of the Highland regiments

The Second Surge of the Sea

and maybe he's calling out in Gaelic. Then I thought that maybe you would be able to understand him."

"I'll try," I said, pulling on my coat.

I found the patient, thrashing his head from side to side with two orderlies holding him down.

"I'm so glad you've come, Miss. He's making his injury worse and upsetting everyone else. We could have given him morphine, but we thought maybe you could calm him down. I didn't want to fetch Major Fortescue."

I nodded. The Major was notorious for his callous attitudes. I knelt down on the floor by the bed.

'Có thusa?' (Who are you?)

'S'e Coinneach an t-ainm a th'orm. Ca' a bheil mi?' (I'm Kenneth. Where am I?)

"He's asking where he is. I'll talk with him for a while."

He calmed down but he made me promise that I would come back again. He was looking out for me the next morning like an anxious dog. I encouraged him to join in the activities and when he saw another soldier making a small doll wearing a khaki uniform, he wanted to do the same for his daughter. I managed to find some scraps of khaki and tartan. Sewing the tiny clothes together stopped his hands shaking. I told him how fine it looked but suggested that he add a corporal's stripes, to match his own. The old look of panic returned, and he started to tear the toy apart. I put my hand over his to stop him, but he kept repeating that he didn't deserve the stripes and that his Kirsty deserved a better father.

"I find it hard to believe that you did anything terrible. Was it something that you were ordered to do?" He looked at me in horror.

"Tell me about it."

"I can't. The other lads understand but they're all gone – Jimmy Henderson, Jock Cameron, Iain MacPherson, Alec Mac… What's the matter with you, Miss? You've gone as white as a sheet."

"This Iain MacPherson – what did he look like?"

"Dark hair, light eyes, not tall. I didn't know him as well as I did the others. They brought us together from different regiments."

"Would you recognise him from a photograph?"

With my hands shaking, I took it out of my pocket. Kenneth stared at it for a long time, while time stood still.

"Aye, it's him. I wanted to be sure. How do you know him?"

"My brother, missing in action." I took a long, jerking breath. "My Mamma refused to believe that he was dead. He could be annoying, but he would never do something really wicked." I was laughing and sobbing at the same time.

"Give me pencil and paper. I'll draw a map of where we were when I last saw him."

Kenneth was shaking from head to foot.

"Are you sure that you can do this?"

"Aye. It's right that you should know. Maybe I survived for a reason – to meet you. I wanted to die in that battle afterwards. I charged ahead like a madman, to be first at the German guns. I didn't care what happened to me after that terrible business."

I couldn't help shivering at his words.

I have to close the diary and walk away. I want to know but not to know at the same time. I can't imagine what Màiri is feeling. She's so brave and experienced so much, compared to me. I've studied the First World War, learnt about it, but not felt it in my heart and guts.

I hear the sound of a letter plopping through the letterbox. News about Pappa? I can't bear that either, but I run to the door, recognise Granny's writing and tear the envelope open.

My dear Margaret,

I know that you will be worried. Your Pappa is in pain with a badly sprained ankle. I feared that he might have to lose his leg, but the

The Second Surge of the Sea

doctors have put it in plaster and hope that he will recover although he is having morphine. He gave me a row for being so angry with you. He says that you've kept him going since you've been with us. He is determined to get better so that the two of you can together tell me the whole story. God be with you, my beloved grandchild.

Like Màiri, I'm swept off my feet in a tide of emotion.

CHAPTER 44

24 December (cont.)

I went back to see Kenneth, terrified that he might have retreated into madness again, but I saw with relief that he was sitting up in bed and looked calm.

"We were given a few days behind the lines to get over what had happened – as if we could. Some of the officers seem to think we're like dumb beasts with no feelings. I got blind drunk on some gut rotting brandy but that just gave me bad dreams. Then we had to go back to our regiments. I remember Iain saying that he didn't feel scared anymore because he didn't care what happened to him.

Our whole section of the front had to advance up a hill towards a wood and get behind the German lines. We were told that there were no trenches. That was true enough, but they had machine guns. I ran like a madman towards them."

He showed me a drawing of a flat-topped hill and then frowned, "I can't remember the name of it. My brain's shot to pieces."

"Just close your eyes and see what comes."

"There was a village by the stream at the bottom of the hill, but everything had been blasted to smithereens by the guns."

He chewed the pencil so hard that splinters of wood broke off. He spat them out while I clenched my fists with the suspense. I didn't dare speak in case he broke down and fell silent.

"Wait a moment! There was something I noticed as we climbed the hill. One of those things the Frenchies build in honour of a saint. Lot of superstitious rubbish if you ask..."

"A shrine, you mean? A statue?"

"Aye, that's it! There were faded bunches of flowers there and a broken fountain."

"What did you see when you ran up the hill?"

"More rolling hills." He drew them in with a shaky hand. *"And something on the furthest hill – a windmill, its sails still turning."*

He sketched it in. "After that I don't remember. I think I passed out."

"One last question – How many miles away was this place, do you think?"

"I don't know. Not far."

He suddenly grabbed my hand and squeezed my fingers so hard that I nearly called out in pain.

"Go and find him."

Doubts gnawed away at my mind. Kenneth's news was old, and he was disturbed. Was he remembering properly? How could Iain disappear without trace? That sort of thing only happened in old tales about people disappearing to live with the fairies. I stopped believing those stories years ago.

26 December

We made an effort to celebrate Christmas yesterday. The chaplain held a service but not all the patients would take part because he was a Church of Scotland minister and they belonged to other churches. I would have hoped that in wartime we could forget these petty differences but at least those who were well enough enjoyed Christmas lunch. It was a mixture of meat from local farms – chicken, beef and goose and apple tarts instead of plum pudding. Tomorrow I'll see if Kenneth remembers anything more.

27 December

A nasty shock this morning. I arrived at the ward to find Major Fortescue seated at a small table with a pile of papers in front of him. All the patients were out of bed and standing in a ragged line. Some were frozen, others couldn't stand still, their faces twitching, arms flailing or mouths soundlessly working. Kenneth was there, looking better than most of them. The Major stood up and strode down the line, barely glancing at them.

"You're all fit for discharge. You will return to your regiments so that I can ready this space for men who really are ill."

He turned on his heel and marched out.

"It was bound to happen," Kenneth said, "but how can these lads hold a rifle when their hands are shaking all the time?"

"At least you finished the doll. Tell me your address and I'll send it to your wee girl."

My own hands were shaking as I wrote it down. We waved them off and I struggled to hold back the tears. I concentrated on holding up the doll and putting its arm up in a salute. If only these poor men could be repaired with a few stitches, like the toy. Sophie and I returned to the empty ward to clean it ready for the new arrivals. We were too dispirited to talk. We were putting the brooms away when the Major returned.

"The men coming in have real physical injuries, but they are still a disgrace to their country."

He turned on his heel, leaving us puzzled by his words.

We soon found out when a small group shuffled and tottered into the room. Some swung along on crutches, others hopped, wincing with every movement or wobbling along, holding each other upright. The Major strutted behind them.

"These fine fellows have all been shot in the foot. How fortunate for them! Bad enough to leave the trenches but not bad enough to be permanently crippled. How do you think that happened, young ladies?"

I kept my head down and my lips pressed together.

"You don't know? Explain what happened" He prodded a white-faced lad who looked no older than Sandy.

The Second Surge of the Sea

"I...I was cleaning my rifle, Sir. We were all frozen and knee deep in mud. My mate slipped and pushed me so that my gun fired by accident and shot away my big toe."

"And what about you?" the Major asked the man next to him.

"I jumped sky high, Sir, when a shell burst close by and my rifle went off, accidental like."

"Well, young ladies, do you detect a pattern here?"

I closed my eyes. I couldn't bear to look at his red face, distorted with rage, or to see the haggard soldiers with their blood-stained bandages and dejected faces.

"We will clean up your wounds although they should be left to fester. Then you'll be court-martialled."

"What does that mean, Sir?" the first young soldier asked, in a croaky voice.

"You'll be tried and punished. Shot for all I know."

He started to sway on his feet. I leapt forward to take his arm and sit him down on a bed.

"I'll deal with you first." The Major unwound the bandage from his foot and tore off the dressing underneath so roughly that the wound began to ooze blood and pus. He stifled a howl of pain and I could bear it no longer.

"No! We are here to ease a patient's pain, not to cause more."

The Major stared at me, "How dare you speak to me like that."

My knees were knocking, and everyone froze.

"Stop that racket or I'll crack your head open!"

We all turned to see where the commotion was coming from. Three orderlies were clinging onto a huge, bellowing man who was struggling to shake them off, while balancing on his good leg. They wrenched his arms behind his back, making him snarl in pain, tied his hands together and pushed him down onto a bed.

The Major shouted. "Stop causing trouble or you'll be locked up. And you, young woman, MacPherson, is it? will leave at once for the *clearing station. I'll send a letter, recommending your dismissal. I won't allow insubordination."*

My face was red, but I forced myself to look directly at the newcomer. The big man jerked his head up and stared at me with hate and fury on his face. He was like a terrible giant from one of the old stories. He struggled to stand but the orderlies forced him back down. I walked out of the door, my head held high.

CHAPTER 45

28 December

I went back to my room and tossed my clothes into my bag. I remembered that Kenneth's doll was still in my pocket. I would have to leave it with a note for Sophie to send it to his daughter. I sat on the bed, smoothing out the pleats of the toy's kilt until my heart slowed down. Why had that huge man stared at me as if he wanted to kill me? I had never seen him before in my life. I mustn't worry about him. He would be locked up. I needed to think straight. I had a chance now to find this wood, rather than waiting to see Sandy and Mrs Gillespie first. I snapped the bag shut, sprang to my feet, and strode out of the main entrance. Then I headed for the potholed road leading to the Clearing Station.

"Hey, Miss! Where are you going?"

I turned round to see one of the orderlies who had been pinning down the huge man.

"Hello, I'm John. I've just come outside for a breather. We got that brute sent on his way."

"I'm relieved to hear that. He seemed to have taken against me." I tried to smile but couldn't stop shivering. "I don't know why. He's a total stranger."

Suddenly, it hit me, as if someone had pushed me hard in the back. Sandy had talked about how he had killed the dog belonging to the Summer Traveller. Was that him and did the brute see a resemblance between me and Sandy? But we don't look alike, at all. He's tall-ish and fair while I'm small and dark. My friend Isobel at the Bank used to say that Sandy was a Viking while I was a Pict.

"Will I have to start painting myself blue?" I had said, laughing. That seemed so long ago, in a happier world.

But the man had heard my name too. Had he guessed the link with Sandy?

"Don't look so worried, Miss. That brute is behind bars."

"I know."

"You were brave standing up to Major Fortescue. He's a hard man."

"Aye but he's got his revenge. I've been branded as insubordinate, and the Clearing Station won't want me back. Did they call Mrs Pankhurst insubordinate, I wonder."

"How are you getting back?"

"I'll walk but I'm going to try and find this wood first."

I showed him the map. "It was where my brother was last seen."

"Umm." His kind, middle-aged face set into a frown. I could see that he was struggling for the right words. "I don't see how he could still be there."

"But I have to look. Kenneth said that he and my brother had been ordered to do something wrong and it preyed on their minds. I think that Iain must have kept running after the fighting and not stopped until he was well clear of the battlefield."

"If he did that, he would be considered a deserter. He would be court-martialled if he was caught. Listen. I don't think that you should go there on your own. I'll take you on my motorbike to have a quick look."

"Thank you but I can manage on my own and you have to get back to your work."

"I know that you're smart and brave but there are bad rumours about that part of the line. Both sides withdrew and it's not part of the Front anymore. The people who lived on the farms there haven't returned. It's a wilderness, a hiding place for deserters and thieves. It's not safe for anyone who's not armed and certainly not safe for a girl."

I was about to protest but I could see how his kind, rumpled face was creased with concern.

The Second Surge of the Sea

"I understand. Can we go on your motorbike to have a quick look?"

"Very well. I'll go and get a spare uniform for you."

He brought me a uniform and I returned to my room to put it on. The trousers slipped down over my hips and I had to turn up the legs but otherwise it fitted. I tried not to think about it maybe coming from a dead soldier. When I returned, he gave me a cap to tuck my hair inside.

"There. You look like a new recruit now."

"Won't you be in trouble for leaving the hospital?"

He shrugged. "My mates will cover for me."

It was exciting riding on the motorbike, bouncing down the road. I had to put my arms tightly round his waist to stop myself falling off. We stopped to ask a local farmer for directions. He scratched his head in puzzlement until I remembered the word for windmill.

"Moulin?" he said, his face lighting up and pointed to a turning ahead that was almost buried among the trees. We followed the rough track up the hill, ducking to avoid overhanging branches. The path opened out into a clearing.

"Look! That's the shrine or what's left of it," I said.

The statue had been beheaded but the body was still there, pockmarked with bullet holes. The head had fallen into a dried-out stream and the ground rose steeply ahead of us. We dismounted and clambered uphill, picking our way over fallen trees. John pushed the motorbike while looking over his shoulder.

"I can't risk it getting nicked."

"But there's no-one here. It's deserted, like you said."

"We don't know that we're not being watched."

I shivered. The trees loomed over us, drowning out the light. How I wished that we had Bobby with us. He would warn us of danger. When a branch snapped, we both jumped and froze. Then we carried on climbing upwards.

"Look! There's the windmill, just like Kenneth said."

I pointed at the stone building, perched atop the next rise, its sails hanging like broken wings.

"I don't understand it," John said. "In country like this, they would have taken the dead and wounded down with them. There wouldn't be bodies buried in the mud. So, where would your brother have gone?"

"Maybe he was taken prisoner?"

"But it's odd that no one was told. It's as if he disappeared off the face of the earth."

We made our way down the hill, silent and alert. Even though there was birdsong, the woods were threatening, and I was relieved to get back to the road. I felt sure that Iain wasn't dead. When I told Sandy and Mrs Gillespie what I had found out we could come back. I had a feeling that I couldn't explain. A sense that my brother wasn't far away. First though, I would have to face Sister Humphries and Doctor Russell at the Clearing Station. What would they say about my so-called insubordination?

"I need to get back before I'm missed. You look smart in that uniform. Keep it, it might come in useful."

Then he roared off with a cheerful wave.

CHAPTER 46

28 December (cont.)

I saw the ambulance first, turning into the Clearing Station and there was Sandy jumping down from the cab, his legs nearly buckling under him. I ran up to him and his face lit up as he saw my smile.

"You've news!"

"I have, although we mustn't get too excited."

Mrs Gillespie heard us and climbed down carefully. I blurted out the whole story.

"Well, my dear, that sounds amazing. Let's get inside and you can explain the whole thing properly."

When I finished, she frowned, "Well, it's no wonder that Sandy and I had no luck. We were looking in the wrong places. We must be careful now not to rush headlong into action. It could be dangerous, and we need military help if there are lawless men involved. I shall seek advice."

I took a deep breath. "Something else happened too. While I was there some injured men came in and the doctor accused them of deliberately injuring themselves to escape the fighting. One of them was a giant of a man who kept lashing out. When he saw me, he stared with such hatred that my blood ran cold."

Sandy gasped, "Angus Stewart, the Summer Traveller! I killed his dog when it attacked Bobby. He wants his revenge on me. The man is a mad devil."

"But how would he know that I'm your sister? He heard my name, but I don't look anything like you."

Mrs Gillespie smiled, "I don't know why. Was he under arrest? Even a giant can't break through iron bars. You look very tired, my dear. Was it very hard working at that hospital?"

"Yes. I had better tell you. The doctor there was very harsh towards the men with injured feet. He called them cowards for trying to escape the fighting. I said that we should treat them decently because they were our patients. He accused me of being insubordinate and sent me back here in disgrace."

"Well, big sis, you've always been one to speak before you think."

"And you can talk, wee brother – fighting a maniac and putting us all in danger."

Mrs Gillespie held up a hand, "That's enough, children. We need to keep cool heads. We should all rest now while I decide what to do next."

After she left, I burst out laughing, "I'm not really cross with you, Sandy, but I was exasperated with Mrs Gillespie treating us like over-excited children. She means well but Iain is our brother, and we should be the ones to decide what to do."

"We could go and look for Iain ourselves."

"And maybe we need help, but it doesn't have to be soldiers." I bent over to rub Bobby's belly while I thought.

"What about Jules? He brings food to the hospital, and he has horses we could use."

I spoke to him the next day when he appeared carrying a side of mutton and whistling through his teeth. I explained through my stumbling French, sign language and showing him the map. He rubbed his fingers together and I said that Mrs Gillespie would pay him. We slipped out of the hospital early the next morning without being seen by Mrs Gillespie, Bobby trotting along beside us. Jules and his friend appeared out of the mist, riding hairy ponies and leading a third one. Jules indicated that I get up behind him while Sandy rode the third beast, but I pretended not to understand and got up behind my brother. We trotted up the overgrown track towards the mill.

Our mount suddenly neighed and I gasped at the sound of branches snapping. There was a shout behind us and hoof beats. I glanced

The Second Surge of the Sea

behind me and knew that the riders meant us harm. Sandy dug his heels into our pony, and it lurched forward. Our only hope was to reach the windmill first and hope that we could get inside. There was an uproar of snarls, whinnying and swearing.

"It's Bobby! He's snapping at the horses' hooves." The path was steeper now.

"What if we can't get inside?" Sandy said.

As we slowed down, I seized the chance to roll off the beast and run to the door. Bobby lunged at the nearest horse and made it rear up. That's when I heard a shot and a cry of pain.

I turned the page but that was the end of the writing, and I couldn't ask Pappa what happened next. I know that he hadn't planned to go to hospital but this was an ideal way to create suspense! I didn't know when Granny and Pappa would be home but decided I would tidy the house up to get into Granny's good books.

CHAPTER 47

It was a good job that I did too because they returned the next day in an ambulance with Pappa wheeled in by the driver. Granny looked around but couldn't see anything out of place to criticise. I had potatoes ready to boil and a tin of salmon to open which put me in her good books.

'Now, leave your Pappa in peace. He has to rest.'

But he winks at me behind her back and the next afternoon we get a chance to talk.

'Màiri's diary ends when Bobby gets hurt – at least I think he's the one who was shot.'

'Well, it all happened very quickly. Bobby ran towards me, blood pouring from his head. I leaped from the horse, scooped him up and threw myself at the door. Màiri was already banging on it and, thank goodness, it opened a crack so that we could get inside before it was slammed shut. It was a heavy oak door that we could never have battered down. I could feel a hand pulling me inside but at first I was blinded by the sudden darkness. As my eyes got used to the gloom, I saw that the hand belonged to an old man. Bobby's blood had soaked my jacket and he lay in my arms, without stirring. The old man lit a candle, and I took off my jacket to wipe away the blood on the dog's face and gently put him down on the floor. My hands trembled as I felt his skull. It felt whole but then I saw the long tear in his ear. It looked as if it had almost been ripped off. I wrenched off my shirt and tore one of the sleeves to make a bandage to wind around his ear and tied the ends under his jaw. He whined and licked my face. As I stood up, I felt arms around my neck.

"Thank the Lord that you're both safe!" Màiri sobbed.

The Second Surge of the Sea

The old man had disappeared but he came back with two rough glasses. I gulped my drink down and started to choke. Màiri slapped my back and the old man laughed.

C'est du vin fort!

"He's saying that the wine is strong," she said.

"I could tell that!"

The old man gestured that we should follow him. Bobby was asleep so I left him as we climbed up a ladder to the top of the mill. There were chairs and a bed made out of rough pieces of timber. I shivered in my vest as the air was cold. I suppose that they couldn't risk a fire in the wooden mill. An old woman was sitting down, a heavy shawl draped over her shoulders.

"I'll ask them if they know anything about Iain," Màiri asked.

Both shook their heads. The old woman clenched her hands together and looked away. It made me suspicious.

"You know something!"

I ran to the ladder in the corner of the room and started to climb it.

"It's Sandy, Iain! Are you there?"

The old man was surprisingly nimble as he leapt to his feet after me but my sister stood in front of the ladder and pushed him back hard.

"Make a noise if you can hear us!" she called out.

There was a banging noise from the ceiling, and I ran up the ladder. I found myself in a tiny, dark space. I nearly tripped over the edge of a narrow bed and I could sense that someone was there. The bed creaked as the figure shifted and the blanket seemed to come alive. Dread filled me as I reached up to pull down the edge of the blanket. There was a thin face with a ragged beard – no-one I recognised. My shoulders slumped in disappointment. I peered into the gloom again. His eyes were sunken but there was something familiar. He gasped and reached out. I stumbled forward and put my arms around him. He felt as frail as a bird under my hands, and he had a terrible unwashed smell that made me want to retch.

"Sandy?" The voice was faint.

"Iain! It is you. Can you get down the ladder if I help you? I'll go first and guide you down."

I shouted down to Màiri, "Watch the old couple while I bring him down."

"Bobby and I have got them. Can't you hear the growling?"

I saw that the brave wee dog had the old man cornered while his wife cowered, wringing her hands. Màiri found some rope near the empty sacks and pushed the old man down hard onto the chair, pulling his arms roughly behind him.

"Don't be too hard on them," Iain said. "They brought me back here when I was wounded and cared for me."

"Some caring! You're a prisoner."

"It's a long story and a strange one.'"

CHAPTER 48

'We were all stunned, sitting together on the bare floor. Màiri gently removed the blanket and cradled Iain's head in her hands.

"Are you injured?"

"Only my ankle." He pointed to where his right leg lay stretched out. "I can't bend it properly since I broke it."

"I'll check all's quiet outside," I said.

"And I'll find you some water," Màiri added. She came back with wine, hard bread and a lump of smelly cheese.

She told Iain how we found out about the windmill.

"I can't tell you what I did. It's too terrible," he said as he sucked on a piece of wine-soaked bread.

"You don't have to, Iain. The first thing is to escape from here. We were chased by a group of deserters."

Iain grinned.

"I can't get over how you've grown up, wee Sandy. I suppose war does that. The old man has a rifle of his own and he took mine. We can hold the deserters off with those, but we need to escape."

Iain fell asleep, leaving Màiri and I to make plans.

"We could sneak out at night, but Iain is too weak to walk far. Do you think those men will be back?"

I nodded.

"Mrs Gillespie might raise the alarm but how soon? Maybe we could send Bobby with a message?"

I shook my head.

"I won't risk that, unless I go with him."

Màiri shivered and I knew that idea terrified her.

"You must obey my orders!" Iain was shouting but he was asleep. "Present arms! Aim for the white cloth!"

"Should we wake him up?" I asked.

"Corporal, go and check the prisoner."

"Sir, it's a …". He let out a terrible scream and sat up.

"You're safe now, Iain. It's only a dream. Tell us about it," I said.

Màiri took his hand, and he gripped it so hard that she winced.

"I can't!"

"Whatever you did, I'm sure that it wasn't your fault. You were under orders. We know that you tried to get yourself killed in the next battle."

"I didn't get that right either. I was shot in the ankle and passed out. The fighting moved on and when I came round, I couldn't move. The old man found me and put me in a cart, brought me here."

"But why keep you a prisoner?"

"I'm not sure but I think that their son was killed, and the old woman thought I was him, back from the dead. Untie them now. They meant no harm."

Màiri opened her mouth as if to disagree, but then she paused and said, "You're suffering from shellshock. I've nursed soldiers who have it – men who've seen too many terrible sights, men who can endure no more."

"But I can still shoot straight. This is what we should do. Sandy, when it's dark you leave with Bobby. Màiri and I have the guns to hold them at bay."

So, we waited for darkness. Time limped by. I was proud that my big brother trusted me, but I was terrified too. I had convinced myself that Angus had escaped and was out there.

Luckily, the new moon hardly pierced the darkness. The night air carried the sounds of snuffling and scraping, and I kept stopping to listen. Where did the deserters go at night? Did they

The Second Surge of the Sea

have a dog? The rhythm of running steadied my breathing. The ground was starting to level. Not too far now. They wouldn't dare to come too near a hospital, would they?

I stopped to lean against a tree for a moment and get my breath back. What was that click?

"Hands up or I shoot!"

CHAPTER 49

'I braced myself for the shock and pain and when nothing happened, I opened my eyes warily.

"I'm from the hospital," I said, my voice squeaky.

The man moved closer, and I could see that he was clean shaven and in uniform.

"My sister works there with Mrs Gillespie."

I saw him lowering his rifle and breathed again.

"The deserters that hide in the woods came after us when we went to find my brother in the old mill. He's trapped there, with my sister. We need to rescue them. Their leader's mad. He wants to kill anyone who knows me because I killed his dog."

"Right, lad. You're not making much sense. Let's see what the Commanding Officer says."

I followed him on wobbling legs, hoping that I could convince the officer. He listened carefully and by then I was making more sense. He ordered six men to get horses and I persuaded him to let me come as I knew the way. As we got closer, I could smell burning and see smoke. Were we too late?

The soldiers dismounted and crawled closer.

"I'm Lieutenant Hopkins, British Army. Put down your weapons."

A shot rang out and one of the soldiers returned fire. They stormed the door, and it was opened. Was that Màiri, standing there with a rifle tucked under her arm? Soon the men came out again with their captives.

"One with a burnt head, another shot in the leg and two others," he said.

"What about the giant?"

"Shot dead when he made a run for it."

I felt lightheaded with relief but sad for Mrs Stewart. He was her son, whatever he had done.

"What about my brother? He was kept a prisoner?"

"The one with the injured ankle? He's with the other deserters."

"But he's not a deserter!"

"The top brass can sort that out."

"He's injured."

"We'll put him on a horse."

When I caught up with Màiri she was ablaze with excitement.

"It was like the Middle Ages! I risked throwing some burning wood down in a bucket on their heads."

"But they've arrested Iain. They think he's a deserter."

"Mrs Gillespie will stop all of that."

I could see that she was still exultant from the battle and I just hoped that she was right. First, I had to tell her what had happened and face Mrs Gillespie's disapproval.

"I can't believe that you took such a silly risk. That was very irresponsible of you, Sandy. Imagine putting your sister in such danger!"

As if I could have stopped her, I thought, but I kept my mouth shut.

She drove the ambulance straight up to Army HQ and demanded to see Major MacDonald. She was like a warrior queen from history.

"You must release that man at once. He was a prisoner, not a deserter like the others. And he needs urgent medical attention."

"He will be court-martialled with the others."

"We Canadians know how to treat people in a civilised way. He will have medical treatment and if he has to go to trial, he will be represented by my son who is a lawyer."

"We are not heartless, Madame. I will ask the MO to examine him."

When he'd left, I asked her, "What will happen if Iain is court-martialled?"

"We will put up the best possible case for him. Hector will do that."

"But it's serious, isn't it? What if he is found guilty?"

"We will prove that he's not a deserter."

She sounded very confident. I glanced at Màiri and saw my doubts reflected in her face.'

CHAPTER 50

'Were we pleased to have Mrs Gillespie on our side! She went to track down the Commanding Officer while we found Iain, propped up in bed, shaved and clean but looking frail.

"Watch you don't bang my leg. They had to break it again to re-set my ankle. The bones knitted crooked."

"That wicked old couple should have got help for you instead of keeping you prisoner," Màiri said.

"But I couldn't escape from them. That should help with the court-martial."

"I can't believe that they're treating you as a deserter."

He squeezed her hand.

"Look, here's Mrs Gillespie. She'll know what we can do."

"I've told the Commanding Officer that he must agree to Hector representing you. He will be here in a few days. Meanwhile, they are trying the deserters. They deserve to be shot. Now, young man, you concentrate on recovering."

After she had swept out again, Iain said, "Having her on our side is as good as having a whole regiment."

"You will have to tell Hector the whole story about the firing squad," Màiri said.

Iain looked haunted and put his face in his hands.

Soon we were helping him walk on his crutches.

"Come on. I know it hurts but you must try."

Iain and I smiled at her brisk nurse's tone. We heard footsteps and turned round. Màiri's face turned pink.

"Good day to you all. I'm Hector Gillespie. You must be Iain."

I could see that my brother was impressed by the tall, confident officer with the ready smile.

"We need to get down to business at once because the Army wants to have the court martial quickly. It makes me think that they have something to hide. I already have a statement from your Commanding Officer, Iain, praising you, twice mentioned in dispatches for risking your life in no-man's land rescuing comrades. I need to speak to the Duvalls at the mill, too."

"And what about the other men in the firing squad with Iain?" Màiri asked. She had stopped flushing.

"A good idea if I can track them down. And both of you can give statements about how strange Madame Duvall seemed. I'm sure that the doctor here will confirm that Iain couldn't escape with a badly broken ankle."

"I don't want you to talk to the others in the firing squad," Iain hissed.

Hector looked at him hard but didn't speak. After he left, my sister took a deep breath, "I know that you're wondering about Hector and me. We became friends when I nursed him. He wanted to marry me after the War is over, but I said, 'No'. I don't want to go to Canada or marry anyone. I want to train as a doctor."

"But lassies always want to get married," Iain said with a grin.

"Not this one."

I could see that steam would soon be coming out of her ears so I said, "I've plans for when the War is over, too. I want to go to Art College."

"There we go, wee brother. We'll both break the mould.'"

CHAPTER 51

'Hector was back three days later, waving a wad of papers.

"Time for a council of war. The doctor confirms that Iain would not have been able to escape from the mill with his injuries. Madame Duvall, poor soul, was convinced that he was her dead son, returned from the War. Her husband went along with her delusions and agreed to keep Iain as their prisoner. I have a translation of both their statements."

I shivered.

"What's wrong, Sandy?" Màiri asked.

"It reminds me of that old woman who tried to keep me prisoner because I reminded her of someone else."

"Hurry up, Hector. We're desperate to hear your news," Mrs Gillespie sounded impatient.

"I've also tracked down one of the other soldiers from the firing squad."

Iain gasped and looked terrified.

"This has to be said, my friend. Shall I explain or do you want to?"

"I must do it. I'm the one who's responsible."

"Take your time."

"When we were in the camp, a young lieutenant with a straggly moustache and a spotty chin came for us. He hopped from foot to foot and his Adam's apple kept bobbing up and down."

"Listen, men. We all have to do things in wartime that we would rather not do. Follow me."

"He marched ahead, trying to look the part of an officer while we grinned at each other. We passed the ammunition stores, the rows of carts, the camp kitchen. A horse whinnied, someone shouted, crows flew overhead. Another ordinary day starting, except that it wasn't an ordinary day. Dread was gnawing at my belly. We dragged our feet."

"Get a move on, lads!" said the sergeant. But every part of me resisted.

Then "Halt!" We juddered to a stop, but time came rushing forwards.

"Present arms!"

They always say that one of the rifles is unloaded in a firing squad so that every man can believe that he didn't fire the fatal shot. The soldier was already tied to a post and wearing a blindfold. There was a white cloth on his chest to aim at. I aimed wide and the soldier slumped forward. The officer punished me by making me check if he was dead. I opened his shirt to see if there was a heartbeat…."

Iain's breath was ragged, and he closed his eyes. His whole body was shaking and Màiri seized his fluttering hand.

"It was a lassie we killed."

"How could that be?" My sister whispered.

"I don't know. I staggered over to the officer and told him to look. He turned as white as a sheet and ordered us to bury her at once. I couldn't get her out of my head, and I didn't want to go on living."

"It wasn't your fault!" Màiri cried out in anguish.

"The soldier I spoke to gave me the same account," Hector said.

"So, if Iain tells the court what happened…"

"No! Màiri, I won't!"

"And we have no proof. The Army destroyed the evidence."

"But listen, Hector. The lassie was wearing Army uniform. How did that happen? And why didn't she speak up to save her life?"

The Second Surge of the Sea

Màiri was frowning in concentration.

"This terrible war makes people do mad things. Maybe the uniform belonged to her young man or her brother and she had some insane idea of coming to the battlefield and finding him still alive?"

"And that name was used for her when she was buried. It could be the name of the soldier who had already died and whose uniform she was wearing. So, the same name would appear twice in the records."

"You're brilliant Màiri! If we find that evidence the Army won't want this terrible mistake to become public knowledge and we can use it to secure Iain's release. I shall ask for a postponement of the court martial while I go through the records at Army HQ with a fine-tooth comb."'

CHAPTER 52

'We knew that Iain's life hung by a thread and the waiting was agony. Two days later Hector was back. He lifted Màiri off the ground and swung her in the air.

"You were right. You're a marvel! James Andrew MacFarlane died three months earlier. The same name and number appear as the soldier shot by the firing squad and the date matches too. That proves that someone else was wearing his uniform. I'm going to prepare the papers as the court martial is set for the day after tomorrow. Iain is locked up now, so I'll tell him the good news."

Later he came to find us. His good spirits had drained away.

"Your brother refuses to testify on his own behalf. He says that he is guilty of killing the young woman and won't speak of it."

"And that could badly weaken his defence?"

"I'm afraid so, Màiri. He seems to think that he should be punished for being part of the firing squad."

"Can we go and speak to him?" I asked.

"No. Only I can see him now."

"But you could give him a letter from us?" Màiri pleaded.

"It's worth a try."

So, that's what we did. I had always hated writing at school, but this letter was a matter of life and death. How could I make my words strong enough to convince him? I would speak from my heart.'

Pappa took out a scrap of paper.

'This is the rough copy of it that I kept.

The Second Surge of the Sea

My dear Iain,

I cannot let you throw your life away. I know what it's like to believe yourself a wicked person because of a terrible mistake. That's what happened when I hit Mr Graham, the bullying school master, and thought that I had killed him. I ran away because I felt such shame. Now I know what heartache I caused our parents. I should have told Mamma and Dadda what was happening and spared them all that pain.

You were ordered to join the firing squad. How could you refuse? And you shot wide, so your bullet wasn't the fatal one. I can't bear to tell Mamma about your death if you are found guilty. She has endured too much pain already.

I want to go fishing with you again when this war is over.

Your ever-loving brother,

Sandy.

When Màiri had finished writing we read each other's letters. She kept a copy too,

My dear brother,

I know that you are tormented by the death of that poor girl but nothing we can do will bring her back. It was a terrible mistake, but it was not your fault. Your needless death will help no-one but only break your family's hearts.

All we can do is try to repair some of the damage. That poor girl's family don't know what happened to her and they deserve to know. I can't believe that they would want you to die too. When this war is over, I will do everything I can to help you find her family and tell them.

Your ever-loving sister,

Màiri

"Well done, Sandy. Let's pray that Iain follows our advice."

Her voice was firm, but her hands were shaking. Bobby came and stood between us, pressing his head against each of us in turn.'

CHAPTER 53

'It was the Wednesday morning when Hector appeared with shining boots and a confident tilt to his head.

"You can't be present at the court martial, but I want you to accompany me to the waiting room," he said, handing each of us a pile of papers, tied up with ribbon.

That seemed so strange, as if they were presents and it struck me that they were life-giving presents, with the power to prove Iain's innocence. We followed him into the room where the court martial would take place but there was no sign of Iain. Three men in uniform turned to look at us. They had red flashes on their collars and cuffs and looked even smarter than Hector.

"Here are Corporal MacPherson's brother and sister. They both work at the hospital and it's thanks to their courage and persistence that I recovered from my injuries. You will find their testimonies among these papers."

We both held our heads high as we put the papers down on the table. Then we walked out through the heavy wooden doors that were closed behind us. A sentry stood guard so there was no chance of eavesdropping here.

"Let's go and walk in the woods while we wait," said Màiri.

"I suppose that much of a soldier's life is like this – waiting, full of fear, not knowing what will happen and dreading the worst."

"But we must stay hopeful," I said, throwing a stick for Bobby.

After a while we stopped by a large oak and sat down, with our backs against its trunk. I closed my eyes and tried to still my racing heart. I must have fallen asleep and tumbled into a nightmare. I could hear Scar, Angus Stewart's hell hound, growling in my ear and smell his rotting breath. He caught my arm in his jaws and shook it. I woke with a jolt.

"We should go and find out what's happened."

It was my sister shaking me. I rubbed my eyes and felt relief that it was only a dream but being awake was just as terrifying. Màiri smoothed down my hair, took a deep breath and we set off. The sun glinted through the trees, Bobby trotted along with his nose to the ground and artillery thudded in the distance. I could hear running footsteps but didn't dare look round. Hector was heading towards us. What was he saying?

"Iain's free! Found not guilty!"

The three of us spun round in a circle, faster and faster until we were breathless. Bobby weaved between our legs, barking with excitement.

"Iain agreed to say what happened after he read your letters. The prosecutors looked grim after they heard my evidence. They didn't want to believe it and adjourned while they discussed it. I didn't threaten to make the young woman's death public, but I think they knew I would reveal it if I had to and if I didn't, my mother certainly would. I swore on my honour that I would keep it secret if they found your brother innocent. His excellent war record helped, and he said that he hoped to return to active service when he was better.'"

Pappa sighs and falls silent.

'I'm so relieved that Iain was found innocent but there's so much I still want to know, especially if they ever found out about the girl who was shot by mistake,' I say.

'Aye, they did get some answers, when the war was over. Iain, Màiri and I went to Caithness, a strange, flat land where we met Mr MacFarlane. We trudged across the fields to his cottage, Iain's leg still dragging a little.

"Come away in," a voice called out as we knocked on the door. I was shocked when I saw the speaker. He wasn't old, only middle-aged but his hair was white, his shoulders slumped, and his body withered. He gestured to the chairs in front of the empty hearth. Ashes crunched under our feet and a cloud of dust rose from the cushions as we sat down. A scrawny sheepdog nuzzled his hand.

"The place has suffered since my wife died."

"I'm sorry to hear of your loss," Màiri said.

He nodded and closed his eyes. We waited in silence while the dog whimpered, the wind howled, and he coughed. I wanted to run away.

"Kirsty Macleod was her name. She was an orphan from further south. We took her in to help around the house when she was thirteen. We did our Christian duty and gave her a home."

Again, the silence hung heavy while he closed his eyes. Then he lifted his head and frowned.

"But she was a thief. She stole our son, Jimmie."

I sensed Màiri gasp, wait and then she asked gently, "How did that happen?"

"He was already spoken for to marry our neighbour's daughter, Ella, when they were old enough. They were both only children and the two crofts would be joined together, but that Kirsty got her claws into him."

My sister was biting her lip to stop herself from saying anything.

"When they turned seventeen, they told us that they wanted to get married. There was a terrible row when we refused to allow it."

He fell silent and looked at his feet.

"What happened next?" My sister kept her voice soft.

"They ran away and got married. When they came back, they thought we would forgive them. How could we? So, they left for good. He joined up and was reported missing. My wife, Jessie, never got over it. She lost the will to live and faded away."

"I'm sorry that you lost all your family," said Màiri.

"But Kirsty, the cause of all our heartache, still lived. They sent his uniform and medals to her. She had the cheek to come here and ask us if we wanted them. We showed her the door, of course."

"So, after that she went to France?"

"Aye, lassie." She joined a group that went out to entertain the troops. She always liked singing and showing off." He spat into the empty fireplace.

"Then she must have put on his uniform when she went looking for him?"

He shrugged, "I don't know or care. All I know is that she stole my son and killed my wife."

"That's not true. She loved your son so much that she couldn't live without him and went to find him. She cared so little about her own life that she kept silent when she could have spoken and been saved."

Màiri stood up and walked out, without a backward glance. Iain and I followed, leaving Mr MacFarlane gazing into the empty hearth.'

'So much waste of life,' Pappa says.

'Shall we save the rest for tomorrow?' I say, realising that I don't want the story to end.

CHAPTER 54

I have that feeling when I'm near the end of a book I've really enjoyed and I delay reading the last chapter because I know that I'll have to say goodbye to the characters I have got to know so well. Equally, I want to know what happened to them. So I wait impatiently for Pappa to be ready for our walk.

'I really want to know what happened to all of you afterwards,' I tell Pappa.

'Well, it's grand to be so much in demand,' he says as he struggles into his shoes.

'Iain had some peace at last. The terrible nightmares got less when we went home.

"I'm glad that we came to Caithness. I can see now that Kirsty's death wasn't my fault," Iain said as we returned to the car.

"I will think about her. She won't be forgotten. How strange that she was with one of those troupes of entertainers. She might even have been in that troupe I met," Màiri said.

I turned the starting handle.

"I suppose I'll have to sit in the back with Bobby?"

"Aye!" my brother and sister said in unison.

"It was kind of the doctor to lend me his car today. I think I'll accept his offer to be his driver. I wouldn't be much use on a boat with my stiff leg," Iain said.

"That's good news. It means that you can afford to marry that nice Morag MacPhee you've been courting on the quiet," Màiri said. His face reddened.

"How do you know? Have you been spying on me?"

"I just have eyes in my head. You should marry her although she's too good for you."

"Thank you for your permission. You might even get to be a bridesmaid, unless you're off to Canada to marry Hector."

It was Màiri's turn to blush.

"Never! He's only a good friend and Mrs Gillespie would make a very bossy mother-in-law. Come on, drive us home."

"Aye, Madam."

Bobby looked at our laughing faces, sighed and closed his eyes.'

Pappa falls silent. After a while I ask, 'What happened to everyone after that, Pappa?'

'Màiri went to Canada – to train as a doctor, with Mrs Gillespie's help. She never married, was well respected but died some years later caring for typhoid sufferers. Iain and Morag married and went over there too. Iain joined the Canadian army in the Second World War and was killed.'

'What about you, Pappa, and your plans to go to Art College?'

'After the others left, I felt that I couldn't go away too and leave Mamma on her own, so I stayed with the fishing.'

'What about the Stewarts? They were important in the story.'

'Well, I think you have met Mrs Stewart's granddaughter?'

'So I have! I'll find her and tell her all I know. The whole story must be written down and kept.'

'Aye. That's the job of the ones who don't go away. But first we must tell your Granny the whole tale so that she doesn't think that we've been keeping secrets.'

'And what about Bobby? What was the rest of his life like?'

Pappa laughs, 'More peaceful. He lived to a good age and founded a family that lives on. You've met one of his descendants.'

'The naughty Dileas who we took back home,' I say.

'That's the one.'

ACKNOWLEDGEMENTS

I owe a debt of gratitude to my publisher, the Islands Book Trust, for their unfailing encouragement. Also, huge thanks to Linda Henderson and my husband Steve for their invaluable help in untangling the twists and turns of the narration as the story flowed between past and present.

Some of the characters in the story have been inspired by my own family history and photographs, such as the images shown on the back cover of my grandmother Dolina MacRae (née Nicolson), her brother Murdo Nicolson, and the iconic Skye terrier.

The title is a reference to 'An Ataireachd Ard' ('The Surge of the Sea'), a beautiful Gaelic song about the pain of exile and loss that hails from the Isle of Lewis in the Western Isles.

Anne Lorne Gillies writes in 'Songs of Gaelic Scotland' how 'the sea, since time immemorial a source of sustenance to the people, also took people away, never to return.' 'The second surge' refers to the power of story telling to return the tide of memory.

The Islands Book Trust

Based in Lewis, the Islands Book Trust are a charity committed to furthering understanding and appreciation of the history of Scottish islands in their wider Celtic and Nordic context. We do this through publishing books, organising talks and conferences, visits, radio broadcasts, research and education on island themes. For details of membership of the Book Trust, which will keep you in touch with all our publications and other activities, see https://islandsbooktrust.org/, phone 07930 801899, or visit us at the address below where a good selection of our books is available.

Islands Book Trust, Community Hub, Balallan, Isle of Lewis, HS2 9PN. Tel: 07930 801899

https://islandsbooktrust.org/